Jaggers, the dog, was unhappy. He had gone to fulfill one duty, and now found himself shut out from fulfilling another. He could not protect Peter now, nor even provide distraction. He lay with his nose against the bottom of the door, his tail quiet. Of the voices he could now hear no more than their rise and fall, the hiss of accusation, the suppressed fury of Peter's angry retorts. Surely soon he'd come out again?

But he didn't, and the curve of the voices became a continually rising one, not in volume but in intensity. Jaggers heard chair springs go—they were no longer sitting but were confronting each other standing up. The curve continued upward, the girl's voice like a whiplash with words of scorn and accusation. Jaggers was considering barking when he heard a tremendous thump, a shattering of glass, and then another bump—to the floor, on the other side of the room to the door. Then silence . . .

—from Robert Barnard's "Dog Television"

Elizabeth Peters Presents *Malice Domestic 1*
Mary Higgins Clark Presents *Malice Domestic 2*
Nancy Pickard Presents *Malice Domestic 3*
Carolyn G. Hart Presents *Malice Domestic 4*
Phyllis A. Whitney Presents *Malice Domestic 5*
Anne Perry Presents *Malice Domestic 6*

Published by POCKET BOOKS

MARY HIGGINS CLARK

presents

MALICE DOMESTIC

2

An Anthology of
Original Traditional
Mystery Stories

POCKET BOOKS

New York   London   Toronto   Sydney   Tokyo   Singapore

An *Original* Publication of POCKET BOOKS

POCKET BOOKS, a division of Simon & Schuster Inc.
1230 Avenue of the Americas, New York, NY 10020

Copyright © 1993 by Martin Greenberg

ISBN: 1-4165-0703-5

This Pocket Books paperback printing September 2004

10 9 8 7 6 5 4 3 2 1

POCKET and colophon are registered trademarks of Simon & Schuster Inc.

Printed in the U.S.A.

Copyright Notices

Contents

Contents

As It Was in the Beginning

Mary Higgins Clark

Writers in the mystery/suspense genre are frequently asked, "Why do people read mysteries? Is there something in human nature that inexorably draws us to tales of murders, kidnappings, assaults, blackmail, robberies, burglaries and similiar unpleasant deeds?"

My theory is that yes, human nature is the culprit and it all began in the Garden of Eden, the setting of the first suspense story. Think about it. There were Adam and Eve without a care in the world. They didn't have to work. They didn't pay taxes. No snow shoveling. No allergies. They had only one small restriction on their activities. They were not to eat the forbidden fruit.

Enter Satan, in the form of a snake, who persuades Eve to eat the apple and pass it on to Adam, thereby committing the first recorded felony. You know the rest of the story. Paradise lost. Eve gave birth to Cain and Abel. Cain murdered Abel. Murder in the first degree and the first example of Malice Domestic.

Mary Morman, one of the founders of Malice Domestic, explained it well: "The root of the word 'domestic' is the Latin *domos,* meaning 'home' or 'house.' Books and stories that fit the Malice Domestic genre involve the protagonist not in a professional capacity but through home relationships. They involve sisters, brothers, friends and lovers. In addition to home relationships, Malice Domestic often breaches the sanctuary of the home itself. Bodies in the bathtub, corpses on the hearthrug . . ."

These, gentle reader, are the kind of stories that await you within the following pages. The emotions we hope to evoke from you include shivery delight, a clutch at the throat, an urge to double-lock the door. In short, we hope you enjoy reading the stories as much as our writers enjoyed writing them.

For a long time there was an attitude that novels of mystery and suspense were unvalued stepchildren in the literary world. Only fifteen years ago, on a national television program, I was asked if I ever hoped to write a "good" book someday, one that wasn't in the *suspense* genre? I replied that I had no idea about my own work, but a few mystery/suspense stories were hanging in there. For example, *Oepidus Rex, Hamlet* and *Macbeth*.

Fortunately that kind of question isn't asked too often anymore. There is ever-increasing awareness that books are and should be judged on their individual merit, and some of the best of the best are found in the mystery/suspense genre. The annual Malice Domestic Convention is a joyous gathering of writers and readers who celebrate the genre. The Agatha, a teapot emblazoned with skull and bones, is the sought-after award presented to the writers who brewed the finest mystery tales of the year. Join us sometime—but reserve early. We sell out fast these days. You'll have a good time with us and with our legendary ghost of honor.

Mary Higgins Clark

MALICE DOMESTIC 2

Who Shot
Mrs. Byron Boyd?

Amanda Cross

Mark Stampede wrote the most macho books that could still pass for crime fiction, at least as most of the other members of the Crime Writers Association of America defined it. Mariana Phillips's mystery novels, while far from what anyone could call ladylike or, heaven forfend, romantic, deprecated male violence and brought into fictional disrepute the male vision that classed women, in E. M. Forster's immortal words, with motorcars if they were attractive and with eye flies if they were not. Mark Stampede worked out in a gym, with the result that the muscles in his upper body were highly developed while his protruding belly betrayed his vociferous appetite and ready thirst. Mariana Phillips, who possessed neither biceps nor belly, tended to place women at the center of her fictions, pleasant, kindly men at the periphery of her plots, and macho men either as villains or, preferably, dead. How the two of them turned up on one platform in a very large hall during the course of a rather high-flown fiction writers' series was a question no one would answer, either when asked politely at the beginning of the event by Mariana Phillips, with considerably less gallantry during the course of the event by Stampede, and with no courtesy at all by the police as the evening wore on.

Mariana Phillips, a woman of honor and a scholar of sorts, had read at least two of Stampede's books before the panel to see what she was up against—and out of courtesy. Stampede had never heard of Phillips's books, considered courtesy an effete maneuver to enslave men, and would not have read a syllable Phillips had written if no other words were available on the proverbial desert island.

The event or panel never did end, leaving forever unresolved the question of how in the world anyone was going to get out of this unfortunate confrontation; rather it was interrupted, after both panelists had disagreed with one another on every possible subject in an atmosphere growing increasingly unpleasant, by a gunshot. For whom the bullet was intended was unclear: Indeed, establishing that was the first priority of the police and the unfortunate institution sponsoring the event. What was unhappily obvious was whom the bullet hit: an elderly woman who had been persuaded at the last moment to moderate the panel. Perhaps, given the youth-worshipping qualities of our culture, "middle-aged" was the kinder description of the victim, although, as Michael Stampede had earlier made clear in tones that reverberated throughout the acoustically alive hall, dames over thirty-five were like Australia: Everyone knew it was down there and nobody gave a damn. The original moderator had been held up by a personal crisis, and the dead woman, Mrs. Byron Boyd (as she preferred to be called), had been persuaded to preside in his place at the latest possible moment. She was on the "hostess" committee, and near to hand when the telephone message announcing his inability to appear was received from the original moderator.

The police assumed that the gun person, as the officer in charge said with a sneer, was mad, personally connected to the victim, or possibly both. Everyone else in the hall assumed that an alter ego of Mark Stampede's had supposed himself (or herself) to be aiming at Mariana Phillips and had shot another female non-sex object by mistake. If women are all the same in the dark, older women are all the same in the light. That seemed the readiest explanation, if explanation it could be called. No one was prepared to believe that someone in the audience had shot Mrs. Boyd out of frustration with the evening's event. Audiences have been known to snarl at and desert speakers; they do not usually shoot them, having easier means of revenge to hand, such as refusing to buy or even read the speakers' books and advising everyone they know to the same course.

The police, while permitting no one in the audience to leave until names and addresses could be recorded and probable witnesses identified, searched the premises and found the murder weapon in a wastebasket in the women's room. Since that room had, it eventually transpired, been deserted at the time of the shot and immediately afterward, this did not necessarily point to a woman murderer. The gun itself was the sort that can be illegally purchased in all states, and legally purchased in most. It had been wiped clean, although the chance of a gun bearing identifiable prints is, detective fiction to the contrary, small.

The police settled down to the long process of listing all those present. Mark Stampede, clearly identified and innocent, since in the sight of all those people he certainly did not wield a gun, nor could he have shot anyone on the platform from the position on the platform he himself occupied, was allowed to depart. Mariana Phillips, who might have chosen to leave on the same grounds, remained out of sympathy with the dead woman and because she had an abiding interest in other people, their actions and reactions. So she stood for a good while just looking on, and finally subsided into a chair some member of the audience, now standing and swirling about, had deserted.

"The general idea," Kate Fansler said some days later, having been called in for consultation by her friend Mariana Phillips, "seems to be that whoever shot the gun was aiming at you."

"But why? I may not be universally loved, but I'm hardly hated enough to justify murder." Mariana smiled, indicating that the thought of being worth murdering was not wholly unpleasing. "Thank you for coming to talk about it. It's remarkably hard to think about anything else. Maybe you can help me to talk it out. Maybe," she added, "you can even figure it out. In my opinion, the whole thing was a miserable fluke, an unpremeditated, unmotivated, therefore undetectable crime."

"The general impression I get from the newspapers," Kate said, "suggests that admirers of Stampede, or the creature himself, are so distressed at losing sales to 'the mob of scribbling women,' as Hawthorne called them, that they are gunning down the competition—the manly solution to all such problems."

"Stampede is the one person who couldn't have shot her, except for me," Mariana said. "The angle was all wrong; anyway, we would have been seen by five hundred people."

"A hit man," Kate said with a certain satisfaction. "I haven't come across one before, not in what is so charmingly called real life. I thought they operated only in spy novels and Mafia warfare. Was the poor woman's family there?"

"No. I think the police were trying to get onto her husband. Her children are grown and scattered."

"Did you know her at all well?"

"Not really," Mariana said. "You know how it is. She arranges the reception that always follows these events: wine, cheese, cookies. She's the one who sees that the books of the speakers are available for purchase and autographing. She stands about being gracious. Very old-fashioned; this is her form of good works. I don't even know her first name; I just always said, 'Hello, Mrs. Boyd,' and passed right along. Wait a minute, I do know her first name: It's Marilee. She did mention that our names were alike. Do you suppose she was a secret admirer of Mark Stampede? She certainly can't have taken to me; I've never had a character in any book who called herself by her husband's name; I'm not her sort at all, really."

"People have an infinite capacity to enjoy books while ignoring the message they find provocative. Someone once said of Shaw's plays that they were revolutionary messages covered with chocolate, but that the audiences licked off the chocolate and left the message. They always wanted Eliza to marry Higgins despite all his efforts, and still do: Remember *My Fair Lady?*"

"Where do you pick up all this miscellaneous information?"

"I've been a magpie from birth. Here's another example. I just read that Anna Freud, who liked detective novels, only admired books with male heroes—in fact, only fantasized herself as a male hero. But later in life she was willing to read even detective novels with a female detective. See what I mean? Now tell me more about last night."

"Well, after a while I went back up to the stage and looked down from there. The body had been removed, and the police had finished protecting the area. Whoever the murderer was, he or she had certainly not been on the platform when the shot was fired."

"Did you see anyone else on the platform when you went back there?"

"Yes. A young man named Elmer Roth. I never imagined anyone was named Elmer anymore, and I used to watch him as though he'd come from another planet. He stood about with us—that is, with me and Stampede—while they hurriedly recruited Mrs. Byron Boyd, and he tried, with little success, to make conversation. Well, hardly conversation: chitchat. 'We are an ill-suited pair,' I said to Stampede, trying to be minimally friendly. 'I didn't know who else would be on the program when I agreed to appear, did you?' Stampede answered that question succinctly with a howl of dismay. It occurred to me that Stampede was literally frightened of postnubile women; either he was with the boys or anticipating a good lay. Any other situation was filled with terror."

"Is Mark Stampede married?"

"Not that I know of. Anyway, Elmer Roth said to me sort of plaintively, 'I thought it would be a real discussion.' I had the feeling he had decided to explain it to me in anticipation of explaining it to the world. 'I thought you both might read a bit from your works and then discuss the function of gender roles in crime fiction. It doesn't,' he added ruefully, but then everything he said was rueful, 'seem to have been one of the century's great ideas.'"

"It was a good enough idea," Kate said. "He just picked rather extreme examples of the possible points of view. My own feeling, though I'm a friend of yours and therefore hardly unbiased, is that you were prepared to be courteous at least, but Stampede responded like a man in a brothel who's been forced to perform with the owner's grandmother. Outraged, I mean. Not getting his rightful deserts. That, at least, was what I gathered from the account in the *Village Voice*. He apparently told someone he was tired of being 'pussy-whipped.' Quite a pungent phrase, that."

"Anyway," Mariana went on, "Elmer was clearly worried that everyone would remember that it was his idea and blame the whole thing on him. I didn't even realize it was his idea, so I told him not to worry."

"After all," Kate said, "there have been unpleasantnesses on other platforms before this, but no one was shot."

"Poor Elmer said he kept thinking the whole thing was a joke, and that Mrs. Boyd would get up and walk away. I knew exactly what he meant. Do you think someone could have planned a joke and a real bullet got into the gun by mistake?"

"I'm not sure that's possible, but it's an interesting suggestion," Kate said. "I'll ask Reed; husbands who know about guns come in handy."

"Elmer said he felt awfully guilty because I'd agreed to be on this panel as a favor to him and I might very well be dead."

"Poor baby," Kate said. "I feel sorry for him. I have to admit it's a bit harder to summon up some real compassion for Mrs. Byron Boyd." This was due, Kate realized, to a certain unreality about the lady or, if it came to that, a certain impression that the whole episode was some trick with mirrors that would ultimately be revealed in all its contrivance. It still seemed imaginable that Mrs. Byron Boyd had sat up in the mortuary van and said, "Well, that joke worked rather well."

Not that the accounts in the papers allowed any such fantasy. Mrs. Byron Boyd's obituaries were lengthy, as were the articles about the shooting. Mrs. Boyd, the newspapers reported, had been shot through the chest and had died within moments. She had, quite literally, never known what hit her. Unlike soldiers and gang warfarers, she had never braced herself for attack. People in her world were never shot.

"Reed," Kate asked him that evening, after she had told him about her talk with Mariana Phillips, "is it possible that someone could have been shooting a blank to create drama or for whatever reason and killed her by mistake because someone else had put a bullet in the gun?"

"It's possible, the way it's possible you'll win the New York lottery," Reed said. "Apart from all the technical problems—and they are many—the chances of the bullet hitting her in the chest, apparently in the heart or lungs, when shot by someone not really aiming and perhaps not able to aim that precisely—I've lost the end of the sentence; I'll leave you to finish it."

"That's what I thought you would say," Kate sighed.

"How much does Mariana know about Mark Stampede?" Reed asked.

"I asked her that," Kate said. "She doesn't know much of anything—nothing that everyone who reads mysteries and hears talk of crime novels doesn't know. He's supposed to be a pretty rough character, and certainly his remarks that night bear that out. But maybe it's all a public image, and at home he's an angel boy with a cozy wife and five adoring children, all kept strictly out of the limelight. I did ask her if she knew anyone who knows him. She finally came up with someone she knew on a Crime Writers Association commit- tee who had actually mentioned that Stampede also served on it."

"And you got his name and plan to go to see him."

"Of course," Kate said. "Not that anything will come of it. But I do have to find out more about Stampede. I don't even suppose that can be his real name. As it happens, Larry Donahue has agreed to see me tomorrow. He's a mildly unsuccessful writer, happy to exchange what information he has for a few drinks, like all of his happy breed. And after all, writers can't just stand around and watch each other be shot."

"Good luck," Reed said.

"Stampede is his real name," Larry Donahue said as he was served with his second martini. Kate could not decide if he had never heard that hard drinking had gone out or if he had reverted. He was a young man in his thirties, and Kate had long since noticed that members of his generation often lived as though the decades between the fifties and the eighties had never been, to say nothing of earlier history. "Somebody asked him at the committee meeting. I think it may have inspired him in some sort of way. He's not a bad guy, really, if you're willing to judge men by their camaraderie with other men and not their professed opinions of women. His were simplistic: Young women were rated one to ten; older women were not a fit subject of conversation or contemplation. But you had the feeling this was all an act he had tried on for size and fit into perfectly. Who knows how many he might have tried on before?"

"How old is he?" Kate asked.

"Middle to late fifties, I would say."

"It wasn't easy to find a picture of him," Kate said.

"There's a picture on the book jackets of his recent books, if you can locate a hardcover copy. He's developed a real style. Gold chain, open-necked shirt with sleeves rolled up. I think he dyes his hair. He's definitely on the muscley side, though heavy. Was that what you wanted to know?"

"If I knew what I wanted to know, I'd be better off. You weren't there that night?"

"No—I don't go to those writers' series things much.

Mostly I just sit there alternately bored and envious," he said frankly. "I take it the police haven't got anywhere."

"One can hardly blame them," Kate said. "My husband was with the D.A., so I have something of an inside track. The obvious suspect, Stampede, couldn't have done it, and the slightly less obvious suspect, Mr. Byron Boyd, turned out to have been attending a Republican fund-raising dinner in the presence of at least two hundred people." Kate did not bother to add that her favorite suspect, the scheduled moderator who had canceled at the last minute, had spent the operative time at the bedside of his son, who had been in an automobile accident. "We seem to have the perfect crime," she said, "which leads to the uncomfortable conclusion that some lunatic decided to see if he or she could shoot someone in public and get away with it, did shoot, and did get away with it. Are Stampede's books very successful?"

"Madly so," Larry Donahue said, looking at his empty glass.

"Would you like another?" Kate asked. Whether Larry Donahue would be more informative drunk or sober was a neat question. Apparently Donahue, considering it, decided to compromise.

"I'll have a beer," he said. She ordered them each a beer. "Money was what it was all about, Stampede always said. Anyone who said any different was either a liar or a fool, and doubly so if a writer of crime fiction. His novels sold to the movies and television, and he loved to sneer at the whole crazy process of filmmaking, but he always said you didn't make much money from movies and TV. I never knew whether to believe him or not."

"Is he married?"

"Legally, I think, but he's frank to say he just stays married to protect himself from having to marry someone else. If his wife doesn't mind, why should anyone else? is my thought." To Kate's relief he sipped at his beer slowly.

"What is he like at meetings, for example?" she asked.

"There have only been one or two—about nominating people to the board of the Crime Writers Association.

Stampede got on to see we didn't get too many women. His ideas were not well received, so I guess he probably won't come anymore. He liked to say that the best rules for detection were laid down by a priest, and that only Roman Catholics truly understood deception. It's hard to tell whether he's serious or just trying to make a point in a tongue-in-cheek sort of way."

"Do you think he's crazy?"

"Not a chance. He's one of those people, like stand-up comics, who insult everyone and say things no one is supposed to say. He wants to make an impression and he certainly does." And Kate got nothing more of interest out of him.

Kate had met Mariana Phillips in graduate school, shortly before Mariana abandoned her pursuit of a doctorate in history for the more immediate rewards of popular fiction. Mariana had felt it natural to consult Kate after the crime, and was not amused when Kate pointed out that this was more Mariana's kind of crime than hers. After talking to Larry Donahue, Kate settled down to contemplation of the police report on witnesses that Reed had allowed her to see. These were not very helpful, to put it at its most gracious, which was hardly how Kate put it to Reed.

"That, my dear," he responded, "is why they let me waft them before your eyes. All amateur insights welcome, if suitably anonymous. I trust you will have some." Kate stuck out her tongue at him.

"There's nothing here about Stampede himself," she said.

"That probably means he doesn't have a criminal record. I'm sure they ran it through the computer."

"Haven't they put together anything on his life?" Kate asked. "Mariana tells me they've been asking around about her, or so she gathers from her friends' reports. I'd even like to know when and where Stampede was born, and all that sort of thing."

"I'll see what I can do," Reed said. "I'm sorry I referred to amateur insights."

"Don't be. I'm beginning to think that's exactly what's

needed here." And she winked. It always worried Reed
when Kate winked.

"Do you tell the police or do I?" Kate asked Reed some
days later. It was a rhetorical question; Reed would, of
course, tell them, if there was anything to tell. Kate had her
own ways of announcing things.

"You've solved it, figured it out, discovered how it was
done?" Reed said.

"Certainly," Kate said. "Whether they have enough to
arrest him on is another question. That, I am glad to say, is
not my problem. I'm a detective, not a lawyer, and as you so
truthfully pointed out, an amateur detective at that."

"Whom might we be thinking of arresting?" Reed asked,
rather against his will.

"Stampede, of course," Kate said. She told Reed all about
it, and he, editing her deductions down from their literary
heights, told them at the D.A.'s office. They had no trouble
with the prosecution; Stampede turned out to have left a
trail the rawest of detectives could follow. It was all circum-
stantial evidence at first, of course, but whatever the police
might say, that was the kind of evidence they liked best.

"Explain it to me carefully," Mariana Phillips said. "I
thought Stampede was the one guy who couldn't possibly
have done it. Any more than I could."

"Exactly. So either he didn't do it, or he wasn't standing
next to you on the platform."

"As you say, 'exactly.' So?"

"Have you ever heard of Ronald Knox?"

"I think so; didn't Evelyn Waugh write his biography? I
remember he said in the introduction that since the clergy
are notoriously longer lived than the laity, Waugh never
expected to survive Knox and be his biographer."

"Correct. Knox was a Roman Catholic priest."

"Kate, are we both in the same conversation?"

"In addition to being a priest," Kate continued, ignoring
this, "Monsignor Ronald Knox wrote several detective
stories, and the 'Ten Commandments of Detection' for all

other such authors of detective fiction. Let me read you the tenth." Here Kate paused for emphasis, holding her text in front of her. She read:

"Ten (written as a Roman numeral, naturally): *'Twin brothers, and doubles generally, must not appear unless we have been duly prepared for them. The dodge is too easy, and the supposition too improbable. I would add as a rider that no criminal should be credited with exceptional powers of disguise unless we have had fair warning that he or she was accustomed to making up for the stage. How admirably is this indicated, for example, in Trent's Last Case.'*" Kate stopped and look at Mariana in triumph.

"Had Stampede been accustomed to make up for the stage?"

"No. But he has been involved a great deal lately with movie making, both for television and the larger screen. It was child's play to pick up the tricks and maybe even the actual makeup from around the various sets."

Mariana looked so bewildered that Kate went on without waiting for her to speak.

"Making someone up to look like Stampede was easy, when you come to think of it. He looks like every tough Irishman you've ever seen in a theater, complete with beer belly and gold chain. A travesty, of course, but that's what Stampede was after. Much easier to make two chaps look the same if they're both travesties."

"And which one was really Stampede?"

"The one who shot you, of course. He meant to shoot you, but he probably wasn't following the events on the stage too closely, and when he chose his moment the wrong middle-aged woman was at the podium, introducing a new stage in the proceedings. I think you better dedicate your next book to the memory of Mrs. Byron Boyd; she died in your place. No doubt a man capable of the extreme remarks Stampede liked to bellow forth couldn't tell one dame from another."

"But why did he want to shoot me?"

"You represent the mob of scribbling women. He's one of those men who like to think women are ruining the comfortable world men have made for themselves. They can't believe they haven't a divine right to the center of the stage and the making of all the rules. There are up to ten of them in any academic department in any university. They've all dreamed Stampede's dream, believe me. His was supposed to be the perfect crime, and symbolic into the bargain. He reckoned without me, however, poor man. The hope is that he will never know I had anything to do with finding him out."

"Couldn't the police have done that?"

"Not really. They all think, like Monsignor Knox, that invention cannot attempt what life rarely offers. Stampede had the perfect alibi, and that was that. They undoubtedly would have attributed the shooting to a homicidal maniac, if I hadn't happened to know you."

"No wonder the Stampede on the stage never mentioned any of my books. That would have been too great a demand on the actor's abilities. Insults are easier to deliver convincingly."

"Now you see how it was done."

"How long do you think he had been planning it?"

"Quite a while, I would say. At least it explains why he agreed to so unlikely an event as a panel with the two of you discussing gender roles in detective fiction."

"Poor Elmer Roth."

"Poor Mrs. Byron Boyd," Kate rather perfunctorily said.

"But wasn't Stampede in danger of being blackmailed by the fellow on the stage impersonating him?"

"I doubt it. The actor probably didn't know why he was there, and even after the shot, he may not have suspected. Even if he did, Stampede had only to tell him to go ahead and publish. Who was to know which of them fired the shot or thought the whole thing up? Nothing to stop Stampede from saying it was the actor's idea in the first place. After all, as Ronald Knox so carefully pointed out, what would Stampede, who never had any stage experience, know about makeup?"

"The poor man must be mad."

"Mad enough to kill with a gun, not any of the more subtle weapons available to saner men who resent women.

But his resentment was easily recognizable to any academic woman with feminist leanings. You should never have left the world of higher education, my dear Mariana, if you wanted to know all there was to know about motives for murdering aging or uppity women.

"Are you or are you not going to offer me a drink?"

Dog Television

Robert Barnard

The cat flap was a success from the start. For the first week
or two the Perspex door was secured up, and Gummidge
was convinced that this hole in the door was God sent and a
secret known only to her: She used to look around to see if
anyone was watching before jumping through it, preening
herself on the other side, knowing that her secret was still
safe. When the flap was let down she was suspicious and
resentful at first, but she soon learned to pat it with her paw,
like a boxer being playful, and march through. Now her
attitude to it changed: This is for *me,* she seemed to say. It is
mine, and *mine alone.* She looked with pity at Jaggers. If he
had had a flap of his own it would have taken out a quarter
of the door. So much better to have the petiteness and
delicacy of a cat.

But in fact the cat flap was a godsend to Jaggers too. He
began to sit on the doormat, his head on his paws, gazing
through the Perspex at the human, animal, and ornitho-
logical cavalcade that changed minute by minute, making
the back garden a fascinating, endless soap opera: Garbage
men came, and postmen, both to be barked at; birds

swooped down on the bread crumbs left out for them, fought each other endlessly over the nut holder, dive-bombed the rough vegetable patch, and bore off worms; male cats came in search of Gummidge, who was on the pill but still retained vestiges of her old attractions. There was always something going on. It was like one of those endless wildlife programs on television.

And in this case the screen image could literally leap into your living room. One day when Jaggers was not on sentry duty a tom leapt through the flap in search of Gummidge. Then there was mayhem. Peter was not at home, so the pursuit went on, with barks and feline shrieks, for all of half an hour before the tom found his way out of the flap again. When Peter got home from school he found the living room so impregnated with tomcat smells that no amount of open windows or deodorant sprays could make it habitable for days.

The flap was wonderful for inspecting callers too. This was the North, and the front door was for "special" callers, the back door for everyday. Jaggers could crouch and size up the dark blue trousers of gas or electricity meter readers, the bare legs of children wanting to be sponsored for this or that or singing carols at Christmas, and the varying garb of political canvassers. All were barked at, but the barks were subtly graded, from the downright threatening for garbage men to the joyful welcoming of children.

Was it a child, that evening in March? The legs were bare and thin, and rather dirty too, and the skirt was above the knees. Still, the heels of her shoes were higher than children wore, except in play. Jaggers barked on, a middle-of-the-road, could-go-either-way kind of bark. Anyway, the ring of the door got Peter up from the pile of exercise books that he was marking in the front room to open the door.

"Oh, hello," he said. Friendly—yet somehow guarded. Jaggers wagged his tail tentatively.

"Hello again. Long time no see."

The tone of the visitor was cheeky, with an undertone of aggression. Jaggers recognized it. There was a Jack Russell that came to the park who took exactly that tone. It tended to run around, barking and snapping. This girl—woman—just stood there with her hands on her hips. Jaggers couldn't see her face, but he always judged more on body than on face.

"Come on in," said Peter.

They went through to the living room. Jaggers had realized by now that he had smelled the girl before. Not recently, but many seasons ago, when she had really been a child. Now she was dirtier, smelled stronger and better, but it was still the same human person. He wagged his tail and got a pat, but no more acknowledgment. The woman sat on the sofa, waiflike but not weak, not begging. The aggressive stance was still there, hardly hidden by any social veneer.

"I'll make a pot of tea," said Peter.

"Haven't you got anything stronger?"

Jaggers's master paused for thought.

"I've got a bottle of beer . . . Oh yes, and there's still some gin left over from Christmas."

"Gin, then. With whatever you've got."

Social gestures, then, were being made, however reluctantly. Jaggers wagged his tail—*thump,* and then *thump* again. He was rewarded by a caress of his ears, which was an acknowledgment of his presence that always delighted him. She wasn't a bad girl. He remembered that she had caressed him often, those times she had come before. Peter had liked her too. They had gone upstairs together.

Peter came back with the gin and a little bottle of ginger ale. He put them down on the table beside her chair. She raised her eyebrows at the single glass, but Peter shook his head. He wasn't having anything, didn't want to make that social gesture. He sat tensely in his chair and waited. The girl-woman filled her glass from the bottle and drank half of it down. Then she slapped the glass down loudly on the table.

"You put me where I am now," she said.

"Where are you now?"

"On the streets."

"I did nothing of the sort."

Jaggers, his nose on the carpet under the table, was

exploring her feet, delicately. They certainly were like no feet he had ever known before. He had known and appreciated Peter's feet after he had come back from a walk across the Pennines, or after a strenuous game of rugby, but these were different—or, rather, *more so*. Much, much dirtier. Layer upon layer of dirt—a dirt that extended, less concentrated, up her legs. It was on the feet that weeks, months, of living outside, living rough, showed most tellingly. Jaggers thought they were wonderful.

"It started upstairs here. It was my first time."

"You were as eager as any girl I've known."

"What kind of schoolteacher is it that takes his pupils to bed?"

"What kind of schoolkid is it who drags her teacher upstairs to bed? A slut—that's the answer. You were determined to be a slut."

"I'm on the streets. I'm not on the game."

The voices were getting raised. Jaggers no longer thumped his tail. He removed his head from under the table, to be ready if anything happened. The girl was shouting, accusing. She could attack Peter, throw herself at him. It had happened before, with other women.

There was a lull. The girl began jiggling her empty glass on the table. Peter sighed, got up, and took it for a refill. Jaggers experimentally licked the feet, but got no answering caress. He lay there, unhappy at the situation.

"I want money."

"You'll have a job—getting money out of a schoolteacher!"

"You inherited this house—you told me. You can raise money on it."

"I've no intention of doing so."

"I'll take a hundred pounds."

"You won't. A hundred would only be a start."

"It might. But if I don't get it I'm going to your headmaster. If he doesn't listen I'll go to the press. And if they don't listen I'll go to the police."

The row didn't get any louder, but it got more intense. They somehow shouted at each other in voices that were hardly raised above a whisper. Jaggers found it unsettling. Peter was getting red in the face, and the girl was too, and her voice kept breaking as if she were going to sob.

Eventually she shouted: "What's a girl have to do to get a drink in this dump?"

When Peter went for her second refill Jaggers made a mistake. He looked at the girl to see that all was well, and then went to check up on the cat flap. It was a good hour since he had barked at those dirty legs. Dark had come, and there had been no birds around for hours. Now there was only the odd luminous eye of a tomcat, on the prowl in hopes of an amorous encounter with Gummidge.

When he had done his couple of minutes on sentry go, he went back into the hall and found the living room door shut.

Jaggers was unhappy. He had gone to fulfill one duty and now found himself shut out from fulfilling another. He could not protect Peter now, nor even provide distraction. He lay with his nose against the bottom of the door, his tail quiet. Of the voices he could now hear no more than their rise and fall, the hiss of accusation, the suppressed fury of Peter's angry retorts. Surely soon he'd come out again.

But he didn't, and the curve of the voices became a continually rising one, not in volume but in intensity. Jaggers heard chair springs go—they were no longer sitting, but were confronting each other standing up. The curve continued upward, the girl's voice like a whiplash with words of scorn and accusation. Jaggers was considering barking when he heard a tremendous thump, a shattering of glass, and then another bump—to the floor, on the other side of the room to the door. Then silence.

Jaggers whined, unhappy. Glass—he knew the sound of breaking glass. But what he'd heard wasn't like a breaking wineglass; it was something heavy, thick. . . . The thick gray glass ashtray, which had sat on the mantelpiece since Peter had given up smoking.

Still silence. Jaggers's nose was firmly inserted into the tiny crack along the bottom of the door, as if by smell alone he could understand what was going on. He was just thinking that he might understand when Peter came out the door and shut it firmly behind him, then leaned his head against the doorjamb, sobbing.

The brief moment that the door was open had told Jaggers. It had given him the whiff of something he came across now and then in his walks in woods and moorlands, a phenomenon that was sometimes exciting, sometimes disconcerting. It was Not Being. An End to Being. Lying there without Being.

He went to the front door, whining, and lay there on the doormat. He no longer wanted to be near the living room.

Peter stood by the door, still sobbing, otherwise motionless, for some minutes. Then he went upstairs. Jaggers heard the lavatory flush, then water running in the bathroom. When Peter came down he was looking more normal, but Jaggers could tell from the way he came down the stairs that he was still tense. He looked in the mirror in the hall, to see that he did look normal. Then he fetched Jaggers's lead from the kitchen.

A walk at this hour! Unheard of! He was more than usually beside himself because he was happy to get out of the house. The air outside was fresh and . . . free from that blight that was now pervading indoors. They walked to the Jug and Bottle, and Peter took him into the saloon bar.

"Have you got such a thing as a bottle of whiskey I could buy? And I'll have a half of bitter while I'm waiting."

Jaggers curled up contentedly by the brass rail around the floor of the bar. He saw no need to behave other than ordinarily.

"Having a party?" asked the landlord when he came back from the cellar.

"Not really. An old rugby friend rang up—may drop in later. Likes a drop of Scotch."

"Show me a rugger player who doesn't," said the landlord. "When they've tanked up on beer."

On the way back Jaggers showed signs of reluctance. He didn't want to go back into the house. But where else was there to go? Peter let them in the front door, then shut Jaggers and the whiskey in the dining room. Jaggers sat listening. Peter didn't go into the sitting room. He went to the kitchen and soon returned with a jug of water and a glass. He poured whiskey, then water, then sat at the table drinking. Jaggers sat close, watching him, waiting for some sign, some revelation of intention. Occasionally he wagged his tail; occasionally a hand would come down and caress his head. He was still unsettled. It was a comfort.

It was well after midnight, when the whiskey bottle was a third empty, when Peter made a move. He got up, only a little unsteady, and left the room. Shutting the door behind him. Jaggers sat by the door, straining his ears. The house was surrounded by a tremendous night silence. Peter opened the back door, leaving it open, and Jaggers heard his steps go to the garden shed. Something taken from it—two heavy implements that clanged when he let them come together.

He was going to the vegetable plot—that large oval that he turned over every year but somehow never seemed to do very much with. Jaggers jumped up against the bookshelf under the back window, peering into the darkness. Yes—he was forking over and then digging. He was in condition—he kept himself in condition. Jaggers lay down on the floor again, waiting.

After what seemed like an eternity Peter came back into the house. He came back into the dining room, chucking Jaggers's ears. Then he went to the whiskey bottle, pouring himself a stiff one. He took his time drinking it—getting his breath or summoning up courage. Then he went out, shutting the door. Jaggers heard the sitting room door being opened. That was where the Not Being thing was. He heard something heavy being dragged. That would be It. Little clinks as bits of glass knocked together on the floor. Peter dragged It into the hall. It seemed heavier than he had expected, or perhaps now he was tired. He had difficulty dragging it around from the sitting room through to the kitchen and the back door. He bumped into the dining room door and it came off the latch. Jaggers watched, giving the tiniest thump of his tail, but did nothing.

The unmistakable sound of the back door being closed. In a second Jaggers was up and nosing at the dining room door.

That was the first trick in the book. A moment and he was through it and on his haunches in front of the cat flap, on duty again.

Peter had something in his arms. It. By the time he got to the vegetable patch they were nothing but shapes, but Jaggers could see that Peter had put It down. There was another, a new shape there. A mound. That must be it. A mound of earth. There were tiny, distant sounds. More digging. Peter had found he needed more digging. Then Jaggers saw the shape of Peter come around the mound, take up It, then lay It down, right in the hole.

Again he saw Peter come around the mound, spade in hand. He stood by the mound and, using the spade with strong, practiced motions, he began rapidly filling the hole. Shovelful followed shovelful, the man powered by alcohol and desperation. In ten minutes the mound was nearly flattened again.

In the kitchen Jaggers still kept watch. His tail went *thump, thump, thump* regularly on the linoleum floor.

What had been buried cried out to be dug up again.

Goodbye, Sue Ellen

Gillian Roberts

"I don't want a lifetime supply of chewing gum! I want *stock!*" Ellsworth Hummer looked around the conference table, pausing to glare at each of the other directors of Chatworth Chewing Gum, Incorporated.

Neither Peter Chatworth (Shipping), Jeffrey Chatworth (Advertising), Oliver Chatworth (Product Control), Agatha Chatworth (Accounting), nor Henry Chatworth (Human Resources) glared back. Instead, each adopted a rather sorrowful expression. Then they turned their collective attention to the chairperson of the board, Sue Ellen Chatworth Hummer.

Sue Ellen looked at her red-faced husband. "We've told you before, honey," she said in her sweetest voice, "Daddy didn't want it that way. This is the Chatworth *family* business."

"I'm family now, aren't I?"

His response was a mildly surprised widening of six pairs of disgustingly similar Chatworth eyes.

"You're my *husband* now, honey, but you're a Hummer, not a Chatworth," Sue Ellen said, purring. "Besides, you should be happy. After all, you're president of the company."

Ellsworth Hummer's blood percolated. She made it sound like playing house—You be the mommy and I'll be the daddy. Only Sue Ellen's game was, You play the president and I'll be the chairperson for real. His title was meaningless as long as Sue Ellen held the stock in her name only.

He'd received the position as an extra wedding gift from his bride, six months earlier, but all it had yielded so far was a lot of free chewing gum. And now, for the sixth time in as many months, the board had voted him down, denied him any real control, any stock, any say.

Ellsworth stood up. The chair he'd been on toppled backwards and landed with a soft thunk on the thick Persian carpet. "I'm sick of Daddy and his rules!" he shouted. "Sick of Chatworths, one and all! Sick of chewing gum!"

"You can't truly mean that." Cousin Peter sounded horrified.

"I do!" Ellsworth shouted.

"But, honey," Sue Ellen said, "chewing gum has kept the Chatworths alive. Chewing gum is our life! How can you possibly be sick of it?"

"What's more," Ellsworth said, "I am not interested in anything else you have to say, or in any of the business on the agenda today or in the future." And he left, slamming the heavy door behind him, cursing the fate that had brought him so far, and yet not far enough.

Once home, he settled into the lushly panelled room Sue Ellen had redecorated for him. She called it his "study," although she'd been unable to tell him what important documents he was supposed to study in there, so he used the room to study the effects of alcohol on the human nervous system. It was the most hospitable room in the rambling, semidecrepit mansion Sue Ellen had inherited. The place had gone to seed after Mrs. Chatworth's death and Sue Ellen had been too busy being his bride—she said—to begin renovations yet. So Ellsworth spent a great deal of time in his study. Now he poured himself a brandy and considered his options. Sue Ellen owned the house. Sue Ellen owned the company. And Sue Ellen owned him. That was not at all the way things were supposed to have worked out.

Divorce was not an option. He had signed a prenuptial agreement because, long ago, Sue Ellen's daddy had reminded her that she'd better not forget that husbands were outsiders, not family. All a split would get him was a one-way ticket back to his mother's shack or, God help us all, to a nine-to-five job. Ellsworth shuddered at the thought of either possibility.

There was only one logical solution. Aside from what she made as chairperson of the present-day company, Sue Ellen was rich in trust funds and the fruits of earlier chewing gum sales, and he was Sue Ellen's legal heir. Ergo, Sue Ellen had to die.

He sighed, not with distaste for the idea itself, but for the work and effort involved in it. This was not how he'd envisioned the happily-ever-after part. He sighed again, and squared his shoulders. He was equal to the task and would do whatever was necessary to achieve his destiny.

All he'd been gifted with at birth was a well-designed set of features and a great deal of faith in himself. His mother, poor in every other way, was rich in hope. Her favorite phrase had always been, "You'll go far, Ellsworth."

And as soon as it was possible, he had.

He'd kept on going, farther and farther, until he finally found the perfect ladder on which to climb to success: Sue Ellen Chatworth, a plain and docile young woman who had spent her life trying to atone for having been born a female.

The elder Chatworths, including the much revered Daddy himself, had never paid attention to Sue Ellen. She was regarded as a bit of an error, a botched first try at producing a son. All their attention was focused on the point in the future when they would be blessed with their rightful heir.

After two heirless decades, during which time the daughter of the house attempted invisibility and was by and large raised by the servants, it finally dawned on the Chatworths that Sue Ellen and chewing gum were to be their only products.

Upon realizing this, Mrs. Chatworth quietly died of shame.

Given that Mr. Chatworth's entire existence was devoted to chewing gum, he was naturally made of more resilient material than his spouse had been. He came home from his wife's funeral and looked toward the horizons. As soon, he made it clear, as a decent period of mourning was over, he'd start afresh with a new brood mare.

But before he found a woman with the look of unborn sons in her, Ellsworth Hummer appeared and became the first human being to take Sue Ellen seriously. She was, understandably, dazzled. Her father took a dimmer view of the courtship.

He was not for a moment enchanted when Ellsworth appeared at his office door and formally asked for Sue Ellen's hand. "Blackguard!" he shouted. "Fortune hunter!"

Ellsworth merely grinned. "Now, now," he said. "You won't be losing a daughter. You'll be gaining a son at long last."

Mr. Chatworth was unused to either irony or defiance in even the most minute dosages. His veins expanded dangerously. His face became mauve, a color Ellsworth had never particularly cared for. Short of breath, he waved his fist at the young man on the other side of his desk. "You'll get *nothing!* I'll change my will!" he shouted. "If you and that daughter of mine, that—"

"Sue Ellen," Ellsworth prompted him. "Sue Ellen's her name, Pop."

Mr. Chatworth was now the color of a fully mature eggplant. "I'll see that you don't get what you want if it's the last thing I—"

"We were thinking of having the wedding in about two weeks," Ellsworth said mildly. "I'd like you to give your daughter away, of course."

"You'll marry over my dead body!" Mr. Chatworth shouted. And then he toppled, facedown, onto his desk and ceased this life thereby, as ever, proving himself correct and having the last word on the subject.

Grateful that the gods and high blood pressure had conspired to pave his way, Ellsworth sailed into marriage and a chewing gum empire. But a mere six months later, he recognized that his triumph was hollow. A sham. All he'd truly gotten was married. Very. And Sue Ellen thought that meant something, wanted to be close to him, seemed unable to comprehend that she was merely a means to an end, to the stock, to the money.

At each of the six monthly board meetings, Ellsworth wheedled, cajoled, charmed, argued, and pontificated about the necessity of his being given some real control. During six months' worth of non-board meeting days, Ellsworth suggested, hinted, insinuated, and said outright how much more of a man he'd feel if Sue Ellen would only treat him as an equal.

"Oh, honey," Sue Ellen would giggle from her pillow, "you're more than enough of a man for me already!"

Today's board meeting had been his last attempt. Now there was no remedy left except Sue Ellen's death.

But how?

Every eye in the impossibly tight-knit family would be on him. He needed a rock-solid alibi. No amateurish hacking or burying in the cellar would work. The cousins detested him as actively as he disliked them. He had to remain above suspicion.

"Hi, Ellsworth," Sue Ellen said brightly, interrupting his dark and private thoughts. "You working in here or something?"

"What work would I be doing?" he said. "What real work do I have to do?"

"Still sulking? Oh, my, honey, you don't want to be so glum about everything. After all, we've got each other and our health."

He was not cheered by being reminded of those truisms. "You and your cousins take care of all your business?" he asked tartly.

She nodded.

"Anything special?"

She lit a cigarette. "Oh, the company picnic plans and . . . you know, this and that. Ellsworth, honey, you yourself said you weren't and never would be interested in the kind of stuff that concerns the board, and I respect that." She inhaled deeply.

"Those cigarettes will kill you," he muttered. But too slowly, he added to himself. Much too slowly.

"Aren't you the most considerate groom a girl could have?" she chirruped. "I know I have to stop, but maybe in a bit. Not right now. I'm a little too tense to think about it."

"Your family would make anybody tense," he said. "I hate them."

"Yes. I know that. But I like them." She had been leaning on the edge of his desk, but now she stood straight, then bent to stub out her cigarette in his otherwise unused ashtray. "I'm going to visit Cousin Tina this afternoon," she said. "She's been feeling poorly."

There was nothing newsworthy about either Tina's health or the weekly visit. Sue Ellen saw her crotchety cousin every Saturday afternoon. "Goodbye, Sue Ellen," he said.

"See you," she answered with a wave.

Studying the effects of more brandy, Ellsworth listened as his wife's car pulled out, beginning its way over the mountain pass to her cousin's. And he smiled, because Sue Ellen had just helped him decide the method of her death. She would meet her end in a tragic crash going down that mountain. A little tinkering with the brakes and the car would be too far gone after plummeting over the side for anyone to bother investigating.

Ellsworth had one week left before he became a widower. For seven days, he was almost polite to his wife, providing her with fond final memories of him. He kissed her goodbye on the morning of the last day.

"Goodbye, Sue Ellen," he said, and he repeated the words to himself several times during the day as he lay dreaming of how he'd spend the Chatworth fortune. He smiled as he dozed, waiting for the police to arrive and announce the accident.

"Ellsworth!" The voice was agitated, feminine and definitely Sue Ellen's. He opened one eye and saw her. The dull, drab, infinitely boring, and incredibly rich Sue Ellen was intact.

"You'll never believe what happened to me!"

"Try me," he said slowly.

"I was going over the pass and suddenly I didn't have any brakes! I just screamed and panicked and knew that I was going to die!"

Ellsworth sat up. So far, it was exactly as he'd planned it. Except for this part, with her standing here, very much alive. "What did you do, Sue Ellen?" For once, he was honestly interested in what she had to say.

"Don't laugh, but I lost my head and screamed for my daddy. 'Daddy! Daddy! Help me!' like a real idiot, I guess, or something. But then, like magic, suddenly I could *hear* him, clear as day, a voice from beyond shouting and impatient with me the way he always was. It was mystical almost, Ellsworth, like he was right there with me screaming, 'Don't be such an all-around idiot, girl, and don't *bother* me! Get a grip and leave me out of this!' It almost makes you believe, doesn't it?" She looked bedazzled.

"Well, what good is it to be told to get a grip?" Ellsworth asked.

"What good? Well, I always did what my Daddy said. So I got a grip—on the steering wheel. I stopped waving my arms and being crazy, that's what. And to tell you the truth, I think that's what my . . . my heavenly *vision* meant, because what else could I have gripped? That message from my dear daddy saved me, because I hung on, racing around those curves until finally I was on flat ground again, and then I just ran the car into Cousin Tina's barn to stop it." She finally drew a breath.

Ellsworth tilted his head back and glowered upward. He felt strongly that supernatural intervention—even of the bad-tempered kind—violated all the rules.

Sue Ellen's bright smile flashed and then faded almost immediately. "I pretty much wrecked it, though," she said.

"The barn?"

"That, too. I meant the car. I think they're both totaled. I have Cousin Tina's car right now."

Ellsworth mentally deducted the cost of a car and Tina's new barn from the inheritance he'd receive as soon as he came up with a second, more reliable plan for her disposal.

He was appalled by how few really good ways there were to safely murder anyone. He studied mystery magazines and books about criminals and was depressed and discouraged by the fact that the murderer was too often apprehended. It seemed to him that the most successful homicides were those semi-random drive-by shootings that seemed to happen in great uninvestigated clusters, but they were so urban, and Ellsworth and Sue Ellen lived nestled in rural rolling hills, not a street corner within shooting distance. Gang warfare would be too much of a stretch in the sticks.

The problem was, once the crime grew more deliberate and focused, there were horrifyingly accurate ways of identifying the culprit, right down to matching his DNA from the merest bit of him. It was Ellsworth's opinion that forensic science had gone entirely too far.

However, accidents in the home seemed more likely to pass muster. People clucked their tongues and shook their heads and moved on without undue attention or speculation. So one Monday morning, before he left for another day of sitting and staring at his office walls, Ellsworth carefully greased the bottom of the shower with Sue Ellen's night cream. Then he dropped the jar and left. Sue Ellen was fond of starting her day a bit later than he began his. She was "not a morning person" in her own clichéd words, and she required a steamy hot shower to "get the old motor turning over." This time, he hoped to get more than the old motor and the clichés twirling. He was confident she'd slip and either be scalded to death, die of head injuries, or cover the drain in her fall and drown. That sort of thing happened all the time and didn't even make headlines.

This plan had some latitude, and he liked it.

He was downstairs, drinking coffee and reading the

morning paper, when the old pipes of the house signaled that Sue Ellen's shower was going full blast.

"Yes!" he said, raising his buttered toast like a flag. "Yes!" Soon he would call the police and explain how he'd found his wife's body in the shower, too late, alas, to save her.

And then he heard the scream. Yes, yes! He waited for the thud or the gurgle.

Instead, he heard a torrent of words.

Words were wrong. Words did not compute. Whole long strings of words were not what a slipping, sliding, fatally wounded woman would utter.

The words came closer, toward the top of the stairs. Two voices. Ellsworth tensed.

"I don't care if you're new!" Sue Ellen was behaving in a shrill and unladylike manner, to put it mildly. Her daddy would not have approved. "Somebody must have told you my routine. I *need* my morning shower!"

"But, miss, I wanted to make it nice. It was all greasy in there."

"That's ridiculous! It was cleaned yesterday afternoon. That's when it's always done. Well after I'm through."

"Messy. Greasy. But it's nice now."

And then the voices softened. Sue Ellen had a temper when crossed, but it was morning and she wasn't "up to speed" as she would undoubtedly say, so she made peace and retreated to her unslick, horribly safe shower.

Ellsworth refused to be discouraged. He decided to poison her instead, and he chose the family's Memorial Day gathering as the occasion. With forty relatives on his patio, there would be safety in numbers.

Cousin Lotta, according to Sue Ellen, was bringing her famous potato salad, just as she had every other year. Ellsworth had never tasted it, but he decided its recipe could nonetheless be slightly altered. He'd offer to help bring out the covered dishes. It wouldn't be difficult to make an addition in the kitchen.

The plan was brilliant. Many Chatworths would be sickened, but Sue Ellen, her portion hand-delivered by him and specially spiced, would be sickened unto death. And if anyone came under suspicion, it would be Lotta.

He sang all through the morning of the party. In his pocket were small vials of dangerous this and lethal that to be sprinkled over the potatoes, and a special bonus vial for his best beloved.

"I'll bring out the food," he told his wife later in the day.

"Oh, thank you." She spoke listlessly and looked pastier than ever. Her makeup barely clung to her skin. Unwholesome, he thought. Definitely unappetizing. "I'm feeling a bit woozy. I'd be glad to just sit a while longer. Thank you."

It was amazing how easy it was to doctor the salad with no one noticing.

Except that Sue Ellen didn't want to eat. "I'm not really feeling very well," she murmured.

Ah, but unfortunately, left to her own devices, she eventually *would* feel better, he thought. Or was she suspicious? He felt a moment's panic, then relaxed. She was merely being her usual uncooperative, dim self. "It's hunger," he insisted. "You know how you get when you forget to eat for too long. You need something in your stomach. Sit right there—I'll prepare a plate for you."

"Oh, no, I don't think . . . I really do feel quite odd."

"You're overexcited by this wonderful party, these wonderful people," he said. "Relax and let me take care of you."

He watched happily as she ate Gert's ribs and Mildred's pickled beans and Lotta's quietly augmented potato salad. He had known that if pressed, Sue Ellen wouldn't dare hurt her cousins' feelings by refusing to eat their offerings. He could see the headlines in tomorrow's papers. "Tragedy Stalks Chatworth Barbecue: Chewing Gum Heiress Bites Potato Salad and the Dust."

Maybe he'd give the reporters Sue Ellen's wedding portrait. She looked almost good in it. "Goodbye, Sue Ellen," he whispered.

Suddenly, she stood up, horror and pain distorting her features, and she ran, clutching her mouth, toward the woodsy spot behind the house. He followed until he heard the sounds of her being violently ill. And then, slump-shouldered, he walked back to the party.

"Stomach virus," the doctor said later. "Comes on all of a sudden, just like that. Going around. Let her rest a few days. She's plumb cleaned out inside."

"I told you I felt awful," Sue Ellen murmured from her bed.

A few of the cousins also felt poorly. Too poorly to drive home, in fact, and Ellsworth spent the night in his study, trying to lock out the noises of people being sick all over the house.

He could not believe that of all the world, he alone was a failure at murder. He went upstairs and stared at Sue Ellen. She managed a faint wave of greeting.

"I'm so ashamed," she said. "Getting sick in front of everybody like that. Ruining the party. I could just die!"

Fat chance, he thought as he watched her drift back to sleep.

Finally, Sue Ellen regained her strength and began to visit her cousins again. They had a new source of conversation besides each other and chewing gum these days. Now they could review the Day the Chatworths Got the Stomach Flu. They also had a new project. While in residence, several of the cousins had noticed that the house could use some modernization and loving care. Sue Ellen had also become aware of needed work while she was on the mend. "Falling apart," she would now say.

"Not at all! It's a fortress! They built strong and sturdy places back then," Ellsworth insisted. The sort of remodeling she had in mind would cost a fortune—*his* fortune. Even talking about prospective expenses felt like being robbed, or having a favorite part of his body amputated.

Nonetheless, Ellsworth did not have any more of a vote in the future of his dwelling or his inheritance than he did in the chewing gum empire, which is to say he had none. The house was going to be thoroughly redone. Sue Ellen had developed a yen to "do it right," to use her unoriginal phrase. She wanted someday to be featured in *Architectural*

Digest. The prospective tab was astronomical. Ellsworth suffered each planned purchase as a physical pain to his heart, and eventually he refused to listen.

"Let me tell you about what we're going to do up in the—" Sue Ellen would say.

"Not now. I don't understand house things, anyway. Besides, I'm busy," he'd answer.

And he was. He was constantly, frantically, obsessively busy with plans for shortening both the span of his wife's life and the duration of her spending spree. He had failed with the car, with the shower, and with the poison. His mother had always said that bad things come in threes. Perhaps that included bungled murder attempts.

People were dying all over the world. Was it asking too much for Sue Ellen to join them?

But their town had no subway for her to fall under. Their house had no large windows for her to crash through. Sue Ellen seldom drank or took even prescription drugs, and when she did, she was careful. A faked suicide was ridiculous, since she was so unrelentingly cheerful—aside from a bit of a temper tantrum now and then, of course.

He thought he would go crazy formulating a new plan. He read accounts of perfect crimes, but couldn't find one that didn't hinge on intricate coincidences or isolation or strange habits of the deceased that had earned them a slew of enemies, all of whom could be suspects.

One evening, over dessert, Sue Ellen and Cousin Tina chattered away as Ellsworth mulled over murder and watched the women with disgust.

Sue Ellen lit a cigarette.

"You ought to stop smoking," Tina said. "It'll kill you."

"But not for *years.*" Ellsworth had not meant to say it out loud.

Cousin Tina's spoon stopped midway to her mouth and she looked intently at Ellsworth.

"Sweet Ellsy," Sue Ellen said, "trying to keep me from worrying about my dreadful habit. But Tina's right. I should stop."

Ellsworth watched his wife's plain little face disappear behind a smoke screen and he suddenly smiled.

The next day Ellsworth carefully disconnected the positive battery contact in the upstairs smoke alarm. The change was nearly invisible. Nobody, even a fire marshal, would notice—and if he did, it would be chalked up to mischance. Ellsworth lit a match, held it up to the alarm, and smiled as nothing whatsoever happened. And then he waited until the time was right.

The time was perfect three nights later, when Sue Ellen stood in the living room in her stocking feet, contemplating her brandy snifter. They had just come back from an early dinner with Cousin Peter and his wife. They dined out frequently these days as half the house, including the kitchen, was pulled apart and chaotic. Besides, it was the housekeeper's evening off, and neither Sue Ellen nor Ellsworth was much good at figuring out what to do in a servantless pinch.

"I'm exhausted," Sue Ellen said. "Between the office and the remodeling, I feel like I'm spinning. Can't wait till we get past these practical things and to the fun stuff, like new furniture and wallpaper and things. I just hate even talking about the plumbing and the wiring and the replastering and—"

"Then don't," Ellsworth said. "Why don't you toddle up to bed instead, and get yourself some well-deserved rest?"

"You mean you're just as bored as I am about all that retrofitting and rewiring stuff?" Sue Ellen asked with a yawn. "I thought men liked that kind of hardware store thing. Why just today—"

"Tell me tomorrow," he said. "You must be completely exhausted."

Thirty minutes later, he tiptoed upstairs. Sue Ellen lay, snoring softly, in the pink and repulsively ruffled chamber she insisted on calling the master bedroom, although it made the theoretical master ill. It was symbolic of the many ways in which he was ignored and undervalued. Sue Ellen's pet husband. He looked down at his sleeping wife and felt not a single pang at what he was about to do. Her brandy snifter sat, drained, on her bedside table, next to an ashtray with one stubbed-out cigarette.

Ellsworth took a fresh cigarette from her pack and lit it, then placed it carefully on the pillow next to her. Then he tiptoed out, leaving the door open, the better to let the currents of air flow up the staircase and fan the fire.

He stretched out on his study's sofa and waited. When the smoke reached all the way to him, he would rush to save his bride but, tragically, it would be too late.

Just as everybody had told her—even her own relatives— smoking would be the death of her.

Ellsworth grinned to himself. "Goodbye, Sue Ellen," he said, and closed his eyes.

The howl hurled down the stairwell, directly into his skull. How had she awakened? Smoke wasn't supposed to do that to people—in fact, it was supposed to do just the opposite. The sounds from upstairs were loud and harsh and he closed his eyes again. In five minutes he'd go up far enough to burn his jacket. Then he'd call the fire department.

"Ellsworth! Ellsworth! Wake up!" The voice reached him from outside the study, but then, there she was. Without so much as a singed hair and in her nightgown.

The scream continued from upstairs.

"The house is on fire!" she said. "Upstairs. I already called the fire department." She helped him up. "You look so confused," she said. "You must have been sleeping very soundly." Then together they went and stood outside on the lawn.

"Sue Ellen," he said slowly, "somebody is still up there."

She shook her head. "There's only the two of us home tonight."

"But I heard screaming. In fact, I can still hear it."

"Screaming?" She looked puzzled for a moment, then she chuckled. "I tried to tell you! The contractor said our old alarm was unsafe. He made me light up directly under it and puff into it and he was right, Ellsworth. It didn't even make a peep. That's incredibly dangerous! So he put in these new electronic ones, and now we have them all over the place." She looked back at the flaming roof. "Had," she said. "We had electronic ones."

They both sighed. But then Sue Ellen brightened. "We should look at the bright side, though. Maybe we lost some of the house and a lot of time and hard work, but we have our *lives*. Isn't it lucky that contractor was so sharp? And what a miracle—he put the new ones in today and they saved our lives tonight! It really makes you think, doesn't it?"

Ellsworth nodded dully. The thoughts it made him think were unbearable and endless, and only the whine of approaching fire engines finally distracted him.

"Oh, Ellsworth," Sue Ellen shrieked, "I'm a mess! The whole fire department will see me in my nightgown. I could just die!"

"Stop saying that!" he shouted.

He began to smoke himself shortly thereafter, needing to do something besides pace the floor through the long nights. He searched wildly for a solution to his problem. He considered hazardous sports, but they made him nervous and Sue Ellen was, by her own admission, rather a klutz.

He pondered whether a fish bone could be wedged down somebody else's throat.

He considered disguising himself as a robber and shooting Sue Ellen dead as he entered the house. But he couldn't figure out how to arrange a good alibi for the time since the only people he knew in town were her doting relatives.

He wept a great deal, lost weight, and bit at his bottom lip until he had a series of small sores there.

Then one fine Sunday, thirty-two days after Ellsworth had first decided that Sue Ellen must go, Sue Ellen herself provided him with the answer. "Oh," she gasped with excitement as she peered out of his study's window. They had been sleeping in the small room, living in much too close surrounds while the upstairs was repaired. "Look," she said. "We have a perfect day for it."

"For what?" he asked, although he had long since lost all interest in his wife's babble.

"For the board meeting!"

"What does the weather have to do with anything?" he asked. "Besides, it's Sunday."

"You left that last meeting, honey, so you didn't hear. We decided to have the next one on the river. Picnic lunch and all. Kind of combining business and pleasure."

"Well, then," he grumbled, "since I am finished with your kind of business, in that case, I'll see you tonight." The fact that it was time for another monthly meeting was incredibly depressing. *Tempus fugit* but Sue Ellen didn't. An entire month gone and nothing had changed. Nothing whatsoever. He was still Ellsworth Hummer, possessor of nothing except a meaningless title, and the status quo might last forever.

"Nonsense!" Sue Ellen said. "We need you there. Oh, I know you had your little snit, but you are still the company president. Don't ruin everything. Besides, it'll be fun." She pursed her mouth and burst into an ancient and boring song, "'Cruising down the river . . . on a Sunday afternoon—' I can't remember any more of the words," she said.

Wait a second, he thought. Rivers were good things. People drowned in them. And with a little help, so would Sue Ellen, this very day. "Goodie," he said. "A family picnic. What a treat."

He whistled as he drove. The river, he knew, turned and curved romantically between banks laden with trees. If he could get a head start and place their canoe beyond a curve, away from the relatives, he could push Sue Ellen into the water and hold her there long enough to finally do the job. A few minutes were all that were required—probably even less. A person could only hold her breath for so long. Then he'd release her, flounder around, and call for help. Her whole family would witness his desperate attempts to save her.

After a hearty lunch, Peter asked whether they wanted to hold the business meeting now or later.

"Later," Ellsworth said. "Always later and later."

"Ah," Peter said. "Are we then to take it you haven't had a change of heart toward chewing gum concerns or board matters? Is that how it still is?"

"I have the same heart I always had. Why change it?" Ellsworth said with a mean smile.

The seven board members headed for the river and climbed into canoes. Agatha said she'd rather paddle by herself, and the rest, including Ellsworth and Sue Ellen, divided up into pairs.

Ellsworth was younger and stronger than his fellow board members, so it was easy and fairly quick to get himself a wide lead and to station his canoe in the arc of a blind curve. He could hear the cousins laugh and call to one another just beyond the trees. This was good, because he'd be able to summon them quickly.

"Isn't this nice?" Sue Ellen said dreamily. "Wasn't this a great idea?"

He nodded and grinned.

"I'm so glad we had today together this way," she said. "For once you don't seem angry about the business or how we're running it."

"Well . . ." Ellsworth said, positioning himself. "Things change. People learn. Finally, I think I really understand what can be and what can't be and what must be. So goodbye, Sue Ellen."

Her Chatworth eyes opened wide. "Why, Ellsworth—" she began.

Quickly, he stood up in the canoe, but Sue Ellen instantly followed his lead, and her motions overturned the boat, throwing them both into the water.

The dive into the river was unplanned, but it didn't discourage Ellsworth. However, the hard clap on his head from Sue Ellen's oar definitely did.

As he sank, he heard her shouting. For help, he hoped. But then, he could hear nothing more as the pressure on his head grew heavier and heavier. Was little Sue Ellen really that strong? he wondered.

Then that and all other concerns left him forever.

Sue Ellen shivered as she climbed into Cousin Aggie's canoe.

Cousins Peter and Jeremy smiled at her from their boats and then Jeremy finally released his oar from Ellsworth's submerged head. "Went well, don't you think?" Jeremy said as he righted the overturned canoe and, with help from Henry, pulled the inert form into it.

"Exactly as planned," Peter said. "Ellsworth was wrong, you know."

"Dead wrong," Aggie said with a chuckle. "He should have stayed at that last meeting, don't you think?"

"He should have given chewing gum another chance," Henry said.

"He blew it," Aggie said. Her voice took on a chillingly Ellsworth-like quality as she mimicked him. "'I have the same heart I always had. Why change it?'" She shook her head. "No turning back after that."

"We have a *good* board and we work well together. Look how smoothly this decision was implemented," Peter said. "Quite a pity that he never learned to appreciate our strengths or how the system works."

"Your daddy was right, Sue Ellen," Oliver of Product Control said. "The family can handle everything by itself, just like he always said."

"We'd best get back to report the unfortunate accident," Jeremy said.

"Yes," Sue Ellen agreed. "But first, I have to tell you one thing I surely can't tell the police. I'm positive that Ellsworth knew just what we were going to do and that he *approved*. He knew that he didn't fit in. He didn't belong. But in the end he understood. The last few weeks, he's been so kind to me, so concerned, so *serene*, you know? Why, it's almost like he knew the plan and accepted it. Especially today. Because just before I toppled us into the water, you know what he said, real sweetly? He said that he understood what must be—honest and truly, just like that, he said it. And then he said, 'Goodbye, Sue Ellen.' Makes you wonder, doesn't it?"

And with contented strokes she and her cousins and uncles and aunt paddled back to shore. Once she looked over at her late husband, nestled in his canoe.

"Goodbye," Sue Ellen whispered.

Even Steven

Taylor McCafferty

I feel real bad. A lot of folks around these parts have told me that what happened wasn't my fault, but I know different. I can't help going over it and over it in my mind. Maybe if I just hadn't won that dumb trip, nobody would've ended up dead.

Of course, at the time I won, I'd been tickled pink. When that AM radio station in Louisville called out my name over the air as the grand prize winner of their three-day, two-night, all-expense-paid trip for four to Las Vegas, I started jumping up and down right there behind the counter at the Crayton County Supermarket.

It was about seven thirty in the morning, and I had quite a few folks in line at the cash register, waiting to have their coffee and doughnuts rung up. But I didn't let that bother me. As soon as that disc jockey said, "The winner is Arbidella Calvert of Pigeon Fork, Kentucky," I screamed and started doing me a little dance right in front of everybody.

"I won, I won, I won!" I sang, waving my arms over my head like some fool. I'd picked up a little weight in the last few months, so with my white apron on, I probably looked like the Pillsbury Doughboy in drag. I didn't even care. You see, last year I became a grandmother for the fifth time, and here lately I've pretty much resigned myself that I might as well look it. I reckon my philosophy these days is pretty much the same as Popeye's. I am what I am. I'm a little too wide, a little too gray, and a little too far on the down side of fifty.

What's more, I've actually discovered that there's a certain kind of freedom in having a philosophy like this. For one thing, if you've got something to celebrate, you just go ahead and let loose. Without worrying what you look like to all the folks standing around staring.

"Hallelujah, hallelujah, hallelujah!" I yelled. "I'm on my way to wonderful, beautiful, glorious Las Vegas!" Actually, I'd never been to Las Vegas in my life, and I couldn't rightly have told you if Las Vegas was wonderful, beautiful, *or* glorious. Frankly, all I really cared about at that moment was that Las Vegas was someplace far, far away from Pigeon Fork, Kentucky.

Not that Pigeon Fork is all that bad. Don't get me wrong. As small towns go, Pigeon Fork—population right around 1,500—would rate right up there with the best of them. In the last few months, though, I'd been a tad depressed. What I needed—no doubt about it—was a change of scenery. Not to mention, as the sole proprietor of one of only two groceries in town, I hadn't had me a vacation in almost five years. I reckon that's why I sent my name in to that radio contest in the first place.

As soon as I finished doing my jig, I started ringing up everybody standing in line real fast. I was trying to clear everybody out of there so's I could get on the phone and spread my good news. Getting rid of the folks in line, however, turned out to be harder than I thought. Everybody in line—and, it seemed like, every warm body in the store—wanted to shake my hand and say congratulations.

It sounds downright unfriendly, but by the time I'd shook my last hand and heard my last congrats, it was all I could do not to act testy. By then I was all but jumping out of my britches to tell my news to the three people in the world that my news ought to make happiest—the three people I intended to take with me.

I hadn't had to think twice to decide who all that was going to be. No doubt about it, it had to be Glynnis Duffy, Irma Hatler, and Delia Bischoff, my three best friends since high school. Back in our Pigeon Fork High days, they'd started calling us The Four Musketeers—that's how much we hung around together. Fact is, we've been hanging around together for well over forty years.

Lord. You'd think you'd really know a person after forty years.

Today, of course, I realize that's not necessarily so. No doubt this should've occurred to me a whole lot sooner, being as how all three of them Musketeers started surprising me right off the bat.

The first was Irma. I said what I had to say and waited for the kind of reaction I'd had myself when I first heard my name over the radio. What I got instead was, "Las Vegas? Oh, my Lordy, no, I couldn't possibly go there," Irma said. "That place ain't nothing but a den of iniquity!"

Actually, that sounded like my kind of town, but I thought this might be a bad time to mention it. "Irma," I said. "Maybe I haven't made myself clear. This is a *free* trip out of town. For *all* us Musketeers. Understand? It's the trip we've always talked about making!"

This last was all too true. Irma, Delia, Glynnis, and I had been dreaming out loud about us all taking a trip together ever since we were in the ninth grade. Over the years, though, what with all of us getting married right out of high school—and, after that, what with one or the other of us always having a kid on the way or needing the money for something else—there never had seemed to be a good time for the four of us to get off by ourselves. Until now.

"Irma, it's a dream trip of a lifetime!" I finished.

There was a clicking sound on the line. I thought for a second that something had gone wrong with my phone until I realized it was Irma clucking her tongue. "Las Vegas is a modern-day Sodom and Gomorrah, Arbidella." Irma's voice was so solemn, she could've been quoting from the Bible. "That's what it is, a modern-day Sodom and Gomorrah!"

Too late I was remembering what a sanctimonious blue-nose Irma could be. Back in high school, the woman was already dressing as if she were the age she is now.

"Las Vegas is not neither a Sodom and Gomorrah!" I was losing patience by the handful. "It's just a fun vacation town, that's all."

Irma humphed. "Well, *sure,* if your idea of fun is gambling away your life savings, or being mistaken for a wanton woman! Why, I hear tell, in Las Vegas, if a woman stands still for five seconds in a hotel lobby—"

Irma went on and on. At this point, I think I should mention that Irma is as skinny as a stick, she wears glasses thicker than the bottoms of Coke bottles, and her short-cropped hair is almost as gray as mine. In spite of all this, Irma constantly acts as if all the men in the world are trying to talk her into doing obscene things in the backseats of their cars.

I heaved me a sigh. "Irma," I said, "I don't think the folks in Las Vegas force you to sell your body unless you really want—"

Irma interrupted me. "Why, if I ever went to a place like Las Vegas, I'm sure Jimmy would roll over in his grave—"

Jimmy Hatler was Irma's husband. They'd been married only a year when he'd been killed in a car accident. That was over thirty-seven years ago. Irma almost never talked about Jimmy—once she'd even admitted to me that she couldn't rightly remember what he'd looked like—and yet, if Irma doesn't want to do a thing, she always drags poor Jimmy into it.

I gritted my teeth. "You know, Irma, I bet Jimmy wouldn't mind a bit if you were off enjoying yourself," I said.

Irma didn't seem to hear me. "Arbidella," Irma said, "Las Vegas just *isn't* the sort of place decent folks go!"

Once she'd made that little proclamation, it took me a

good ten minutes to get Saint Irma to agree that if Delia and Glynnis were indecent enough to take a free trip to Las Vegas, she would stoop that low, too.

I was feeling a mite weary when I hung up and started dialing Delia.

Delia's reaction to my news had Irma's beat all to pieces. At first, anyways. "Oh my God, I can't believe it!" Delia screamed. "I'm a-going to Las Vegas!"

I was really enjoying Delia's enthusiasm until it occurred to me that Delia was pronouncing the words as if they were spelled "Lass Vaygers." Which made me wonder if Delia even had the vaguest notion where exactly Las Vegas was.

Delia also seemed to be a little unclear on something else. "This is so exciting! Steven and me have never been to Lass Vaygers before!" Delia's voice was shrill with excitement. "Arbidella, Steven is a-going to be *so* thrilled! This is *so* nice of you to invite us!"

Steven was Delia's husband. He was only about five eight, he weighed only about one fifty, tops, and yet, the way Steven acted, you'd have sworn he was twice that size. The man always had to be in charge. I don't know if it was on account of him being the manager of that big Shell station just outside of town and him having gotten a tad too accustomed to giving orders, or if it was on account of him trying too hard to make up for being on the small side.

Whatever the reason, if you went anywhere with Steven Bischoff, you were going to end up doing *exactly* what he wanted to do. The thought of my spending three days with Steven marching me and the rest of the Musketeers through Las Vegas, seeing only the sights *he* wanted to see, made my stomach hurt.

"Uh, Delia?" I said. "I'm just asking *you*. Not you and Steven."

The hysterics over the phone abruptly stopped. "Just me? But, Arbidella, you *did* say it was a trip for four, didn't you?"

"That's right. But I'm intending it to be a trip for just us Musketeers. It's going to be the trip we've all been talking about taking ever since—"

Delia, at this point, started doing a fair-to-middling imitation of Irma. She humphed and interrupted me. "Arbidella, I think it's real mean of you to call up, a-teasing me like this. You know very well I can't go." At this point Delia sounded near tears. "You know very well Steven won't let me!"

Hearing a grown woman say that somebody won't "let" her do something has always gotten my goat. While it was true that in the last few months Steven *had* gotten to be awful possessive when it came to Delia, I was pretty sure Delia was a big girl—fact was, she was almost as big as Steven—and the way it looked to me, Delia didn't need Steven's permission to do anything.

"Nonsense," I said. "You can go if you want to."

Delia acted as if I hadn't said anything. "There's no way on God's green earth that Steven's a-going to let me go out of town all by myself—"

"You won't be all by yourself," I said. "You'll be with me and Irma and Glynnis."

In spite of what I said, I did know, of course, exactly what Delia meant. In Steven's eyes, if Delia wasn't with him, she was alone. Steven hadn't always been like this, but in the last few months he must've started going through some kind of weird male menopause or something, because all of a sudden he hardly ever let Delia out of his sight.

When it had first started happening—and Steven had begun insisting on personally driving Delia to things like our weekly Women's Auxiliary meetings and the post office and the grocery—Delia had actually acted as if Steven were paying her a compliment. "I reckon Steven knows what he's got, and he's just keeping an eye on it," she'd said.

Delia always has been a tad uppity about her looks. To hear Delia talk, you'd think she still looked the same as she did when she beat me out for "Best-Looking" our senior year. To be honest, I reckon I'd have to admit that today Delia is still "Best-Looking" among us Musketeers. Of course, she's had more time to devote to keeping herself up than the rest of us. Glynnis works at the dry cleaners and Irma at the school board. Delia's the only one of us without a full-time job. If you're home all day, it's a lot easier to take the time to put all that dye stuff on your hair and to go off to aerobics classes three times a week.

In a way, though, I kind of admire Delia. She sure isn't about to throw in the towel. She still flirts with every male within a twenty-five-mile radius. Up until Steven started shadowing her, anyways.

Delia actually appears to think she can hold back the clock. In fact, I do believe this was why Delia was so all-fired pleased at first with Steven's sudden attention. She saw it as positive proof she wasn't slipping after all. Even if she and Steven *had* been married almost forty years, Steven was just as jealous of her as he ever was.

Of course, that was before Steven got to where he wouldn't let Delia so much as stick her nose out the door unless he was with her. By that time Delia had stopped thinking it was flattering and had started thinking that Steven was a pain in the neck.

Now, over the phone, Delia wailed, "It won't matter who I tell Steven I'm a-going out of town with, Arbidella, he's not a-going to let me!" She took a shaky breath. "Lordy mercy, sometimes it just seems as if I can't breathe, what with him a-hanging on me all the time!"

I had a solution. "Just tell him you're going, and that's that."

Delia actually laughed. Like I'd said the most preposterous thing she'd ever heard. "Arbidella," she said, "obviously it's been a real long time since you had yourself a man around."

Which, I do believe, was a right unkind thing to say.

Six years ago my Frank, God rest his soul, up and finally had that fatal heart attack that I'd been warning him about for years. That's right, *years*. But—just like a man—Frank never did listen to me. He just kept right on puffing away at them cigarettes, and practically inhaling them thick slices of country ham and four eggs for breakfast every day of his life, and not getting himself a lick of exercise.

Until finally the inevitable happened.

Delia knew very well how much I missed Frank. Lord

knows, I'd told her enough times. This, however, was just like Delia. To say something thoughtless just because things weren't going her way.

"Look," I said, and my voice was real clipped now, "call me back and let me know if you can go, okay? Because if you can't, I need to ask somebody else."

Which, yes, was a little nasty to say, but I couldn't help it. Sometimes you can get real tired of Delia's self-centered ways.

I hung up before Delia could say another word, and started dialing up Glynnis.

After talking to Irma and Delia, I was feeling downright hesitant about talking to Glynnis. Here I'd been expecting Irma and Delia to be delighted, and look at the reactions I'd gotten. Glynnis, I knew, hadn't exactly been a barrel of laughs lately, so there was no telling what in the world she was going to say.

Glynnis, of course, did have good reason to be down in the dumps. In fact, the last few months I'd felt particularly close to Glynnis, being as how she and I now shared something in common.

Just six months ago Glynnis's husband, Jake, had had himself a heart attack just like my Frank. I'd been there when she'd found him, and it still made my throat tighten up when I thought about it.

That Wednesday night we'd been to our usual Women's Auxiliary meeting over at the First Baptist Church. Us Musketeers always took turns driving, and that week had been my turn. So I was driving everybody home just like always.

Well, no, not exactly just like always. Usually Delia would've been with us, too—Steven had not yet started driving her himself—but on this particular Wednesday, Delia had called me up and told me she'd come down with the flu and she wasn't going anywhere. So it was just the three of us—me and Glynnis and Irma. Glynnis had invited me and Irma in for a cup of coffee before we headed on, and as soon as we all walked in Glynnis's front door, I saw Jake.

He was all stretched out on the couch. Asleep with his eyes open.

I think I knew the second I saw him. I drew up short, just inside the front door, and stared. I couldn't seem to pull my eyes away. I mean, here was a man I'd known since seventh grade. I'd watched him become a star quarterback for Pigeon Fork High, I'd been a bridesmaid at his wedding, I'd known him about as well as you could know anybody.

And his life had all come down to this.

Beside me, Glynnis had gone rigid, her pale blue eyes getting like saucers, her round face going white as ash. I think she, too, already knew. After all, Jake had had himself a heart condition for a couple years by then.

Glynnis always was a real reserved sort of person, always real concerned about acting proper. Her short, frosted blond hair was always perfectly combed, her makeup always perfectly applied, and up to then I don't believe I'd ever heard her, in all the years I'd known her, raise her voice in public.

That Wednesday night, when Glynnis moved to Jake's side, she started carrying on like somebody gone crazy. Screaming and wailing and hollering. It had been a pitiful sight.

Now, over the phone, Glynnis didn't sound a whole lot less pitiful than she had that night. "H—Hello?"

The minute she spoke, I realized she'd been crying. Moreover, judging from how quivery her voice sounded, I guessed she'd been crying for some time.

"Glynnis?" I said. "You okay?"

There was the longest silence before Glynnis answered. "Yes, I'm okay. I—I've just been packing up Jake's things. Getting his clothes ready to give to the rummage sale over at the Women's Auxiliary."

I winced, remembering that little chore myself. Cleaning out the closets, packing away the familiar-smelling shirts and pants. I wasn't surprised that Glynnis had put off doing this for as long as she had. It wasn't a fun job.

I blinked my own sad thoughts away, and said, "Aw, Glynnis, I know how you feel, hon."

Her answer was strange.

"Nope," she said flatly. "I don't think you do."

For a second, I didn't know what to say. Because, of course, I did, too, know. I was pretty sure I understood why Glynnis said what she did, though. When you're grieving, sometimes you can't rightly imagine that anybody has ever felt as bad as you do.

"Listen," I said, changing the subject altogether, "the reason I called is to tell you some great news." I made my voice as cheerful as I could. "I won me a free trip to Las Vegas, and I want you to come along!"

As a matter of fact, I wanted Glynnis to come on this trip worse than any of the other Musketeers. In my opinion, she needed a vacation worse than any of us, the way she'd been acting lately. Ever since Jake had died, Glynnis had been walking around like she was in a fog. Sometimes, when I came over to visit, she looked as if she hadn't run a comb through her hair the whole day.

"So what do you say?" I finished. Welcome Wagon ladies couldn't sound any more inviting.

There was another long pause. "Um, I don't think so, Arbidella," Glynnis finally said. "The mood I'm in, I'd just be a burden."

"Nonsense," I said, "it'd do you good!"

"I said no," Glynnis said. "Understand?" With that, she hung up on me.

I stood there, staring at the receiver, wondering if maybe I should call her right back. When I finally did hang up, my phone rang almost immediately. I picked it up, sure that it was Glynnis calling *me* back. No doubt apologizing for being so abrupt.

It wasn't, though. It was Delia. "Arbidella?" she said, "I talked to Steven, and I can go after all! Isn't that wonderful?" Delia sounded as if she were about to jump right through the phone, she was that excited. "Steven's a-going to pay his own way hisself. That way *all* us Musketeers can go! I'll share a room with Steven, of course, but this way I'll still get to go with the rest of you! Isn't that great?"

Great wasn't exactly the word for it, but if this was the

only way all four of us were going to get to take a trip together, well, then, so be it. Maybe putting up with Steven for a few days wouldn't be so bad. "Great, Delia," I said. "That's wonderful." I think I even sounded halfway enthusiastic.

Now, mind you, this right here is, without a doubt, one of the reasons I feel so bad. Because at this point I could still have easily backed out. I knew at the time that I really didn't want to go with bossy Steven tagging along. So I could have just called everything off. I could have just turned around and given my prize trip to my two sons and their wives. I could've done that. And none of the rest of it would've happened.

But I didn't.

I called Irma back. And in ten minutes I'd convinced her to be just as indecent as the rest of us.

After that I called Glynnis back. This time I was determined. I wanted real bad to do something nice for her, and I was going to do it. Period. So I said, "Look, Irma is going, and Delia, and Steven, too—he's going to pay his own way, so's all us Musketeers can have the prize trip—so come on, how about it? A vacation'll do you good."

Glynnis didn't even pause. "Okay," she said. "I'll go. Are you happy now?"

From her tone I believe I could assume that Glynnis was just agreeing to satisfy me, but I didn't care. Because, matter of fact, I *was* happy.

I stayed happy, too, right up until the very morning we arrived in Las Vegas. I stayed happy even though, sure enough, as soon as we got off the plane, Steven started telling us what time we were to go to bed ("no later than midnight") and what time we were getting up ("no earlier than eight"), and choosing which restaurants we'd eat at.

"I don't like Chinese, so that's definitely out," Steven said. He'd dressed for the occasion in white slacks, white shoes, a loud print shirt, and a white Panama hat. I reckon he wanted us to think that he was wearing that hat just to complete his casual ensemble, but I couldn't help but notice that it also covered his bald spot right nice. "Mexican is out, too," Steven went on. "In fact, we'll just have burgers for lunch. For dinner, though, we need to find us a nice steak place—nothing fancy—" Steven could've been giving last-minute instructions to his troops, but surprisingly enough, it didn't bother me. I was so happy to be in Las Vegas that I hardly even heard him.

I even found it easy to ignore Saint Irma. When our plane landed, they told us it was a hundred degrees in the shade, but Irma, like Steven, had also apparently dressed for the occasion. She had on a purple turtleneck with long sleeves and a purple print skirt reaching to her ankles. I do believe I've seen nuns dress more provocatively.

Nuns, however, probably wouldn't have been nearly as outraged as Irma when she got a load of all the slot machines lined up in the airport. Irma's face went almost as purple as her turtleneck. "Just look at that," she said, clutching her straw purse tighter, "these people here got no shame. They want you to start throwing away your money the second you get off the plane!"

The color of Irma's face deepened when she got a gander at the magazines advertising burlesque shows in the newsstands we passed. "Why, I never! If this ain't Sodom and Gomorrah, I don't know what is," she said, giving me a look. Irma kept it up, too, all the while we were waiting for our luggage, and getting ourselves a taxi, and heading toward our hotel. I reckon if I heard the words *Sodom and Gomorrah* once, I heard them a thousand times.

I might've been able to ignore Irma, but Delia evidently couldn't. When Irma came to an abrupt halt just inside the front door of our hotel and openly gawked at all the slot machines in the lobby, Delia elbowed her in the back.

"Irma," Delia said, "for God's sake, if you so much as mention either Sodom *or* Gomorrah one more time, I'm a-going to hit you."

Now, this reaction wasn't all that surprising from Delia. Delia has never been one to hold her tongue.

What *was* surprising was Glynnis. Her frosted blond head jerked around and she glared at Delia. "Look," Glynnis snapped, "if Irma wants to talk about Sodom and Gomorrah, she can! Who are *you* to tell her what to do?"

Well, you could've knocked me over with a feather. Like I said, Glynnis never raised her voice. Delia looked every bit as surprised as I was. "Well, uh, I was just—" Delia sort of stammered.

Steven, of course, was no help whatsoever. He just looked amused by the whole thing.

Saint Irma, if anything, looked triumphant. She moved closer to Glynnis and said, "This *is* a Sodom and Gomorrah, isn't it?"

Glynnis's answer was another surprise. "Irma," she said, "will you shut *up?*"

That pretty much did the trick as far as closing Irma's mouth for a while.

My mouth, of course, was hanging open. At first. And then it was all I could do to keep from applauding Glynnis. I mean, I knew she was being a tad testy and all, but this was such an improvement over the way she'd been acting. At least Glynnis wasn't walking around like some kind of grief-stricken zombie anymore. I was trying real hard not to smile as I followed the others through the lobby. This trip was doing what I'd hoped it would. It looked like Glynnis was finally coming around.

After that little scene, Irma confined herself to just giving all them slot machines in the lobby a real hard stare as we went by.

The lobby *was* a sight to behold, I have to admit. I reckon I had never seen the like. Hundreds and hundreds of them slot machines were all lined up, side by side, flashing and clanging and making the biggest racket I'd ever heard in all my born days. Over in the corner you could see a few roulette wheels, and some blackjack tables, but mainly the lobby was a maze of wall-to-wall slot machines.

I couldn't resist putting a quarter in one as we passed by on our way to register for our rooms. Right away that fool machine started beeping and flashing and spewing out money. In all, twenty whole dollars in quarters came rattling out of that thing!

Now, this is yet another thing that I feel real bad about. Sometimes I can't help but wonder what would've happened if I hadn't been so lucky almost the second we arrived in Las Vegas. Because my winning that money so quick sure made us all real interested in gambling.

Right away we had something to do that kept us out of our hotel rooms for hours.

That must've made things awful easy.

After I'd won all them quarters, even Saint Irma seemed to get hooked, believe it or not. Her tiny eyes got real round behind her glasses, and she said, "You mean to tell me you got all that money just from putting in one little bitty quarter?"

I noticed that Irma did not object whatsoever when Steven said, after we'd got our rooms, "We got us some time before lunch, so we'll spend it downstairs in the casino."

The hotel had given us four rooms right next to each other, and we were all standing in the hall, waiting while the bellmen unlocked our doors and took in our luggage, when Steven said that.

According to Steven, we were to stow our luggage in our rooms, get ourselves freshened up, and meet back at his and Delia's room. Then we'd go downstairs to play the slot machines. *All* of us.

That was the plan at first, anyways.

Until Steven discovered the dirty movies on his TV.

Irma, of course, did a lot to help Steven discover them. Glynnis and I were already knocking on Steven and Delia's door when Irma came flying out of her room, her face purple again. Apparently she'd been in there looking for things—other than gambling—to confirm her Sodom and Gomorrah assessment. It hadn't taken her long.

"You know what they got on this here TV?" Irma waved a colorful brochure in our faces just as Steven opened his door. "Filth! Disgusting filth! And all you have to do is just punch in the right number on your remote control and it's right there. Right in front of you! X-rated filth!"

I did notice that Steven didn't look anywhere near as dismayed at such a prospect as Irma. While Glynnis and I were trying to look real shocked so's Irma wouldn't rant and rave forever, Steven started saying, "You know, I think that plane ride has tired me out more than I thought. Maybe I'll take me a little nap—"

In back of him, Delia—no surprise—did not beg him to join us. "Why, that sounds like a real good idea, hon," she said.

"You'll stay with the other girls, won't you?" Steven said to her, but even as he said it, he already seemed a tad distracted. I do believe old Steven was reaching for the remote control even before us four Musketeers had closed the door behind us.

What happened after that I remember real clear, being as how I had to go over it so many times with the police and all.

Delia, Irma, Glynnis, and I all went downstairs to the lobby and started on the quarter machines. Pretty soon, though, Delia said, "I'm not having a bit of luck—I'm a-going to try the next row over." And off she went.

Shortly after that, Glynnis said, "I think I'll try the dime machines. Maybe my money will last longer." And she moved away.

Right after that, Irma said, "I'm out of quarters. I'm going for change."

So's after about a half hour, it was just me feeding quarters into that slot machine. All by myself.

I won several times, once getting me a payoff of fifty whole dollars in quarters, so, of course, I kept sitting there. Feeding that machine. You get almost hypnotized, watching them little lemons and cherries and things dancing before your eyes. Before I knew it, two hours had passed and my hands were gray from handling so many quarters.

I probably wouldn't even have stopped then, except my stomach started rumbling, reminding me it was getting close to lunchtime. That's when I went looking for the others.

It didn't take any time to find them. Delia was in front of one of the quarter machines toward the elevators, Irma was in front of one of the nickel machines near the front door of the hotel, and Glynnis was around the corner from me, about three rows over, working a dollar machine.

Delia and Irma were as empty-handed as me, but the tray in front of Glynnis's machine was brimming with silver coins. As soon as I walked up, Glynnis turned and grinned at me. I stared at her, realizing this was the first smile I'd seen on Glynnis's face since Jake had died. "I've been real lucky," she said, scooping up all those silver dollars and letting them slide past the pink tips of her fingers into the tray again.

All that money clanging against the side of the tray made a most impressive racket.

Irma gasped. "Oh, my Lord! How in the world did you manage to win all this?"

Glynnis's grin grew larger. "Just sitting here, feeding this here machine for a couple hours," she said. "That's all."

Delia looked downright envious. "You lucky duck!" she said. "I lost every dollar in my purse. Steven's going to kill me!"

As it turned out, though, Steven was in no condition to do any such thing.

Looking back, I could swear Delia started screaming even before she got her door open all the way. But, then again, all it took was one quick look at Steven to see how bad it was.

Irma and Glynnis and I were down the hall, opening our own doors, but when Delia screamed, we rushed right over. And then we all just gawked, standing there in the doorway.

In a way, Steven reminded me of Jake, lying there on the big double bed, his eyes wide open. Of course, there was a slight difference. Unlike Jake, Steven had a knife protruding from his chest and an awful smear of red spilling across the front of his loud print shirt.

Next to Steven's hand was the remote control, and on the TV screen the X-rated movie was still going strong.

For a long moment, all four of us just stood there in the hall, as if we were in some kind of awful trance. Then Delia ran to Steven's side, feeling for a pulse that clearly wasn't there. And crying and carrying on.

Irma started moving, too. She ran for the phone and

started calling up the police, and the hotel security folks, and an ambulance, and anybody else she could think of, I reckon.

So it was just me and Glynnis left in the hallway. Neither one of us seemed to want to move inside, so we just stood there. At first, I was mainly looking at the door to Steven and Delia's room, noticing how there didn't seem to be any signs of forced entry. The police would say later that Steven's wallet was missing, and that the murder weapon was just an ordinary kitchen knife. The kind you could get anywhere. But I didn't know all this then, of course.

After a while I started looking down at my own hands. I reckon, on account of my wanting to look anywhere but over at poor Steven.

My hands, I noticed distractedly, were still gray from playing the slot machines.

It was then that I remembered Glynnis downstairs, letting all those coins slide slowly over her fingertips.

Her *pink* fingertips.

My throat went dry.

"Glynnis," I said. My voice sounded downright strange. "If you were playing the slot machines downstairs all that time, how come your hands aren't gray?"

If Glynnis's hands hadn't been gray before, her face was now. She lifted tired blue eyes to mine.

"Delia killed my Jake," was all Glynnis said.

I took a couple of steps away from her. Not wanting to hear any more.

But Glynnis moved closer. "She did! Delia knew Jake had that heart condition, and yet she kept right on with him. She lied to us about having the flu that night, Arbidella! She was in bed with my Jake the Wednesday night he died!"

I just stared at her. Had grief unhinged her mind? "Glynnis, you're wrong," I said. "My God, whatever made you think such a thing?"

Glynnis didn't answer right off. She just reached down into her purse and pulled out a wrinkled letter. It looked as if it had been read maybe a million times. And judging from the smeared writing, as if it had been cried over some, too. "I found this in one of Jake's jeans pockets when I was getting his clothes together for the rummage sale," Glynnis said. "Along with a bunch of other letters he'd written her."

I swallowed hard and made myself look at the letter. No wonder Glynnis had sounded as if she'd been crying the day I'd called her. The letter had been dated the day Jake died. "Dear Del—" Jake had written, "please, darling, one more time? Tell the other Musketeers you're sick and meet me tonight. All my love, Jake."

Glynnis snatched the letter back. "Jake told *me,* his own wife, that we couldn't have a love life no more, on account of his heart. But he made an exception for *her.*"

I just looked at Glynnis. A thing like that could make you awful mad.

"But, Glynnis," I said, "why—why Steven?" I could barely get the words out. And yet, as much as I hated to even think about such a thing, it seemed to me that if you were in a killing frame of mind, it made a whole lot more sense to kill Delia, not Steven.

Glynnis looked at me as if I were not real bright. "It's an eye for an eye," she said, real calm. "Delia killed *my* husband, so I killed hers." She gave a little shrug. "This evens things up."

I just looked at her some more.

Even Steven.

Lord.

When the police arrived, Glynnis didn't even try to deny what she'd done. Fact is, she actually seemed to enjoy admitting it. She particularly seemed to enjoy admitting it, in a very loud voice, in front of Delia.

Delia let out a wail that probably could've been heard all the way back in Kentucky. "You're lying!" Delia yelled. "I never done nothing with Jake!"

Nobody believed her.

Nobody still believes her. When I finally got back to Pigeon Fork—after talking to the police for what seemed like years and getting Glynnis a lawyer who says he might be able to get her off with a plea of temporary insanity—I found that the news of Steven's demise had gotten back before me.

I also found that everybody had already made up their mind. Of course, Irma had done her part in helping everybody remember how possessive Steven had been those last days. And what a flirt Delia was. According to Irma, Steven no doubt had found out about Delia's affair with Jake and was keeping a real close eye on her. Saint Irma uses the phrase "the wages of sin" a whole lot lately. It's real irritating.

I've been telling everybody that Irma is wrong about Delia and that I believe every word Delia says. Delia, bless her heart, seems right grateful for my support.

Of course, I haven't told Delia that I'm pretty sure Irma *is* right about one thing. Steven probably *had* heard about the affair. No doubt Glynnis herself had told him.

I haven't told Delia something else, either. Or, for that matter, anybody else.

Fact is, I keep waiting for it to occur to somebody to ask why Jake still had all them letters in his possession. Wasn't he supposed to have given them to Delia?

I'm also waiting for folks to wonder if maybe Jake could've been writing to somebody else besides Delia. Somebody else whose long name Jake had shortened to just a nickname.

From Arbidella to just "Del."

I reckon I would never have succumbed to Jake's flattery if it hadn't been for how much I was missing Frank. A woman can get awful lonely when she's lost her husband, and Jake was suddenly there, telling me how he'd always been attracted to me. Even though I was a fifty-seven-year-old grandmother of five.

Who knows? Jake could've been telling me the truth. Or he could've been trying to feel like a young stud again, making a new conquest.

I want to be real clear about one thing, though. The Wednesday Jake died, we hadn't been together. At least, not in the sense Glynnis meant. The guilt about what we'd been doing had finally caught up to me, and I'd gone over to Jake and Glynnis's house early that afternoon—while Glynnis was still at work—to give Jake back all the letters he'd ever written me. Including the one he'd left in my mailbox that very day.

I'd been telling him that we had to end it, and I was finally doing it.

I was finally doing what was right.

Surely my doing what was right couldn't have made Jake so upset that it brought on his—no, surely that couldn't have happened.

Of course, I never will know for sure. All I know is how guilty I feel. About everything.

My feeling guilty, of course, was why I'd wanted to give Glynnis that Las Vegas trip in the first place. I was trying to make things up to her. A little.

It sure didn't turn out the way I'd hoped.

Like I said at the beginning, I feel real bad.

Water

Sally Gunning

When Arnie Huxtover first set foot on Nashtoba Island, he knew this was the place for him. First of all, it was the cheapest waterfront property on the whole New England coast, and second of all, it didn't look like the kind of place that would have the Rockefellers and the Vanderbilts moving in right next door. A little fish like Arnie Huxtover could look like a pretty big shark around here, as long as the Rockefellers and the Vanderbilts stayed away. But Arnie Huxtover was pretty sure the Vanderbilts and the Rockefellers had never even *heard* of Nashtoba. After all, who had?

Arnie Huxtover drove down the shabby little main street, looked over the single-story weathered cottages, the one bank, the general store with the sagging porch filled to brimming with a bunch of useless old men, the market that at most must have had three aisles. He shook his head. If he took a liking to this place, maybe he could do something for it—put in a real supermarket, one of the big chains, turn that penny-ante mercantile into a real, honest-to-goodness department store. Yes, Nashtoba had possibilities, all right.

Arnie pulled his Mercedes off the road in front of Beston's Store and got out.

The obscenely fat man on the left, and consequently sagging side of the porch, ducked his multiple chins in a nod. That was the extent of the greeting Arnie got, but it didn't bother Arnie any. Arnie had learned that in life it was money that talked, and once he arrived on Nashtoba these local yokels would get wind of Arnie's speaking style soon enough.

"How do," said Arnie. "Name's Huxtover."

The fat man didn't so much as blink. For that matter, neither did the reptilian-looking thin one or the craggy-featured medium-sized one. Arnie decided to excuse them, and to explain. "President, Huxtover and Constable Incorporated."

"What's that, some sort of sheriff's association?" asked the fat man.

"Manufacturing," said Arnie tightly. He waited for one of the three men to ask, "Of what?"

Nobody did.

"Not much manufacturing around here," said the craggy fellow.

"You're right there, Evan," said the fat man. "'Less you want to count May's jelly."

"Hell, Ed," the snaky fellow said to the fat man, presumably Ed, *"nobody* counts May's jelly."

Arnie Huxtover, always one to get right to the point, got to it. "I'm looking for some waterfront property. Perhaps one of you gentlemen could point me in the right direction."

"Water's thataway," said Evan, the craggy-faced man. He pointed over his shoulder.

"And thataway," said the man called Ed, pointing straight ahead.

"And for that matter, up thataway, too." This time Evan pointed up the street.

Arnie counted to ten. Slowly. "I'm looking to *purchase* some waterfront property. A realtor, perhaps—"

"Ah. A realtor." The three men exchanged glances.

"We got one," said the man called Ed, "but not so's you'd notice. Over there." He pointed to one of the scruffier shingled structures next door.

Arnie left the porch of the little store with some relief, walked next door, and entered the realtor's office with great anticipation. This was more his arena. This was where he did his best work. This was where he talked deal.

And deal it was. The spot he decided on was perfect—so loaded with conservation restrictions that Arnie was able to use that as a lever to knock the price way down, yet remote enough so that he'd be safe from prying eyes once he went about ignoring those same restrictions. Arnie knew a thing or two about these greenie-type rules. Usually it was only a matter of a fine or two. Once you got in there and did what you wanted to do there was no turning back, after all.

And Arnie did what he wanted to do. He ripped out the beach grass that held the dune in place and replaced it with a real lawn, the kind that needed lots of watering. He bulldozed up the beach plums and the bayberries and put in a hedge that would turn at right angles when Arnie told it to. He cemented a teak deck into the face of the bluff. He installed a squash court out back. On July 1 Arnie Huxtover arrived at his newly completed home, looked around him at the four stories of metal and glass and concrete, and saw that it was good.

And, Arnie Huxtover told himself, he deserved to have something that was good. There were few men who worked as hard as Arnie—at least, not at real work, not at the kind of work that made the world go round. Just today, for example. Arnie had arrived on Nashtoba fresh from a hot, sweaty, exhausting ordeal back in the big city. It was a deal that had culminated with him successfully eradicating a small business that had been like a pebble in his shoe for three years. True, the fellow had sweated and slaved for three years at his piddling little cottage industry and had failed to make the faintest dent in Arnie's balance sheet, but still, it was the principle of the thing!

So why was Arnie wasting time thinking about that little man now? He was of no more significance than those three bums there on the steps of that run-down store. True, those three had been singularly unimpressed with Arnie up to now, but now that his house was up and the whole island could see just what he could do, just what he was made of, just what he was *worth,* things would be a little different on that bench in front of that store. Arnie swung up alongside Beston's porch and got out.

"Hey, Bert, it's Mr. Huxtable," the fat man said to the snaky man.

Arnie, who had been all ready to smile magnanimously at the three wastrels on the bench, pinched his lips. *"Huxtover,"* he said.

"How's the jelly business going?"

Ed banged an elbow into Bert's side. *"Sheriffs,* Bert, *sheriffs.* He's not in jelly."

Arnie strode with purpose into Beston's Store. His masterful stride took him to the back wall of the store in fifteen seconds, but there was nothing inside the store that Arnie could possibly want to buy. He strode out, sweeping past the men on the bench without comment.

Several minutes later Arnie sank into his custom-made teak lawn chair on his deck, looked out at the ocean, and sighed. On this July day the sea was as calm as it would ever get. The surface never rippled, and still, as Arnie watched, it shot a long, slow wave across the beach and sucked a considerable amount of sand back out to sea with it. Arnie smiled, forgetting all about Huxtables and jellies and sheriffs. Yes, this was what Arnie liked about the sea—the power. It reminded him of *him. That* was where he belonged.

Arnie went back inside the glass and steel of his new home, threw on his swim trunks, and trotted down the sweeping set of stairs to the beach. He hit the water on the run. He dove, and surfaced, and struck out with a slow stroke over the surface of the water, as buoyant as a beach ball in the heavily salted sea. Yes, this was what he needed. The sea. Arnie flipped over and floated on his back. The water lapped over him, washing him clean. Not only was this what he needed, this was what he deserved. This was the life for Arnie Huxtover. At last. Arnie paddled to shore, climbed out, and sat on the sand, the salty tingle on his skin making him feel fresh and clean.

Arnie wasn't able to get back to the island of Nashtoba that weekend. A few legalities had cropped up that required the work of his most agile brain. Fortunately for Arnie, legalities weren't the problem they once were—not since he'd been able to persuade his only daughter to get rid of that schoolteacher and marry that judge. But still, it had been a hell of a week. The judge was getting cold feet, Arnie's daughter was talking about leaving the judge, and Arnie'd had to turn a few screws to get those two to come around. Yes, it had been a hell of a week, and by the end of it Arnie was more than ready to get away to his undiscovered island. This time, as Arnie drove down Nashtoba's Main Street, he saw a beat-up TR-6 parked in front of Beston's Store and a striking woman with the tall, solid kind of body he especially preferred leaning against the porch rail. She tilted her head back, sipping a Coke out of a bottle that must have been left over from 1910, and Arnie, who had had no intention of ever wasting his time with those porch sitters again, found himself slowing down. After all, his divorce was almost final, and any day now he could continue to do in the open what he'd had to do in secret for so long!

Arnie hopped up the rickety steps. "Well, hello," he said to the woman.

The woman looked at, and through, Arnie.

"Hey, Mr. Huxtable!" said Ed.

Arnie didn't bother to correct him again. It wasn't as if the fat man was anybody, after all.

And besides, thought Arnie, as he drove faster and faster over the sandy roads toward his home, up close there had been something *wrong* with that woman, something too—well—*tall*.

This time Arnie didn't even bother to sit down on his deck—he just went straight for his swimming trunks and then for the ocean. He'd been dreaming of that water for two weeks, dreaming of the way that slate of sand was wiped clean each time a wave rolled by. He took the steps two at a time. He dove, headfirst. He waited for the water to wash his mind the way it did the shore; he waited for that clean slate. Yes, there it was. But it didn't last long this time. For some reason, the first thing that popped up on its blank screen was that woman at the store. Why? There were plenty of women in the world for men like Arnie—women who were looking for a meal ticket, women who didn't mind being considered just part of the meal. That woman at the store was nothing but trouble—Arnie'd bet his last dollar on it! Well, maybe not his *last* dollar. No woman was worth his *last* dollar! Arnie cut into the water with a rough crawl stroke until he'd drowned his thoughts in the ocean at last. Then he paddled into shore and home.

The next week Arnie left work early. After all, someone had to be trusted to do things in his absence once in a while, and there wasn't much going on this afternoon, only a minor downgrade in a few supply orders: the meat they served in the cafeteria, the safety goggles, the toilet paper. Any moron could handle *that*.

Arnie was on Nashtoba by five o'clock, and realizing the foolishness of wasting time on the steps of some foolish store, he went straight to his house without detours. He hit the waves with a long, hard dive. He held his breath until he couldn't, then rose, slowly, to the surface. He breathed in the pungent air. Yes, the air *was* cleaner here. All of a sudden Arnie remembered the emission control devices he had instructed his engineers to remove from his factory chimneys. Hell, so what? They cost him money, didn't they? Arnie flipped onto his back and paddled in toward shore, watching the sky for traces of black plumes as he went. The sky was a perfect blue umbrella over Arnie's new world. Okay! The air was still clear *here,* and that was all that mattered. It was every man for himself, after all. This place would last as long as Arnie would, and after that, who cared?

Arnie sighed. Yes, this was the life. The ocean helped him, healed him, soothed him every time.

That was when Arnie first heard the voice.

"I'm tired," it said. "I'm tired."

It made Arnie jerk around clumsily in the water, looking for the woman who had spoken those words. There was no woman in sight. The waves seemed a little rougher than they had been, and Arnie watched them, looking for any evidence in them of another human form. He heard the waves crash onto the beach and creep back off again.

"Tired . . . tired . . . tired."

Arnie laughed. Was he hearing things now? Women's voices, when all along it was just a wave, rasping against the sand. Boy, for a minute he could have sworn it was a voice, a woman's voice, and all it was was water!

"I'm tired."

Arnie laughed again. "You and me both, lady!" He scrambled out of the water, but this time he hurried over the sand to his house, shaking himself like a dog to get rid of the excess salt.

Arnie missed two more weekends on the little island—not that he really had to, but his wife wanted to meet with him again about the divorce and Arnie wanted to keep up every appearance of generosity and goodwill. He could afford this gesture, since he had safely squirreled away most of his viable assets in a foreign bank account by now, and had put this new house in his daughter's name.

When Arnie finally hit the island three weeks later it seemed colder to him. It was the end of August, after all, and on Nashtoba summer ended fast and hard and didn't return for a long time. Arnie floated and shivered on his back, looking toward his castle on shore. For the first time he noticed the wide, raw scar that had been ripped through the beach grass to put in his stairs. He made a mental note to get the contractor to fill that gap.

"How? . . . How? . . . How?"

She was back. The woman in the waves.

But this time Arnie knew right away it was just the waves—more strident this time, maybe, but still, just waves.

"Wood chips!" he hollered, and laughed out loud.

The waves rolled in with a roar. They whispered back out. "Tired . . . tired . . . tired. I'm tired of washing away the sins of the world."

Arnie Huxtover took a long, hot shower the minute he reached the house. From inside the high-velocity shower he could hear nothing at all—no waves, no women, no . . . Wait. Wait one minute. Arnie snapped off the shower and got a good grip on himself. Outside the bathroom window he could hear the waves, yes. *Waves.* There *was* no woman. Clearly, it was Arnie who was tired! That was it. Arnie had been working too hard. He was tired. He went to bed early that night, planning to start taking better care of himself. He'd get up early next morning. He'd start a regular exercise regimen. He'd swim.

The next morning Arnie walked down to the beach and tiptoed gingerly into the chilly water. It was so cold it took his breath away! He turned around for the shore, ready to give up, but the shallow sun glanced off all the glass and metal of his new home and half blinded him. The house looked huge! It looked like a monster! With the sun blazing from every surface it looked even taller than its four stories, two of which were illegal, achieved by making a split ranch out of the first floor and dormering the fourth. He turned back to face the cold sea, needing a respite from all the glare. He dove. He began his crawl. One, two, three, breathe, one, two, three, breathe. The cold was winding him. He was tired. He was already tired.

"Tired . . . tired . . . tired."

What was it about this island? Why was it making him crazy this way? Arnie Huxtover chopped harder at the water, trying to make more noise than the surf itself, but it was no use. "Sins," hissed the sea in his ear. "Sins . . . sins . . . sins."

Arnie bolted onto the beach, up the stairs and into his home. "Tired," he heard behind him, just before he slammed the sliding glass door. He showered and changed. As he walked to his car he heard *something*, but he blocked his ears to the sound. *"Your* sins," the water shrieked after him as he sprayed gravel on his way out the drive.

"Afternoon, Huxtable," said Ed. "You're looking kind of tired. He's looking kind of tired, isn't he, Bert?"

"Yep," said Bert. "Tired, tired, tired."

Arnie whipped around to face Bert. Was this some kind of joke?

"You need to take it easy, Huxtable," said Bert. "You let those sheriffs run their own little club for a while. What you need's a vacation. Settle down, relax for a week or two."

Arnie drove home from the store thinking maybe old Bert was right. When had he last taken a vacation, after all? He needed rest. He *was* tired. He needed to get in shape. Mentally and physically. Arnie went to the phone and called himself in a week's vacation right then and there. True, it was going to mean his vice-president would have to postpone *his* vacation, but that was the whole point of being president, wasn't it? He'd take *two* weeks off. He'd stay on the island. He'd sleep right, eat right, swim every day.

He swam the very next morning. He wasn't in the water five seconds when the voice started up again.

"Answer . . . answer . . . answer," whispered the waves.

Arnie stopped swimming. Somehow he'd gotten out over his head. He treaded water. "What the hell are you talking about?"

"Laws of nature," called the voice. "Laws of man. You must answer . . . answer . . . answer."

Arnie struck out for shore. Answer, hell! He'd show them! He'd show them all! Arnie Huxtover had to answer to no one! *No one.* He thrashed against the waves. The sky seemed as bright and gleaming as ever, but somehow the water had blackened, thickened, roughened. When Arnie finally reached the beach he lay on it, gasping like a fish for five minutes before he could summon the strength to mount his own stairs home.

"No doubt about it," said Ed. "It's around **the eyes, isn't** it, Ev? Kind of graylike?"

"Thin," said Evan. "You're looking thin. You took this vacation just in time."

"Maybe what you need's a doctor," said Bert. "We got a good one, far as doctors go."

Arnie Huxtover snorted. As if he'd ever trust his body, insured for five mill, to some local quack! He had a doctor in the city, a top man, who treated him for nothing as long as Arnie tipped him off just before a deal was closed now and then. But maybe he *should* run back to the city and get checked out. "I *am* thinner," Arnie told the men on the porch. "Too much swimming, maybe."

"Too much sinning," said Evan, and Arnie grabbed him by the shirt.

"What did you say?"

Evan removed his shirt from Arnie's fingers. He looked a little surprised. "Too much swimming. I said too much swimming. You better cut down. You look tired."

Arnie sighed. Yes, he *was* tired. He was also hearing things here on the porch, which meant it was definitely all in his head back there in the sea. So good. So what's the big deal? Arnie Huxtover could control his own head, couldn't he? Of course he could! Arnie Huxtover could control the whole *world!*

Arnie jumped into the sea the next morning with confidence. He decided to do the backstroke today, singing to himself as he went. That ought to drown out any other stray sounds. It was a beautiful day, a beautiful sky, and clear, calm water. The beach was deserted. It was the perfect place to bring a woman. But which woman? What the heck, maybe before they got divorced he should get his wife out here for one more fling. Tell her he wanted to try to work it out one more time. Spend a week, then boot her back home . . .

"Under my thumb!" sang Arnie.

A wave knocked into the side of his head, pushing his face under, and Arnie came up spluttering. Now where had *that* come from? The water was still ripple-free, quiet-calm. Arnie flipped over onto his stomach and did the crawl instead, the better to see what was ahead of him. The only trouble was, he couldn't sing so well that way. He tried "under my thumb!" again and swallowed a good swig of seawater. He stopped singing.

"Stop . . . stop . . . stop *you*."

Arnie stopped swimming and looked around. He could *swear* there was someone in this water with him—some woman, some snot of woman who . . .

Suddenly a wave thundered and crashed onto the beach. "Pay! Pay! Pay!"

Arnie slid down into a trough of a wave that completely blocked him from shore, but he could still hear the waves crashing against the beach. "You've made me pay! You've made us *all* pay! I'll make *you* pay! Pay . . . pay . . ."

Arnie raised his head to look for the voice, the woman's voice, and swallowed water. A lot of water. He began to cough.

"Tired!" shrieked the sea. "Tired! Tired! Tired! How long can I last? How long? How long?"

The sea surged around him, black and heavy. Suddenly he couldn't move well. It felt like the floor of the ocean was holding him down. Arnie pushed against the heavy sea, but his arms felt like lead. He *must* be near the shore! He struggled to crest a wave. Where had these enormous seas come from? Wasn't the sun still shining? Wasn't his house, his castle, still gleaming and bright?

Arnie finally pulled himself up to the top of the wave, but he could no longer see his house. He was far out to sea. He could swim no more. He felt the great weight of the sea pulling at him. He was tired.

Tired.

Tired.

He went down.

Bert Barker and Evan Spender looked up from their seats on the bench as Ed Healey labored up the steps of Beston's Store. "Doc says Huxtover drowned," said Ed. "Plain and simple."

"No heart attack?" asked Evan.

"No heart attack."

"No cramp?" asked Bert.

"No cramp. They did an autopsy. Just drowned. And on a nice calm day like that."

The three men sat in silence for a minute.

Over their shoulders, and straight ahead, and up the street, they could hear the sound of the waves as they lipped along the sand.

"Nice calm day today," said Ed.

"Yep," said Bert. "Nice calm day."

You Never Know

Sarah Shankman

"I'm so hot I could die," said Lily Cheri Boisson Davidson, standing at the bus stop at the corner of Royal and Elysian Fields. Eight thirty in the morning, the temperature was ninety. The humidity was the same. It didn't even help to take a shower in New Orleans in July. You couldn't towel off fast enough to keep ahead of the sweat.

Which Lily wouldn't be doing if she were still married to Clark Davidson. Sweating, that is, while waiting for the Royal Street bus to take her from her hot, hot, hot little shotgun house in the shabby but outlaw-chic Faubourg Marigny district to her job at the Levee Bookstore in the French Quarter near Canal.

" 'If you hadn't run off and left Clark you'd be summering down on the Gulf,' " Lily said in an exaggerated falsetto, imitating her mother's voice for her friend Bernard, who was standing with her at the bus stop.

As she spoke, she had a vision of their lovely old beach house, hers and Clark's but Clark's really, low-hipped with porches all around, live oaks dripping with Spanish moss, St. Augustine lawn right up to where the sand started. Oh, the very thought of it made her heart ache, so she interrupted her vision: "Don't I sound exactly like Daisy?"

Bernard laughed, for Lily did. She didn't look like her mother though. Daisy Boisson was every inch the uptown lady. Daisy's hair was tinted blue to match her blood and she was built like a three-cushion sofa. Clothed in white from Memorial Day to Labor Day, she wore Jean Naté and baby powder, which made her smell like lemon cake.

Lily, at thirty-five, was long and lean with flashing black eyes and a mop of dark curls she twisted up and pinioned with a trio of ebony hairpins she'd received in trade for her diamond-encircled gold wedding ring in the ladies' room of Tipitina's juke joint the very next night after she'd come home early from a Nuke Duke fundraiser, back when the "former" Klansman was running for governor. That was when she had found her husband Clark in bed with the wife of his law partner and best friend. Since then Lily'd worn nothing but black. Daisy Boisson told her bridge friends her daughter was in mourning for the demise of her marriage.

"Pure horse twaddle," said Lily, damming a rivulet of sweat on her neck with her monogrammed handkerchief. "Just means clothes are one less thing I have to save for since Clark made off with all our money."

"Unh-huh," said Bernard, thinking Lily could wear an old tablecloth and be the height of chic. Whereas here he was in his head-to-toe vanilla-colored Armani, feeling like something the cats dragged in.

"Plus with black I don't have to wear underwear, which I never understood how women can do in this heat anyway."

Bernard rolled his pale blue eyes behind his horn rims. Ladies' undies were not something he gave a lot of thought to, though there had been that one brief interlude . . .

"Besides, I ask you, how can I mourn Clark if he's not dead?"

Bernard made a cross with two carefully manicured forefingers and held them in Lily's face.

"Don't you start that witch business again with me," she said.

But Bernard had known Lily since their mommas' maids had wheeled their prams down the crumbling sidewalks of St. Charles Avenue, around the roots of the live oak trees, and even then it seemed all Lily had to do was imagine— and *poof!* Call somebody and he was already on the line. Picture someone and there he stood.

Bernard called it witchcraft. Lily called it coincidence.

"Well, if I'm so good," she said now, her hand on her hip in the same pose she'd struck when she was four, "how come I can't make this damned bus come on and get here before we melt into the banquette? Do you think New Orleans buses even have a schedule, Bernard? Or do they just run when the drivers manage to sober up and pull themselves out of bed?"

Charles Robinson, an even six feet of bus driver, was mad enough to spit tenpenny nails. As he was racing out the door, already late for work, his girlfriend Sharleen's momma Dorothy had announced that, thank you very much, she'd love to stay another few days.

Sharleen had already been cranky for weeks, ever since the day the letter announcing Dorothy's impending visit from Alaska had arrived. Dorothy had also sent Sharleen an eight-by-ten glossy of her plaque from the Fairbanks Chamber of Commerce. Minority Entrepreneur of the Year.

"For the only black woman crazy enough to move up there, within shouting distance of the Arctic Circle, to open a twenty-four-hour washateria and tanning salon complete with blues, Dixieland, chicory coffee, and beignets." That's what Sharleen said.

Which is when Charles had offered that Dorothy was so weird she ought to audition for the cast of "Northern Exposure" while she was in the Lower Forty-Eight. Or maybe "In Living Color." Sharleen had just shot him a dirty look. No matter what *she* said, Charles hadn't been allowed to express an opinion about *any* woman, not one word about the entire gender for some time now, not since Clarence Thomas had gone and pissed off all the womenfolk so bad.

As far as Charles could tell, men these days were so evil—and he wasn't denying that there were a lot of mean motorscooters out there, lots of them he was afraid of himself—that every woman in the whole United States had been dubbed a Saint, and he wasn't talking about any football team either. *Black* women went one step further, had their own category: Saints with Attitude.

He had said as much to Sharleen this morning when she and her momma both started in yelling at him. Didn't pick up the dry cleaning or the laundry from Mr. Lee, you'd think he could do some little something to help out around here. Well, he did plenty—lot of the shopping, all the heavy cleaning, most of the cooking, but he didn't have time right now, working a four-to-midnight shift, then turning around and picking up an eight-to-four. Doubling up. Trying to put aside a little bit so they could go someplace cool for a couple of weeks in August. Sharleen didn't make beans at that bookstore where she worked days, went to school at night.

"You want to see attitude? I'll show you attitude!" Sharleen had said, then picked up a handful of books, hard covers, and started chucking them at his head. Wasn't that something? Popped him in the ear with a copy of *You Just Don't Understand*. He bled all over his Regional Transit Authority uniform shirt. Then Sharleen and Dorothy both stared at his bloody collar like he was Jack the Ripper instead of the victim of a book-throwing feminist.

After that there'd been no time for breakfast, and he was the last man in, his supervisor yelling at him, and he'd drawn one of the buses with the on-again, off-again air-conditioning. And his least favorite route. Elysian Fields starting out at the lake—that part wasn't bad. But hang a right on Royal, straight through the Quarter, jammed with tourists clogging up the streets, don't know where they're going, don't have the right change, horse carriages with old uncle drivers dressed up like fools yelling, "Cornstalk Fence Hotel"—it was enough to make a man shoot himself in the foot, try for his disability.

Today even the good part had gone bad. Out in Gentilly, between Mirabeau and Brutus, three kids got on with a boom box screaming dirty rap. Charles said, "You turn that thing off before I rap you—upside your heads." Then an old black lady hobbled up, smelling pretty ripe, talking to herself, not a penny in her purse. Could be his grandma. "Come on, darlin'," he said, "you ride anyway." "Who you calling darlin', you mother-raper?" That was it. The living end. Bottom of his shift, Charles was heading for that bookstore, grab up Sharleen, slap those women silly been feeding her all this women-this, women-that bull, especially the one she's always talking about—that Lily. Charles was a peaceful man, but the time had come to knock some heads.

Lily's friend Bernard walked away from the bus stop for two minutes to buy a *Times-Picayune* at the liquor store. A good-looking man in a blue-and-white seersucker suit carrying a briefcase joined Lily at the bus stop. He nodded Morning, then stared down at her black sandals with the grosgrain ribbon ties and said, "Do you know you have the most gorgeous ankles I've ever seen in my entire life?"

"Bug off," Lily said.

Between Pleasure and Humanity a fat lady got on the bus. She must have weighed three hundred pounds, was carrying another hundredweight of groceries in wet bags. Sure enough, one broke. There were Doritos and Cheez-Its and guacamole dip and chocolate-chip cookies going every which way on Charles's bus. One of the rap kids grabbed up a bag of chips with green onion and sour cream, ripped it open, and dug in. The fat lady got up all her weight behind a pretty good backhand, knocked him forward three seats. "I've had me just about enough of you young hellions," she hollered. "Don't have a lick of home training."

Charles didn't even slow down. He was thinking about the look on Sharleen's face when her momma talked about young white boys growing on trees up there in Alaska.

"I like 'em," Dorothy'd said. "Not set in their ways. Not housebroke either, but who cares—I can train 'em. And one starts getting the least bit sassy, I just toss him out, go get me a fresh one."

Sharleen had looked like that was the best idea she'd heard all day. Like she didn't know a relationship took work, had highs and lows, good times and bad. Like life. "Before my friend Lily cut and ran from her rotten two-timing husband, she chopped his hundred-dollar shirts into little bitty pieces and threw them out the window like Carnival confetti," was what she said.

Lily again.

When Bernard came back with his paper and Lily started talking loud, the man in the seersucker suit hailed a passing cab like he feared for his life.

What Lily said was, "I enjoy being pretty and have as much vanity as the next woman. But couldn't a man just for once get past the how-do-you-do before he starts in commenting on whatever part of my anatomy grabs his squinty little attention?"

"As opposed to your brilliance?" said Bernard. "Well, I'm here to tell you it's your understanding of the future perfect tense I've always been in love with. And your stand on the balance of trade. I'll tell you, if you weren't a woman, I'd marry you myself."

"Oh, shut up, Bernard. It's too hot to tease. But it is true, what I'm saying about men talking on us like we were cows they were thinking about bidding on at the livestock auction. Why, the first thing Clark ever said to me at that party where we met was, 'My God, you have the tiniest waist. Could I put my hands around it?' And like a silly little fool, I giggled and let him."

Then Lily stared off into space, remembering Clark and the good times. How he could and did encircle her with his hands. Strong arms. Long lean legs. All of which she missed.

Oh, the anguish of long, hot summer evenings with no company but Jack Daniel's. The agony of being a single lady in the nineties, when you'd read all the books, heard all the conversations, knew that most men weren't worth killing with a stick. And you missed 'em anyway.

* * *

It was between North Rampart and Burgundy, just before they got to the Royal Street turn, that the smelly old lady who'd called him a mother-raper came up to the front of the bus and stood swaying in Charles's face.

"Ma'am," he said, as patiently as a man could whose bus's air-conditioning had just quit, "you're gonna have to sit down. I can't let you stand up here while the bus's moving."

"Don't tell me what to do," she snapped. Her face looked like a storm brewing out over Lake Pontchartrain.

"Ma'am," he tried again, but didn't get any further as the old lady's shaky brown hand reached into a bag full of bags and pulled out a shiny revolver that she poked in his right ear.

"Turn this bus around," she said. "It's too hot to go shopping. I want to go back home right now."

"Ma'am, I really don't think you want to do this."

She cocked the revolver with a very loud click. "I can't hardly tell you how sick and tired I am of *y'all* telling *me* what *I* want to do. Now don't be doing that no more, okay?"

Bernard said to Lily, "Why don't you just bite the bullet and go *see* Clark? It's only a matter of time. You know you're bound to run into him anyway. Call him up and have a drink at the Absinthe. I bet you'd feel one hell of a lot better, you got it over with."

"I feel just fine, thank you very kindly."

"Unh-huh." Bernard wasn't having any of it.

"Okay, except for a little sleepwalking. The doctor said that's not unusual. Stress. You know. Nothing worse than a case of the mean reds."

"Except they found you out in the middle of St. Roch at four in the morning carrying a quart of milk. Sound asleep as if you were in your bed."

"Just that once."

"Honey," said Bernard, "cop to it. I know he broke your heart. And I know what that feels like, I've been there. All alone, night after night, chewing on the good times like you were a starving man. Waking up in the middle of the night in a puddle of sweat, terrified of you don't know what, worse than the bogeyman when we were little kids. Then you remember it's that you're all, all alone, he's gone, and you wish you were dead."

He tried to look in Lily's face to see how she was taking all this, but she turned her head.

"But you know what? What you're mourning is what *was*, not what is. What Clark may have been back in the sweet days ain't been the reality for a long time now. You see him again, you'll remember that—what a jerk he really is. Besides, I hear he's not nearly as cute, has put on a lot of weight."

"Bernard." Lily turned, her voice as cold as a Dixie beer straight out of the cooler. "What *I'm* afraid of is no bogeyman in the night. I'm afraid if I ever lay eyes on Clark Davidson again I'll kill him stone dead."

"Turn right here," the crazy old lady yelled. "Here, boy!"

Charles turned that wheel hard and did exactly what she said, even if he was headed *up* the boulevard of Elysian Fields instead of down, and definitely in the wrong lane.

"Just close your eyes and imagine Clark fat," said Bernard, who himself was blond and small and elegant, with fine bones and lovely breeding. "Sweat soaking through the pits of his white linen suit, leaving dark stains. His gut straining against his shirt, buttons gaping. His collar too tight, his fat neck hanging over."

"Yuk," said Lily. But she did what Bernard said. She imagined Clark.

And then, as had happened so many times before that she long ago stopped counting, the figment of her imagination appeared in the flesh, *lots* of flesh, hot and sweaty, exactly as Bernard had pictured.

Right *there*, right across from them on Elysian Fields stood Clark Davidson, her ex-husband. The man to whom she had given her virginity, given her love, her trust, to whom she'd whispered her deepest longings, her darkest secrets. The man who'd tossed all that away as if it were a bunch of milkweed he'd admired and cut, brought into the house, and stuck into a blood-red glass vase before he'd thought, Oh, well, they're just weeds after all, and dumped them into the trash.

He was wearing a white linen suit, already darkened with sweat, not even nine o'clock in the morning. Lily waved. Clark lit up. He looked truly thrilled to see her. Now there was his grin, that grin that used to make her heart jump up and down like a puppy. He gave her a big wave.

"Hey!" he called. "Hey, Lily!" Then he glanced to his left, checking for oncoming traffic, and stepped out onto the melting pavement of Elysian Fields.

"Well, lady, I hope you're happy," Charles said to the old woman who was still poking the gun in him even after the bus had squashed the big white man in the big white suit flat as a fritter, right into the pavement.

"Fool should have looked both ways," she snorted. "Now come on, giddyap. Busy woman like me don't have all day."

The Return of Ma Barker

Gary Alexander

The local press named her Ma Barker, but the tag was inaccurate. The real Ma Barker, the 1930s outlaw, was a ruthless killer. "Our" Ma Barker was as sweet as pie. When she robbed a bank, she never flashed a gun or threatened. Her style was to pass a note to the teller, requesting money, mentioning apologetically that she had a weapon in her purse, a weapon she dearly hoped she would never ever have to use. Ma smiled. She said please and thank you.

In the past two years she had hit thirteen downtown bank branches to the tune of eighty grand. If she wasn't dangerous, she was crafty, with a knack for disguise. No two eyewitness descriptions or bank camera tapes exactly matched. Her voice, her speech patterns, and her accents varied too. All we knew for sure was that she was an average-appearing lady in her sixties—average in height and weight with no distinguishing features her disguises didn't conceal. Depressingly average.

She had no known partner. She pulled her jobs at the height of the lunch hour and nobody had ever seen a getaway car. Ma politely took the bank's money and blended into the noontime crush. There had been a few leads, a few possible sightings—Ma on a bus, Ma in a cab, Ma going into a house, an apartment. Every tip was checked, of course, but nothing panned out.

The publicity was giving the police department plenty of heat and the detectives assigned to it fits. I ought to know. I'm one of them. My partner and I recently inherited the headache from Wilson and Blasingame. Wilson took early retirement on account of Ma. Blasingame transferred back into uniform after his ulcer got better and he was able to return to duty.

Paget, my partner, and I were reviewing the case at lunch. Rehashing it was becoming tedious. We kept a copy of the file in the car with us. The folder was six inches thick; Wilson had taken meticulous notes. It was like reviewing a bad book over and over again.

I didn't mind too much today since it was Paget's turn to pick the restaurant. His hobbies were gourmet cooking and gourmet eating. We were at this la-di-da French joint and Paget had ordered escargot. Ma kept my mind off the food.

"I agree that she doesn't use a car," Paget said.

"Does she use public transportation or is she on foot?" I said.

"Good question. She may live downtown, in a condo or a hotel. She's raking in enough bucks to afford the rent. Or maybe she slips into an office building restroom and tosses her costume."

"The acting angle bugs me," I said. "She obviously has a background in theater. Each time, Ma gives us a different look."

"You might be right," Paget said, "but Wilson and Blasingame covered every theater group and drama workshop in town. They came up blank."

Our food arrived. I'd ordered an oversauced crepe whatchamacallit that would pack on five pounds I didn't need. I would've killed for a cheeseburger.

Paget held up a forkful of dead snails. "Superb. Try one."

My beeper beeped. Saved by the bell. I went to a pay phone and called in. Ma Barker had struck ten minutes ago at a bank two blocks from us. We hustled on over. The scene was all too familiar—a superbusy downtown branch on the ground floor of an office tower, the busiest part of the day, Ma vanishing into the sunset with somebody else's money.

A uniformed officer directed us to the teller Ma had robbed.

"It was kind of scary at first, you know?" the young woman said breathlessly. "I guess she could see I was frightened. She whispered at me with this nice smile on her face to be calm and give her the money. She said she wouldn't dream of hurting me. She said please and thank you. She was *so* nice."

I asked for a description.

"Oh, she was a little old lady, you know. She had brown hair, I think. She wore a tan raincoat, I think, and had glasses on. Come to think of it, I remember catching a reflection in those glasses. The lenses might be flat."

She was more help than most. "Anything else?"

"Yeah. I have to call my mom. A TV crew is coming. I'm going to be on the five o'clock news!"

Another officer approached carrying a tan raincoat, a pair of flat-lens glasses, and a brown wig.

"I found them in a garbage can in the alley," he said. "We might be in luck. A guy on the next block thought he remembered seeing a woman walking fast out of the alley. She was wearing a blue pantsuit and climbed on a bus. He made eye contact with her and she looked nervous when he did."

If we were in luck, we were way overdue. We'd gotten this far before, but dead-ended soon thereafter. No discarded clothing could be traced to a purchaser and every possible Ma was eliminated as a suspect after the initial interview. Paget phoned the bus company and got the number and route of that coach. We hurried to our car, called headquarters, and arranged to have the nearest patrol car stop the bus.

We drove in the general direction of the bus route. Headquarters gave us the location of the pulled-over bus, a neighborhood of older homes and apartments. Although no more than twenty minutes had elapsed since we left downtown, we saw nobody on the bus who resembled Ma. One of the passengers did recall a middle-aged woman dressed in blue.

"She was sitting in front of me, so I didn't notice her face," she said. "I do remember her hair. It was gray and kind of messy."

Messy, as if she'd worn a wig over it. We couldn't be that lucky. "Where did she get off?"

"Two or three stops ago. No, two. Eighth and Powers."

"Which direction did she walk?"

"I didn't see her after she stepped off the bus."

The bus stop was right in front of a brick apartment building. I said, "If she wasn't seen again, isn't it logical she went into this building? She didn't walk ahead or cross the street."

"You're just hoping," Paget said. "But we have to start somewhere."

The apartment house had a dozen units plus the manager's. We talked to her, keeping our questions vague. A talk show blared behind her. Guests were shouting and shrieking, arguing the existence of space aliens. The manager's answers were impatient. "I haven't seen or heard anyone come or go all afternoon. Most of my tenants are singles and young married couples who work during the day. Retired folks, you're asking? I only have two. Jane Holmes in one-oh-four. This afternoon's her pottery class, I believe. Edna Bemis in two-ten. She's a retired schoolteacher. She's usually home."

A sixtyish, gray-haired woman with twinkling eyes greeted us. She wore a flowered housedress and a winning smile. Her apartment was modestly furnished and absolutely immaculate. A dust mote would die a quick death around here.

We showed our identification and I said, "Mrs. Bemis, a robbery suspect has been seen in the area. We're canvassing for eyewitnesses."

"Well, come in, and do call me Edna," she said. "I'm afraid I can't be very helpful. I've been too busy to have a cup of coffee, let alone peek out the window. Do you have a picture of your robber? I'll identify him if I can."

"Not him," I said. "Her. You might have heard of her. The newspapers call her Ma Barker."

"That awful woman! She gives us senior citizens a bad name."

I was staring at her, all the while trying not to be too obvious, trying to connect her with the bank camera blow-ups I had studied hour upon hour. I couldn't. If Edna Bemis was Ma Barker, she was a chameleon.

Taking short, quick steps, she led us into the kitchen. "Sorry to be in such a rush, gentlemen. My son and daughter-in-law are coming to dinner. They visit so seldom, I like to put an elegant meal on the table."

The kitchen was hot and fragrant. I said, "Smells delicious. Whatever it is you're cooking."

"Wow!" Paget said, gawking. "This is an impressive layout."

Her kitchen was impressive, even to someone as uncouth as myself, whose idea of a three-course dinner was pizza, chips, and a six-pack. There was a gleaming white range with stovetop grill, a humongous microwave mounted above, stainless steel and copper pots and pans hanging from hooks, and a library of cookbooks inside a beveled glass cabinet. On the spotless counter, next to a cookbook with a marker in it, was a food processor that in shape and size reminded me of an outboard motor.

"Thank you," Mrs. Bemis said. "Do you gentlemen enjoy cooking?"

"Detective Paget does," I said. "He's an expert."

"How nice," she said, opening the oven. "Mr. Paget, please give me your expert opinion. This is my first attempt at Marco Polo Duck."

"Marco Polo Duck," Paget said in awe. "I've always wanted to tackle the dish. I saw them do it on a TV cooking show. With the veal and duck stocks and everything, there are so many steps."

It looked like a half-cooked bird to me, but what did I

know? I casually touched the stove. Hot. Very hot. Edna had been home for a while. Meanwhile, she and my pard began chattering like long-lost friends, comparing tips on cookery. Deglazing, carmelizing, marinating—stuff like that.

I was the odd person out and was feeling lonely. I slipped into a pause in the conversation, asking, "We understand you taught school, Edna. What did you teach?"

"High school," she said. "Thirty-eight years. Home economics and drama."

Paget was scribbling in his notebook, the notebook he normally used to record crime scene descriptions. Now he was recording a tip of Edna's on clarified butter. Suddenly his pen hand froze and our eyes locked.

Paget and I have teamed for five years. After a certain period of time, you develop this telepathy. Insignificant things trigger a red flare. An observation, a sensation, a word. *Drama.*

"Edna, I wonder if I could take another quick peek at your Marco Polo Duck?" Paget said.

"Certainly, young man. We can't leave the oven open long, however. We must simmer."

Paget peered in and tapped the floor of the oven with a finger. When he withdrew it, there was a gray, powdery residue on the tip. Paget was no longer gawking, awestruck, or even smiling.

In a kitchen I was a stranger in a strange land, but my training kicked in. I began doing my job, observing as a detective rather than as a guest of Edna's. Her sink was as empty and spiffy as a sink in a cleanser commercial. For a dish supposedly as complicated to whip up as it would be to fire the duck to the moon, you'd imagine the sink would be piled to the ceiling with pots and bowls and silverware, wouldn't you?

"Edna," Paget said softly. "We'll get out of your hair soon. My partner has to go downstairs to the car. While he's there, I'd be grateful if I could jot down your recipe for the Marco Polo Duck."

"I'd be delighted," Edna said without a change of inflection or the dimming by a single watt of her glorious smile. "I strongly recommend an organically raised duck. On the south side of the city is a butcher who—"

I took my cue and was out the door. Jotting down that recipe would be like jotting down *War and Peace*. Paget was stalling for a bunch of time—enough time for me to browse the file. I didn't need much. I knew what I was hunting for. Paget had a hunch, but he needed solid ground to rest it on. Wilson—bless him and his meticulous notes! I was back upstairs before they'd cleaned their organic duck.

I'd lugged the file upstairs for effect, fifteen pounds of yellowing paper. I sat on the living room couch without being invited and plunked the file on Edna's coffee table. Paget deduced by my bulging eyes and flushed expression that we had something. He flipped his notebook shut, pocketed it, and asked Edna to have a seat. She sat and he read her her rights.

"Oh dear," she said. "Why on earth would I require the services of an attorney?"

I rolled the mass of paper·back to the crucial page and said, "Detective Sergeant Wilson visited you at your home approximately eleven months ago. He was investigating a downtown bank robbery. A woman resembling the person known as Ma Barker was allegedly spotted exiting a bus in front of your apartment building. Detective Sergeant Wilson interviewed you."

"Well, perhaps," Edna said, frowning and stroking her chin. "Perhaps he did. My mind wanders and my memory isn't what it used to be."

"You stated you were home the entire day," I said, paraphrasing Wilson. "Your son and daughter-in-law were coming to dinner. You were preparing pork tenderloin with apple-rhubarb sauce, a complex, time-consuming dish."

"Lemon juice will prevent the apple from discoloring," Edna advised.

Paget studied the finger he had tapped the hot oven with. He hadn't cleaned off the gray residue.

"Edna," he said sadly. "Why do you rob banks?"

"Good Lord," said an aghast Edna Bemis. "Was I hearing correctly?"

"Did your drama classes do well, Edna?" I asked. "I'll bet they put on school plays worth the price of the ticket."

She couldn't resist the praise. "Indeed they did. My kids won district honors every year. Our production of *Death of a Salesman* in 1974 is still mentioned as an example of excellence."

"Led by an example of excellence," I said.

Edna smiled despite herself.

Paget continued to study that finger. He said, "A self-cleaning oven cleans at eight hundred degrees."

He glanced at me for confirmation. The oven in my apartment doesn't self-clean or otherwise. My feeling was that an oven should be properly broken in, with a nice crust, like the bowl of a pipe. I nodded grimly. "Yeah. Eight hundred degrees. Your stove was as hot as a firecracker. Which made your kitchen toasty too."

"Any foreign material is reduced to—" Paget raised the finger.

"To gray dust," I said knowledgeably.

"You couldn't possibly have had your Marco Polo Duck in an oven that hot," Paget said. "It'd be a cinder."

"You were observed in the alley behind the bank today," I said. "You observed the person observing you. Edna, do you have a ready-made alibi in case someone picks up your trail? Do you have an exotic dish that ties you down to your kitchen set to go? Was that the situation eleven months ago with Wilson and the roast pork?"

Edna Bemis did not reply.

"Your kitchen is as spick-and-span as the rest of the unit," I said.

"I hate a mess," Edna said.

"So you couldn't've been assembling the duck thing," I said. "You were establishing an appearance, but where did that duck in the oven come from?"

"The freezer," Edna said. "Partially prepared for such a contingency and heated in the microwave."

"Marco Polo Duck. *Microwaved!*" Paget said, shaking his head, the color leaving his face.

"My husband died several years ago," Edna volunteered. "He had a lingering illness. The bills aren't paid off yet."

"Edna, where is today's loot?" I asked.

"I'm glad you asked," she said. "A careless police search would create a *dreadful* mess. Inside my vacuum cleaner bag."

"There must have been alternatives for you," Paget said.

Edna Bemis's sweet warm smile returned. "I'll admit it—I enjoyed the excitement too."

We called for backup, officers to keep an eye on the place until a search warrant was issued. We took Edna in and booked her, then clocked out before the media arrived. The brass enjoy cameras and microphones. We don't. We went by Edna's apartment to see how the search crew was doing. Naturally they didn't turn up a weapon, but they found racing forms, binoculars, and a clubhouse pass. Could be Edna's problem wasn't a dead husband. It was lame horses.

We stopped off for a drink, to celebrate. Paget ordered a glass of wine. French. I splurged too, going for an imported beer.

Paget sniffed his wineglass. "Woodsy."

"Whatever you say," I said. "It's all sour grape juice to me. How do you think the prosecuting attorney will go?"

"He'll nail her in court and ask for the minimum sentence."

I agreed. "If he wants to be reelected, he will. First thing in the morning, you and I should check to see if the son and his wife were expected for dinner."

"We'll probably find they were. Tonight and the other thirteen dates too."

"She made up the half-cooked meal in advance, threw it in the freezer, and nuked it when she heard footsteps."

"Coinciding with her oven cleanings, so the oven would be preheated on short notice," Paget said. "By the way, where's lunch tomorrow? It's your turn to pick."

"The bowling alley," I said. "They have fantastic chili dogs."

Paget sipped his wine. "There is no god."

A Romance in the Rockies

K. K. Beck

I first met Ursula Destinoy-Pinchot in August of 1927 on board ship. She was sailing to America with her mother, an old school friend of my aunt Hermione. Gladys Destinoy-Pinchot was an American woman who had married a rich Englishman and gone completely English. My aunt said she even rode to the hounds sidesaddle!

Poor Ursula was a dowdy, horsey sort of girl in clothes that were just all wrong for a girl our age. Whether they were too young for her or too old for her it was hard to say; they were clearly designed to make her seem unattractive. Ursula's mother was afraid of fortune hunters, you see.

So of course, on board ship, Ursula, dowdy clothes and all, fell immediately into the clutches of a bogus French count, which, I must admit, managed to do wonders for her complexion.

In any case, I was surprised to see her exactly a year later in the lobby of the Chateau Lake Louise in the Canadian Rockies. Ursula seemed transformed. I first spotted her striding with confidence across the lobby in fashionably boyish and sporty attire—jodhpurs and a vivid sweater and a felt hat at a clever angle that covered what seemed to be bobbed hair.

"Look," I said to my aunt as we stood before the registration desk. "There's Ursula."

Aunt Hermione fumbled for her pince-nez, which she kept connected to a brooch on her lapel with a chain. "Where?" she said.

"Over there," I said, remembering not to point. I used my shoulder to indicate a group of sofas situated in front of a stunning picture window, affording a view of the incredible turquoise lake, the dazzling white glacier, and the looming rocky peaks. "See? She's wearing—"

And then I saw something shocking enough to render me speechless.

"Where?" prompted Aunt Hermione, who had now placed her spectacles on her nose.

"Over there," I said, nonplussed. "Slapping that young man."

Ursula—and I was now certain it was she—had bent over the young man who had been sitting with his back to the window reading the paper, and spoken to him, and when he rose, with a courteous but rather bemused expression, she had slapped his face. There wasn't anything playful about that slap. It was a regular wallop.

He looked, quite naturally, shocked, and stood there with one hand on his cheek, as if to see whether she had actually struck him.

"My goodness," said Aunt Hermione. "Slapping him in one of the public rooms." She shook her head slightly. "Not that it would have been all that much better, I suppose, to have slapped him in privacy."

Ursula was now coming toward us at a pretty good clip. Without hesitation, I stepped forward as she passed. I suppose it was rather forward of me to insinuate myself into her little melodrama, but I couldn't help myself.

"Ursula," I said. "Is everything all right?" Which was, of course, a silly thing to ask. Clearly, everything wasn't all right.

She stopped and her eyebrows shot up with surprise. I

thought I detected the beginning of tears, and her cheeks had bright spots of color in them. "Iris Cooper," she said, startled. And then she asked rhetorically, "Aren't men beasts?"

"Of course they are, dear," said my aunt. "Iris, go with Ursula. Get her a cup of coffee or something. I'll see you later in our room." Aunt Hermione is very kind, and of course she was sincere, but I knew also that she hoped I would get all the grim details about Ursula's little contretemps.

Just then, the object of Ursula's wrath came up to us—rather nervously, of course. Aunt Hermione glared at him and he winced a little, then bowed his head to her slightly and coughed. "I believe, madame," he said, "that there has been a terrible misunderstanding. Are you this lady's mother?" He indicated Ursula with his now neatly rolled up newspaper. There was something rather defensive about the gesture, as if he were prepared to ward off any further slaps with this makeshift weapon. In fact, he seemed like a perfectly respectable young man: fresh-faced with neat hair parted in the center, a stiff collar, and a sober dark suit. He spoke with an English accent.

"Oh really," said Ursula. "Don't be absurd. You've certainly met Mother. How *can* you have forgotten!" She took my arm and hustled me away. In full retreat, I looked back over my shoulder and saw the young man take a tentative step after us, then step back and address my aunt.

A moment later, Ursula and I were sitting on a rustic bench near the lake's edge. Even up close, it retained its remarkable turquoise color. The lake was a jewel in a setting of startling peaks, blanketed partway up with forests of lodgepole pine, then, above the timberline, reaching to the clouds in sheer masses of opalescent rock. Ursula apparently noticed that the natural beauty of the place had distracted me, for she said a little peevishly, "Yes, yes. I know it's incredibly beautiful. That just makes it all worse somehow."

I patted her hand while the poor thing snuffled herself to a stop, and presently I learned what had happened.

Ursula had been here with her mother for several weeks.

She had apparently fallen in love with the young man in the lobby, who was an artist named Hugh Kent. "Not a famous artist or anything," she said rather apologetically, which irritated me, as it implied she thought she deserved a famous one. "In fact, the starving kind. He was living in a tent, in the government tourist park. But we didn't know that right away, because he came up to the hotel in evening clothes one evening, and we assumed he was a guest. Mother said that he was posing as a gentleman, in hopes of meeting some heiress. Mother's always worried that someone will marry me for my money. I believe it's because that's why she married father."

Ursula blew her nose.

"And God knows *they* don't get on. We've been traveling the world for a year now, Iris, and she doesn't seem to miss him in the least. So I suppose I shouldn't let anyone marry me for my money."

"Are you saying you slapped Hugh Kent because he was living in a tent and dressed for dinner?" I said, indignant at such snobbery. "I believe Sargent came here to paint and lived in a tent. I don't know whether he dressed for dinner."

"No," said Ursula, "I slapped Hugh because he stole my pearls. At least, I think he did. He must have. But I haven't told Mother yet. It's all too terrible. I suppose she was right about him. I hate it when she's right."

"You must call the police," I said.

"I can't," said Ursula. "I would have to tell them he was in my room."

"Oh," I said.

"It's not what you think," she replied. "One day we were climbing with the Swiss guides we have here, and then he wanted to change into a lounge suit for the tea dance, and I gave him the key to my room so he could change. My mother found out about it, I'm afraid, and she said he was trying to compromise me. The horrid part is, she also said he could have stolen our jewelry."

"And you think he stole the pearls then?"

"Yes, I do. I hate to believe it, but it's the only explanation. Anyway, the next day he was gone. My mother told me she had offered him money to cease his attentions to me. It was humiliating." She leaned over confidentially. "She did that once before. Do you remember the Comte de la Roche?"

"Yes, but wasn't he engaged to somebody else?"

"Marjorie Klepp, the cotter pin heiress. But Mother offered him money just in case. And he took it. She didn't tell me that until four days ago. She then told me Hugh was also happy to take it. I hate money. It's all anyone ever thinks about. Then, Hugh had the nerve to write me, saying he knew Mummy forbade us to meet but that we should meet secretly and that he wanted to marry me."

"Did you reply?"

"Yes. I didn't tell him I knew he'd taken her money. I told him I never wanted to see him again, that we were from two different worlds, and that surely he could understand that it would be unsuitable for me to be the wife of a starving artist. I was as condescending as I could possibly be."

Ursula began to weep again. "I had to say it, so he wouldn't think I really cared for him. Hugh was wonderful and he did love me. I know it. Underneath it all. But then he allowed Mother to buy him off.

"After I wrote the letter and sent it down the mountain with the bellboy, I discovered the pearls were gone. The cad, pretending to be a pure artist with no thought of crass material things! Oh, Iris, will anybody suitable ever really love me?"

"Of course," I said, patting her on the hand again. I didn't tell her I often wondered the same thing. "But we must get those pearls back. Are they very valuable?"

"Very," said Ursula. "They came from Daddy's family. Three strands of graduated pearls with a diamond and ruby clasp. Oh, Iris, what should I do?"

"Call the Mounties," I said. "Your mother is bound to find out."

"I think I still love him," said Ursula.

I ignored this. "Why weren't they in the safe?" I said.

"I was going to wear them that afternoon. I took them off when we went up the mountain, and Mother asked me about them. I told her that I hid them in the pocket of my peach-colored pajamas in the bottom drawer. The chamber maid would hardly go through all the pockets of my pajamas, would she? The horrible thing is, I had that conversation in front of Hugh."

"Did the room show any sign of having been searched?"

"None. Whoever took them went directly to the pajamas in question and took out the pearls. You see, it had to be Hugh."

"Well, if you won't ask for them back, I will," I said. I actually relished the idea of threatening the louse with the Royal Canadian Mounted Police. I had seen plenty of them, handsome in their scarlet jackets and khaki hats, on the streets of Banff and was sure one or two of them could be summoned to the hotel in short order. Ursula was awfully cavalier about those pearls, I thought. Of course, she'd just said she didn't care about money, but I thought it was horrible to let Hugh steal her jewelry after breaking her heart.

"Oh, Iris," said Ursula, "would you? Do you think you can do it without Mother knowing?"

"Of course I can," I said. It was easier to convince Ursula that I was plucky and clever enough to carry it off than it was to convince myself. "Why don't you go up to your room and bathe your face in cool water. You don't want to get red and blotchy or anything, do you? I'll see if I can corner him and have it out with him and get the pearls back before dinner." It had already occurred to me that he very likely had them on his person. After all, he couldn't exactly sell them in one of the little towns around here—Banff or Lake Louise, or even Calgary—without attracting immediate attention. And surely he wouldn't keep them in a tent.

I went over the phrases in my mind. After confronting him with the theft, I would demand the pearls back immediately, no questions asked. (Not that there were any questions to ask, really.) If he said he had them somewhere else (a hollow log in the forest or something), I would remind him that the Mounties could seal off this place very easily, either by road or rail, and he hadn't a prayer of leaving with the pearls.

I would give him, I decided, no more than a couple of hours to come up with them. The morning train from Banff had already left, and the other wouldn't leave until late tonight.

I also decided to conduct our interview in some public place. If Hugh Kent were a desperate criminal, he'd be perfectly capable of hitting me over the head in order to make good his escape. Which brought up the most obvious question, of course. Why hadn't he made good his escape? Why had he appeared back in the hotel, cool as a cucumber?

I hadn't a moment to lose. After having been slapped, he might be planning to lie low or find some way out by car. I began to wander through the hotel, looking for Hugh Kent.

It is startling to find such a hotel in a pristine, remote spot like Lake Louise. You would expect to find it in the middle of any cosmopolitan city, with its nine stories and its sprawling wings, covering an area the size of several city blocks. Within its large, high-ceilinged rooms, I heard a half dozen languages. Many of the guests were dressed as elegantly and as formally as you would find anywhere, yet others were dressed for alpinism and trail riding. Several examples of the taxidermist's art—heads of buffalo and moose—presided over the rooms where women paraded in beautiful dresses and jewels. And everywhere the spectacular vistas brought into the hotel through huge picture windows dwarfed the mere mortals who had come to worship nature in complete luxury.

When I finally found Mr. Kent, it was outside underneath a gay red-and-white canvas umbrella at a table by the poolside terrace. The pool, which artificially matches the beautifully colored lake, is open to the sky above, but the terrace is enclosed on the sides by elegant arches, where more picture windows keep out the cool mountain breezes but let in the scenery. Mr. Kent, however, seemed oblivious to that scenery. He was having what appeared to be a very friendly tête-à-tête with my aunt Hermione.

When I came to the table, I gave him a cold look, but Aunt Hermione didn't seem to notice. "Iris, dear," she said, "this young man is Mr.—"

"Kent, I believe," I said, narrowing my eyes to let him know I was on to him.

"Yes. Mr. Kent has the most interesting story to tell, and I believe it may shed some light on poor Ursula's curious action just now. This is my niece, Iris," she said to him, and turning back to me she said, "Sit down, dear. We're having tea."

Mr. Kent rose and bowed. "My name," he said, "is Rupert Kent."

"Rupert?" I said, sitting down. "Don't you mean Hugh?"

"That's just it, darling," said my aunt. "Poor Mr. Kent gets mistaken for his brother all the time. They are twins, you see. Just like Charlotte Mannering's adorable babies."

"My brother and I," said Mr. Kent, "are as alike as two peas in a pod." He sighed, as if he weren't particularly pleased about the fact.

"Ursula never mentioned a twin," I said.

"I have only just arrived," said Mr. Kent. "Looking for Hugh, actually. I've been following him all across Canada. I'm afraid Hugh has been a trial to our family, and I'm trying to catch up with him and let him know my father has found him a good position on a coffee plantation in Kenya. We feel it may be just the sort of place where he could find a fresh start for himself."

"Naturally," said my aunt, "Mr. Kent and I are curious as to what made Ursula want to slap him. Not that it is any of our business, actually, but poor Mr. Kent seemed so distressed."

"I'm afraid," said Mr. Kent, "that the resemblance between us has caused all sorts of trouble for me over the years. Stealing fruit from trees, bullying other boys, teasing the girls—so often, I would be blamed." He touched his cheek. "This won't have been the first blow I took for Hugh. But your aunt is wrong. I wouldn't presume to want to know what trouble the young lady may have had. I only hope to have the opportunity to apologize to her on behalf of the family for any ungentlemanly behavior to which she may have been subjected."

"I think you're displaying excessive delicacy of feeling," said my aunt firmly. "You are not responsible for what your brother has done." She turned to me. "What exactly"—she hesitated for a moment, then plunged on—*"has* he done, Iris? Were you able to find out?"

"Yes," said Mr. Kent, who had abandoned his delicacy quite quickly, at least in the matter of discovering what brought on the slap. "What did he do?"

I didn't reveal all the humiliating details about Ursula's mother having bought him off. I considered telling him about the pearls, but then I stopped. Perhaps it would compromise Ursula somehow to say Hugh had been in her room. "Maybe Ursula will tell you," I said.

He leaned forward eagerly. "Do you think?" he said, "you could arrange a meeting?"

"Certainly," said my aunt. "Iris, go find Ursula and make her promise not to strike Mr. Kent again. This one, anyway."

I found Ursula in her room, which was evidently part of a suite she shared with her mother. In fact, that formidable lady was at the open door of the room, snapping at a tall man in striped trousers who appeared to be the hotel manager. "Absolutely absurd," she continued. "I won't hear another thing about it." Gladys Destinoy-Pinchot was up to her old high-handed ways. Aunt Hermione said Gladys had been poor as a young girl, wearing old hand-me-downs, and the bitterness of the experience had shaped her behavior now that she had wealth and position.

Mrs. Destinoy-Pinchot now turned to me, her face still fierce and red. "It's Hermione's niece, isn't it?" she said. "Ursula told me you were here. So nice to know there are respectable people about."

"My aunt was glad to know you were here," I said, trying to inject some warmth into my voice. It occurred to me then that I could use my aunt to decoy Ursula's mother so I could spirit Ursula away to confront Mr. Kent. After a certain amount of maneuvering, I did just that, arranging to go off with Ursula, and telling her mother that my aunt would be up to see her soon.

I told Ursula the story of the Kent twins—one apparently good and the other apparently evil—in the elevator on the way down. She seemed quite taken aback by the whole thing, which is understandable. When we all met again at the table by the pool, she offered Mr. Kent her hand and held his for a while, gazing into his eyes. "It's remarkable," she said.

I explained to my aunt that she must keep Gladys Destinoy-Pinchot occupied for a while, and she agreed. Implied was the understanding that I would fill her in on all that transpired. I knew that *she* knew that I knew all about Ursula and why she had slapped this young man. When I was able to tell her about the stolen pearls and Ursula's mother writing out checks to her daughter's suitors, I knew she'd be even more fascinated.

Ursula, Mr. Kent, and I all sat down rather awkwardly. "I'm sorry if my brother did anything to distress you," he said earnestly. "I am afraid he is often careless. He has the artistic temperament, which I do not have. But he is not really a bad fellow."

Ursula continued to stare at him. "I can't believe you're not Hugh," she said.

He sighed. "I am not," he said. He leaned forward, apparently fascinated by Ursula. "I don't mean to pry, but was my brother paying you attentions that—that is—well, I can understand it, I really can. You're a jolly nice-looking girl."

Ursula gazed right back at him. I cleared my throat to break their mood. "I think you should tell him, Ursula. He may help you get them back."

"Get what back?" said Mr. Kent, looking alarmed.

Ursula gave me a sidelong look. Then she said, "My pearls are gone and I believe your brother took them."

"But how?" he began, looking so genuinely alarmed that I felt instantly sorry for him.

"It doesn't matter how," I said quickly. "Ursula's mother doesn't know, and I propose that you help me find your brother and get them back before there's any fuss. I'm sure you'll do what you can to help avoid having your name connected with any scandal."

"It's impossible," said Mr. Kent. "Hugh would never steal anything."

"You said he stole fruit as a boy," I said.

"Yes, but he's not a thief. He may have led a rather bohemian life—while I chose a more regulated existence in the family firm. But he's not a thief." He fell silent for a moment and looked down at the ground. He seemed to be thinking. "At least I can't imagine him doing anything like that." He passed a hand over his eyes. "This is terrible."

"I know it is a shock to you," said Ursula. She went around to the side of his chair and put an arm on his shoulder. It seemed such a familiar gesture, but perhaps, having known his brother, she thought she knew him.

Presently he straightened up. "It is remarkable," she said. You part your hair in the center, and he parts his on the side, but you have the same little counterclockwise cowlick." She began to sniffle a little.

"Please don't distress yourself, Miss Destinoy-Pinchot," said Rupert Kent. He reached for a handkerchief in his breast pocket and handed it to her. "There must be a way to get those pearls back. Are you sure they aren't simply mislaid?"

"Oh, I don't know," said Ursula. "I'm so confused." It was clear Ursula had taken to him. They seemed to be consoling each other about their disappointment in Hugh and didn't notice at all when I excused myself. I was eager to find Aunt Hermione, but it was some time before we were reunited and were able to compare stories.

As we were unpacking, I told my aunt all about Ursula's pearls.

Aunt Hermione was naturally shocked. "And they haven't called the police?"

"Mrs. Destinoy-Pinchot doesn't even know about it. I told Ursula I'd try and get them back from Hugh Kent, but then he turned out to be Rupert."

"Perhaps Rupert, if he finds his brother, can get them

back," she said. "Such a nice young man. How sad that his brother is such a rascal. In any case, Ursula will have to let her mother know eventually." Aunt Hermione looked a little nervous. "I feel that perhaps Gladys would think it my duty to tell her what I know."

"Oh," I said hastily, "Ursula would be devastated. She told me in confidence, not knowing that I confide so much in you, and I told you in confidence—"

"Naturally I won't say a word," she said. "But I wish the pearls could be found. It would be terrible if Ursula made trouble for the maids, knowing that the young man took them."

"There's more," I said, filling her in on how Ursula's mother had bought off two suitors.

"What a dreadful thing for poor Ursula," said Aunt Hermione. "Even if Gladys felt it were necessary to buy off these men, why on earth would she tell the poor girl? It is humiliating.

"To be honest, Iris, I think she would prefer Ursula never marry. I believe that underneath it all she'd like to keep her to herself so that she might have a companion for her travels. Did you know they'd been traveling around for a year, staying first with relatives and now drifting from hotel to hotel?"

"Not much of a life for Ursula," I said. I love travel, but I was also eager to get back to Stanford in the fall.

"I told Gladys that she must make sure Ursula gets to spend some time with young people. I told her I never allow myself to cling to you and prevent you from enjoying yourself with people your age."

"You are a wonderful aunt," I said.

"And you are a wonderful niece. I never need to worry about you. You are so sensible for a girl of twenty."

I hate it when my aunt says that. I am sensible, but I don't like to have it pointed out too much. It doesn't strike me as a particularly charming quality. Aunt Hermione must have noticed my slight displeasure, because she added, "You don't mind being sensible, do you? I used to worry that you had been cheated of a normal girlhood by early responsibilities. Your father hasn't always understood that."

This was a reference to the fact that my mother died when I was young and I have looked out after my brothers and sisters a lot. But Aunt Hermione had insisted I go away to college, and she's taken me all around the world, too.

"You have done lots to make sure I haven't turned into a hopeless domestic drudge," I said, embracing her. "Father would have been perfectly glad to have me manage the house and help him with secretarial work forever."

"And Gladys, I believe, would be perfectly content to have Ursula be her mousy little browbeaten companion forever," replied Aunt Hermione. "I arranged for us all to dine together. I hope you don't mind. That way, we can set an example of how one chaperones the modern girl." Aunt Hermione pinched some waves into her blue marcelled hair.

"If Ursula is running around getting tangled up with lounge lizards and slapping men in hotel lobbies," she went on, "Gladys is partly to blame. Won't it be nice to have a little sherry before dinner? I understand they had Prohibition here in Alberta too, but wisely abandoned the experiment."

In the dining room, the sherry, the magnificent views (there seemed to be one from every point of the hotel, all visible through the startling huge windows), the five-piece orchestra, and the festive buzz of conversation combined to make me almost forget about the Destinoy-Pinchots and their troubles, but soon Ursula and her mother joined us.

Ursula was wearing a girlish white dress, but now that she was hatless I could see she had indeed bobbed her hair, and she was wearing a little light lipstick, too, and had penciled her brows. All in all, it was a vast improvement over the Ursula of a year ago. Maybe her American relatives had had some influence. Her mother, however, looked like one of Queen Victoria's ladies-in-waiting, in stiff corseting and bottle-green damask silk.

"Isn't this a wonderful hotel?" said my aunt when we were all settled in. "We were for a while at the Banff Springs

Hotel—also very nice of course, quite luxurious—but the setting here is quite another thing, isn't it? Even more remote and lovely, if such a thing is possible."

"We were there too," said Ursula with a sulky little flounce. "Mother didn't like it. She probably won't like it here, either."

"Cheeky, that's what they were," said Mrs. Destinoy-Pinchot gruffly. I imagined she expected a lot of feudal servants pulling their forelocks. I couldn't imagine anything worse than being her traveling companion.

"Really?" said my aunt. "I have found everything in both hotels to have been absolutely first class. Here, of course, it is rather sportier, which I thought might make a change for Iris." I recognized that she had begun telling her old friend how to behave toward Ursula. "It's so important that young people be allowed some scope. Lots of fresh air and exercise and of course wholesome companionship of others their age—"

Mrs. Destinoy Pinchot narrowed her eyes. "Have to be on your guard, Hermione. Plenty of adventurers about. People whom one does not know. Riffraff. Ever since the war, standards have slackened."

Aunt Hermione began to speak, but before she had a chance, Mrs. Destinoy-Pinchot, who appeared to be staring fiercely over my shoulder, began to tremble with anger.

"Ursula," she hissed, "there is that Kent person again. You are to cut him dead, do you hear?"

"Oh, for goodness' sakes, Gladys," said Aunt Hermione without her usual gentleness. "That isn't Hugh Kent. It's his twin brother Rupert. I met him earlier. They are twins but entirely different people. Whatever quarrel you may have had with his brother—"

Mr. Kent bowed rather stiffly toward us, and Ursula, my aunt, and I all waved gaily at him. He smiled rather sweetly and sat down at a table by himself. He had brought a book.

"Oh, look, he's eating alone," said my sociable aunt "Let's ask him to join us."

"Absolutely not," said Mrs. Destinoy-Pinchot. "If he is a relative of that odious—"

"I'm sure he'd rather eat alone than be insulted by Mother," said Ursula brusquely. Her mother gave a grim little smile, as if pleased with her powers to repel.

"I don't know what has passed between you and the young man's brother," said my aunt untruthfully but with great dignity nevertheless. "However, there is such a thing, Gladys, as being too exclusive."

Ironically, it was just at this point that a rather flashily dressed couple came up to our table and greeted Mrs. Destinoy-Pinchot like old friends. Mr. and Mrs. Cutter were Americans in their forties. He wore evening clothes with an exaggerated cut and a lot of brilliantine in his hair, and had a wide and friendly smile. Mrs. Cutter was olive skinned with dark hair arranged in elaborate spit curls, dangling earrings that I supposed were rhinestones, a scarlet dress revealing a lot of décolletage, sheer stockings, and scarlet evening slippers.

To my astonishment, Mrs. Destinoy-Pinchot was actually gracious, introducing them and falling in with their suggestion she and my aunt play bridge with them after dinner.

Ursula gave me a little look of triumph. We could be alone this evening. I hoped to find out more from her about Rupert Kent. Perhaps he could help us find his brother, and the pearls.

"Thank goodness those awful Cutters appeared," she said, when her mother and my aunt had left. "I can't think what she sees in them. They're bridge fiends and she's had them up in our room at all hours playing cards. Now we can talk."

We decided on a stroll by the lake, which was lovely by moonlight. Ursula had plenty to tell me. "Rupert has been so kind. He's appalled at Hugh's behavior and says he can't believe he took the pearls. I also learned more about the Kents. The father is a clergyman and Rupert got a nice job in a bank from his uncle, and I gather he has a pretty solid future." She sighed. "He's just as handsome as his brother, but more respectable."

"Ursula," I said, "it's every girl's dream. A romance with an attractive but unprincipled suitor falls all to pieces, and you get a second chance with a better version of the same man."

She sighed, and fingered the chiffon scarf she wore over her shoulders. "I rather liked it that Hugh was artistic," she said. It was clear from her wistful tone that the pearls were the last things on Ursula's mind.

"It is rather unsettling," she continued, "that they look so alike. It is hard not to believe they are one person. I think Rupert's face might be a little fuller, but otherwise they are exactly alike."

"Mirror images," I said, thinking of the Mannering twins and their bald, fuzzy heads. "Ursula," I said suddenly, "perhaps they are the same person. What was it you said yesterday about his cowlick?"

But she was unable to answer, as Mr. Kent came up to us just then. Ursula beamed happily at him.

There was no point being subtle with these two. "Ursula says you have the same cowlick as your brother. She said it went counterclockwise. Is that so?"

"It's at the back of my head," he said, startled. "I wouldn't know which way it went."

"Twins," I said, "are mirror images of one another. If one twin's cowlick goes clockwise, the other must go counterclockwise. I noticed that on baby twins I know as they were sitting side by side."

Ursula gazed at him, startled. "But it can't be," she said. "His face is fuller."

"An illusion, caused by the center part," I said. "Ursula," I said firmly, "yesterday Mr. Kent offered you his handkerchief. Do you still have it?"

She blushed. "It's in my bag," she said. "I meant to return it." I imagine she had meant to keep it for sentimental reasons. Poor Ursula had fallen in love with the same man twice.

She began to hand it back to him, but I snatched it. "Let me see that," I said. There, embroidered neatly in the corner, were the initials H.K. I showed it Ursula, trying to keep the triumph out of my gesture.

"You should have called yourself Harry," I said, flinging his handkerchief at him.

"How could you?" said Ursula, who had begun to sniffle. He handed her the handkerchief she had handed me and I had just handed him, and she started to wipe her eyes, but then she gazed at the monogram and burst into tears.

"I didn't know what else to do," he said. "Your mother told me to leave you alone, and you wrote me that dreadful letter saying I wasn't good enough for you, just a starving artist, so I came back as myself."

"As yourself?" I said.

"Well, in a way. We're perfectly respectable people and I do work in my uncle's bank, or I will soon. I just took a long holiday living outdoors and painting before I settled down into the bank. But you thought I was so disreputable I thought I might have a chance if I came back transformed somewhat. Stiffer collar, a little less of the bohemian. And I checked into the hotel and abandoned the tent."

His voice took on a little anger, and I liked him for it. "I shouldn't have done it. I'm not ashamed of my painting, or of living in a tent. But I fell in love with you, and you've turned me into a liar and a hypocrite. I suppose it's the influence of that mother of yours. Well never mind, I'll go now."

"What about the pearls?" I said.

"I didn't take her wretched pearls. Do you think I'd be such a fool as to come back if I had?"

"No, I don't think you would have," I said.

"I came back," he said, "because I am disgustedly besotted with Ursula. I suppose I shall get over it." He turned to her and said, "You know, Ursula, you never should have slapped me. How could you have thought I took those pearls?"

Ursula's lip trembled a little. "You were the only one who knew where they were. Besides, that isn't why I slapped you."

"Why," he said, exasperated, "did you slap me? Because I proposed?"

"Ursula thinks her mother bought you off," I said bluntly.

"Did she tell you that?" he demanded. "I think I'll go have a word with the old dragon." And with that, he turned on his heel to leave.

But he hadn't gone more than a step before Aunt Hermione joined us. She nodded at Ursula and Mr. Kent, who both tried to wipe away the intensity of feeling from their features. Being English, they succeeded pretty well.

Aunt Hermione was carrying my Chinese shawl. "Iris, I've brought you a wrap. It's so chilly."

"Aren't you playing bridge?" I said.

"I'm dummy," she said, "so I excused myself to bring you this. But I'm really looking for a fourth to replace me. To be quite honest, I had no idea that Gladys was playing for such high stakes," she said. "Out of my league, I'm afraid."

The stakes must have been high for her to have said that. Aunt Hermione was a terrible bridge player, but she didn't know it. She was always overbidding and blaming the resulting shambles on bad cards.

"It was rather awkward, as Gladys and I were going down badly."

"Ursula," I said, "didn't you say your mother's been playing a lot of bridge with the Cutters?"

"Yes. They were at the Banff Springs Hotel and they played there and they turned up here after we did."

"It's all beginning to make sense," I said. "Has she been losing a lot?"

"I don't know," said Ursula. "I hope not. Father said he wouldn't give her more than her allowance to take care of her bridge debts any longer. They had an awful row about it right before we left England. I think that's why we've stayed away so long."

"I saw the manager up in their room today," I told my aunt. "Now that I think about it, he was probably asking for payment."

"It's so awful," said Ursula, putting a hand to her face. "The manager at the Banff Springs came up to our room and demanded we settle the bill too," she said. "Thank goodness

Mummy's allowance came through the next day, and we left soon after." She turned to Hugh. "This is so disgraceful. What must you think of us?"

"Never mind that," he said. "I happen to be an excellent bridge player. Do you think your mother would consent to accept me as a fourth?"

"A perfect idea," said Aunt Hermione, arranging my shawl around my shoulders. "Come with me and I shall arrange it."

"Don't," said Ursula. "You may not be able to afford it."

"It sounds as if your mother can't either," he said.

"Mother would never allow it," said Ursula. "Remember how horrid she was at dinner?"

"Listen," I said to my aunt Hermione. "I have an idea. If Mrs. Destinoy-Pinchot seems the least bit reluctant, look her in the eye very firmly and say this: "I just saw Ursula in that lovely white dress. It would look so nice with pearls." And then give her a real fish-eye. I think she may just do whatever you say."

Aunt Hermione repeated my phrase. Bless her heart, she had such confidence in my cleverness, she never even asked for an explanation, although I knew she expected one later. She bristled pleasurably at the hint of intrigue and led Mr. Kent away with her.

"Come with me, Ursula," I said.

"Where are we going?" she said. She looked so vague and bemused there was nothing to do but order her around.

"To try and get your pearls," I said.

"Where?"

"Where they should have been all along," I said. "Where your mother said they belonged. The hotel safe."

Ten minutes later, a clerk was handing over a velvet case and Ursula was signing for it. As I had instructed, she said she wanted the pearls her mother had placed there.

"I don't understand quite," she said, opening the case and looking at the pearls. I looked at them too. They were lovely, and if I were Ursula I would never have been so blasé about their disappearance.

"Hugh wasn't the only one who knew the pearls were in the pocket of your peach pajamas. He was there when you told the real thief. Your mother."

"Thank God he didn't take them," she said. It was clear that her mother's treachery wasn't as important to her as Hugh's innocence.

"Your mother was strapped for cash and wanted to bust up your romance. My bet is she decided to kill two birds with one stone. Drive a wedge between you and sell the pearls when she could. She'll deny it, of course." I was probably too blunt, but Ursula may as well know just what her mother was—if she hadn't guessed yet.

"You knew Hugh didn't take them," she said. "I'm so glad."

"Why would he have come back if he had?" I said. "Ursula, I think he cares for you very much. Impersonating himself was the act of a man desperately in love." It irked me a little that someone should do something so thrilling for someone like Ursula, who was nice enough but not terribly bright or anything, but I have noticed that men often fall in love with the dull, helpless sort of girl.

"It is rather thrilling, isn't it?" said Ursula.

"Yes," I said, trying not to appear envious. "I like the idea. The opposite of that Prisoner of Zenda thing. Instead of a double impersonating someone, someone impersonates a double."

"He is awfully clever, isn't he?" she said.

"It wasn't too clever to hand you a monogrammed handkerchief," I replied, "but I hope he is clever at cards."

A few days later, Aunt Hermione and I were having lunch, gazing, as usual, out the marvelous picture window. "Look," I said. "There is Ursula."

But this time she wasn't slapping Hugh. She was walking with him hand in hand.

"Such a nice man. And such a good bridge player. I shall never forget that scene when we went into the room after that bridge game." Aunt Hermione's eyes glistened at the memory. Ursula and my aunt and I had gone into the room just as the Cutters were handing over some crisp bills to Mr.

Kent and a pile of I.O.U's to Mrs. Destinoy-Pinchot. "The look of relief on her face," said my aunt. "I have no doubt the Cutters would have made it very unpleasant for her if she'd had to make them good. I think they are professional card sharps."

"I rather relished the look on her face when she saw those pearls around her daughter's neck," I said. "I was glad to see her squirm. And that transparent story about simply wanting to teach her daughter not to be careless with valuables! Even Ursula saw through that."

"It is better sometimes to allow foolish people such as Gladys to save face. I think she has been humbled a little, don't you? Her opposition to Mr. Kent seems to have vanished. She should go back home and patch things up with her husband. Besides, I think it's extremely likely she won't have Ursula as her traveling companion for too much longer." We looked out the window again. Hugh and Ursula were embracing, as the sun glinted off the glacier behind them and the turquoise water took on olive glints.

Aunt Hermione added, "Of course, she has a lot more money than he does, but taking his mother-in-law into account, it will come out about even." She smiled happily. Aunt Hermione believes things always work out for the best in the end, and I suppose I do too.

Checkout

Susan Dunlap

There's probably not one of you who doesn't have some expectations of the afterlife. Some of you ponder it more than others, of course. But I'll bet most of you are like me: you think of eternity as little as possible, and never as a reality. And yet, even you, if pressed, would come up with some picture of it.

But few of you would have the right one. I sure didn't.

Let me backtrack here, so you know who you're dealing with. I had no particular religious attachments. I'd flirted with a number of theologies in an academic sort of way, so if indeed there were many mansions in Heaven, I could have described a lot of the rooms (like a postmortem version of one of those tacky vacation inns with the Beethoven Bath, the Schubert Suite, the Liberace Lounge). I wouldn't have been surprised to come across a newly painted white hallway with a bright light at the end and a helluva suction. A clutch of departed Tibetan monks ready to lead me on a side tour through the Bardo of the Book of the Dead for forty-nine days before dispatching me into my next incarnation would have given me little more than a moment's surprise. Finding nothing at all wouldn't have shocked me. (Well, really, how could it? What would it have shocked?)

I had considered and altogether dismissed any Final Judgment—sheep baa-ing smugly at disgruntled goats.

Even so, had I discovered myself eye-to-eye with Saint Peter, I would have been prepared to become wing-to-wing with the heavenly host, or fork-to-pitchfork with guys advertising ham spread. Cartoon heaven, I understood. But I never, ever expected this.

Dead. I was definitely dead. How did I know? Once a woman has shuffled off the mortal coil, she knows. Trust me. And where was I? No white hallway, no glowing saint, wizened monk, or prodding devil. I couldn't make out my surroundings at all. I didn't know where I was, but what I was doing was standing in line. Standing in line, of all miserable things. I could have done that alive. I *had* done that alive. It had driven me crazy, queuing up in the bank behind ten other people, squatting down, checkbook on knee, trying to fill out the deposit slip with each check number and amount. All the time I'd be watching for the line to move, and when it did I'd madly scoop up my half-done checks and duck-walk forward, trying to keep the checks from flying (not to say bouncing) all over the bank. I'd perform the whole thigh-killing gymnastic exercise to avoid standing blankly in the line for half an hour with two thoughts slapping at me: Not only was I wasting time here (one), but (two) I'd shot ten minutes before I got here writing out those checks.

But forewarned is not forearmed. If I had ten checks the line moved like lightning and I got to the window with every one unsigned and unnumbered and the teller silently berating me for holding up the line. (I never stopped to consider what the people behind me thought. I'll bet they could have killed me.)

Killed me? Had they dispatched me into the Brinks funeral cortege? I was, after all, dead. But you don't die because you delay the bank line. If you did, CitiCorp would put in a mortuary next to the vault.

In any case I didn't want to waste time pondering how I died. Dead was dead. And I had more pressing problems: these damned lines.

Lines! Lines everywhere! I really did hate waiting in line. And not only in the bank. But the airport. All flights east from California leave at 7:00 A.M., as if there were one big gust of air per day off the Pacific. How many sag-eyed 6:15 A.M.s have I spent behind thirty people accompanied by suitcases with wheels, pull straps, and sections expandable in all directions. They had backpacks, shoe racks, cloth sacks, kiddie strollers, bags of crullers, giant umbrellas. And three carryons apiece, each the size of a ram, unshorn. And every single item was without the name and address labels the agent insisted they spend five extra minutes filling out. They inched forward to the two ticket counters, herding their luggage like flocks of sheep that multiplied as they moved. Our communal 7:00 A.M. departures grew closer. Behind me travelers pressed in tighter as if at the moment of truth proximity to the counter would count. Ahead of me the Bo Peeps, tickets between their teeth, thrust their heads at the airline clerk, and when he'd pulled the sodden tickets free, insisted the entirety of their luggage would fit in the overhead compartments, demanded window seats and a list of the nightshades and crucifiers in the vegetarian meals. "Every seat lands at the same time," I told them, perhaps a mite more curtly than I intended. If they'd paid attention and moved along, they wouldn't have forced me to actual rudeness. But did they ever appreciate my good sense and concern about expediting everyone's wait? Hardly. I know some of them could have killed me; they told me so.

I paused again. I had tickets for New York in my purse right now. Had I died at the airport? But no—no matter how irrational the rest of those travelers were, they weren't likely to miss their planes just for the satisfaction of offing me. Even if it would have meant freeing up a window seat and a special fish plate lunch. No, much as they might have liked, they hadn't done me in and tossed me on the luggage conveyer to eternity.

Anyway, no point in worrying about that now. I didn't

care how I died. What I wanted was to get out of this damned line. Lines, always lines; lines, life's penultimate example of stillness in motion.

The airport is bad, okay, but it's nothing to the true Purgatory: the California freeway. How many hours had I spent waiting in line just to get *on* the freeway, standing behind car after bus after truck waiting for that red light to turn green and admit the next vehicle to the slow lane? Enough people to populate Albania were driving on my freeway, and there was no need for them to be there! They weren't all going to work. Why couldn't those non–nine-to-fivers show a little consideration and stay home at rush hour? They had the whole rest of the day to dawdle on the road. It was bad enough to find the freeway jammed; I'd gotten used to that. I'd learned to force my way into traffic; it was a sport of sorts, eyeing the line of cars, "making" the drivers by how slowly they hit the gas, how far they lagged behind the car in front, how much wax and chrome adorned their own vehicle, and how desperate they were to protect it. Before a waivering wimp could blow his horns I'd spot cut in front with half an inch to spare and brakes squealing. And I'd heard enough hollers, seen enough clenched fists and digital birds flying to know what those wimps would like to have done to me.

Could I have been driving to the airport when I died? Rush hour starts before dawn on these freeways. Had I misjudged and cut in front of a truck without brakes or a lunatic with a rifle? But no. If there's one thing you can count on in rush hour, it's that no one's going fast enough to rear-end you into the hereafter. And freeway snipers don't snipe when they'll be stuck next to your corpse in traffic. No, indeed, my funeral cortege was not a first-gear-only affair in the diamond lane to Judgment.

Why was this question nagging me? It was like having a chatterer right behind you in line—one of those infuriatingly cheerful people who was sure everyone was doing his very best and there was a good reason why we were kept waiting. I dismissed the thought as summarily as I had them.

But neither the bank nor the freeway held the line I hated

most. I took a breath and listened. The air was chilly. I wished I'd died wearing a sweater. My feet hurt. Why couldn't I have succumbed in running shoes, or even sandals? It was like I'd just rushed here on the spur of the moment and stumbled onto line. I hadn't expected it to turn out to be *this* line. I couldn't quite make out the surroundings. Undertakers don't bury you with your glasses on, so in the hereafter reality is a bit fuzzy. Music I couldn't quite place played in the distance. I strained to hear, but the melody was too bland to register. Then it stopped, and a voice said over the loudspeaker, "Attention, shoppers."

Oh no, I was in the most infuriating line of all, the nine-items-or-less line in the supermarket! Nine items to eternity! The loudspeaker still slapped at my ears but I blocked out its words, a skill I'd mastered in life. Instead I focused on the mob in front of me. Clearly, this was not the Lucky markets of eternity where they'd open a new line if more than four people were waiting. There were at least twelve people ahead of me, and some of them were not holding little plastic baskets, but leaning on full-sized grocery carts. Fuzzy-eyed or not, even I could tell there were more than nine items in those carts. I glared at the miscreants. Would there never be justice? How many times had I called for a bolt of lightning to crash down and strike gluttons just like these with ten different edibles in their carts! (Were we too high up for lightning now? Not yet. And I was not likely to be unless long suffering was the heavenly criteria.) The checkout clerks know when customers plunk ten items on the counter. You'd think they'd send them packing to the full-cart line. If those gluttons got tossed out a couple times they'd learn. Which was just what I told a few of them (the ones I couldn't shame out of line. A good, loud voice can pique humiliation in the most callous lout, and the rest of the cowards in line behind are willing enough to form a chorus once they know they're not in danger.) The routed louts sputtered; they glared; a couple have even waited for me outside—

Surely, I wasn't murdered there—not in the supermarket —and dispatched in a cortege of grocery carts. But no, the louts wouldn't have dared—not in public, not and take the chance of someone walking off with their groceries.

Dammit, why did my mind keep coming back to that useless question? My foot was tapping, my blood boiling as it had so many times in lines just like this. There was nothing to do but stand and fume. And glance through the magazines and stick them back in the wrong holders. It had always pleased me, I remembered, to page through those periodicals for free. And here, to my left, was a copy of *Time (Is Up)*. It looked just like old Earth's *Time*. How many copies had I fingered through, glancing at the articles, checking the letters for well-known names, looking at the Milestones to see who had married, given birth, or died. Died!

I gave up. I sighed mightily and turned to the Milestone page and, skipping the happy occasions, moved right to the deaths.

I don't know what made me think I'd find my own passing there. I wasn't famous. But, in fact, there it was: DIED. ANN THOMPSON, 42. That was all! No mention of what I'd done in life to qualify for an obituary there. (Well, obituary was overstating it.) And more irritating yet, it didn't say how I died.

I slapped the *Time (Is Up)* back in the rack in front of a stack of *(Dead) People*. Well, dammit, how did I die?

I pulled free a copy of *Life (No More)* and turned to the index. Ignoring articles on "Pestilence, Familiar and Unexpected," "Plague, the Common Scourge," "War, Tried and True," and "Famine, the Familiar Favorite," I came upon one headed, "New Service at Final Checkout" on page 44.

When I turned to page 44 I almost stumbled back into the cart behind me. Pages 44 and 45, the centerfold, sported a picture of this store, this checkout counter, this very line I was in. And me in it! I turned to the next page. "Shoppers are no longer surprised to find new services available at the checkout," it proclaimed in big black letters. "They've long since become used to price scanners, check cashing, and charging their goods on credit. But never before have they been as eager to be rung up and handed their receipt! And why? Because it's not the receipt they're used to. It's a new, exciting game your grocery is offering just for you, the valued customer. A game so engrossing it's heartstopping! Just guess the answer at checkout and you walk away free and clear." "Free and clear" indeed. I understood what that meant, in the eternal sense.

And if I failed to answer the question? But of course, in true marketing fashion, they didn't spell that out.

They also didn't spell out what the question to be answered was. But I could guess.

I picked up a copy of *Condé Nast Traveler (Styx River Special)*. This time I didn't have to consult the index. The cover article was "How Did You Die? Win a Free Trip to Heaven." As quickly as possible I scanned the rules. (Why hadn't I worn contact lenses; the undertaker might have slipped up and buried me in those.) "Present your checkout clerk with one item and one item only," the rules insisted. "You have the whole market to choose from."

"What do they want—one carton of milk or one gallon of ice cream to signify how I died?" I demanded of the crowd in front of me. But the line that had been twelve somnolent slugs had suddenly dwindled to four beavers busily organizing their few items on the conveyor belt. They didn't have time to be bothered with me.

And I certainly didn't have time to waste on them. Frantically, I looked around for some clue. How had I died? What could possibly symbolize that? A knife from the cutlery department? A pack of cigarettes (even though I didn't smoke)? The aerosol hairspray from the display behind me? A can of cherry cola—that was as close to poison as I could think of.

How could I possibly choose if I didn't even know how I died? Dammit, this was like every contest I'd ever entered —astronomical odds and no way to beat them. Just like the lines—once you queue up, they've got you. Then they don't care how long you cool your heels.

Furiously, I looked around. My eyes lighted on a copy of *Country (No Longer) Living*. I opened it to a picture of a road—a two-laner in the wine country. And on it was me.

The page before was also me—three pictures of me. Me having had to wait for a table for brunch at the Tortoise Winery, me drumming my fingers while the waitress made her eleventh trip to the kitchen before she brought out my mimosa and eggs mercury, me slamming in my chair and stamping my foot till she finally brought the bill. The caption said: "Already half an hour late. Can make up the time on the way back to the city."

I stared at the picture of the country road—the two-lane road.

There were only three people ahead of me in the checkout line now. Had this still been life, my two predecessors would have had twenty-seven items each; they would have insisted on paying with out-of-state, third-party checks; they'd have scratched their heads, stroked their chins, and pondered the earthshaking question: paper or plastic? The man in the business suit would have looked over his array of currency and finally settled on the hundred-dollar bill that would force the clerk to get change from the next aisle. The woman with the purse the size of a watermelon would have poured every last coin into her palms and begun sorting out pennies, counting them, trying to figure out how many she could get rid of here, all the time explaining to the clerk the curse of carrying around too many copper coins. Now, the one time I would have welcomed any of those maneuvers, the man in the business suit slid his credit card through the slot, grabbed his bagged food, and loped into the parking lot.

That left only two people ahead, and the picture of the country road in my mind. The two-lane road nearing the intersection. The intersection with the last four-way stop sign between me and the city.

Suddenly the minute of my death was clear. The intersection was a meeting with another two-laned road. As I neared it, I could see the cortege moving forward. I could see the beginning but not the end. The damned funeral line extended to eternity. And those corteges never let anyone through, as if their getting to the cemetery late would hold up the corpse. If I stopped I'd be here forever. But the stop was a *four-way* stop. I stepped on the gas. A four-way stop is a fool's stop. Four people stop; they sit; they wait. No sense in that, especially not when you're in a hurry. And with liveried drivers like the hearse driver, too many traffic tickets mean unemployment—they obey the laws. Some might have said I'd be cutting it close (some of my former passengers) but I knew there was plenty of time.

The woman with the watermelon purse smiled at the clerk and held out exact change. There was only one person between me and the final checkout. I didn't have time to reminisce about my demise. I had to choose the symbol.

I needed to think, but there was no time. Flinging the magazine down, I raced out of line—I could always cut back in—but I knew if my turn came and I missed it that was it for this line, and for me. There would be no chance to stare down the milk sops behind me and demand to take one of their places. And I certainly couldn't go to the end of the line—no such luck this time.

I raced past the aerosol display behind, ignoring the pictures of cheery green turtles with shiny, lacquered shells, past the deli counter where the egg salad had been laid out longer than I had, and skidded to a stop at the meat counter. There was a special on hamburger. People were lined up three deep for it, blocking access to every other item in the cooler. Was hamburger somehow the answer? Was that why they were all here?

I shoved forward, pushing past lamb chops, pork roasts, filet of flounder. Panic grabbed me; I began to sweat. This was a very ordinary supermarket. Maybe they wouldn't even have my item.

But no, there it was. I grabbed, shoved, raced, and plopped it on the counter just as the clerk was about to set my basket, my empty basket, aside.

"Fowl," the checkout machine read.

The clerk looked at me questioningly. "Are you sure? We've got a special on—"

I hesitated, seeing the rest of my penultimate moment of life. The two-lane road. The four-way stop. My foot moving toward the brake, then hitting the gas. I'd been in the intersection before I remembered that funeral corteges don't stop for red lights or stop signs. Before I realized how big a hearse was, I'd been spinning out of control. My car was splintering before I realized how flimsy it, and I, was.

She who hesitates is last. I stared down at my item on the counter. I'd made my choice—there was no time to second-guess now. "Sure."

I ran my credit card through the scanner.

The clerk punched in the code.

I looked down at my item. It was dead as me. It didn't even quack. After all, when that hearse hit I had been a dead duck.

The checkout buzzer blared.

The clerk shook his head. "I'm sorry, ma'am, your card has been rejected."

Panic filled me. "Rejected? What do you mean rejected? A dead duck—what's more appropriate than that?"

The clerk looked down at me with the scorn he might have shown a shoplifter. "A dead duck indeed. Rather banal, don't you think? You could have come up with the right answer—you could have won—if you just taken the time to look around, if you hadn't been in such a hurry."

From the customers behind me came a murmur of agreement.

Chiding is never pleasant, and decidedly less so at a time like this.

"Shall I show her the right answer?"

The murmur grew louder.

The clerk stepped around the register, took three steps behind me, and plucked from the display of smiling, shiny tortoises a cylindrical can with a plastic snap on lid. I looked at it in bewildered disgust. "Hairspray?"

The clerk shrugged, displaying his disbelief and disdain. "Hare spray—H-A-R-E."

"Hare spray!" I screamed. "Splattered like a dead rabbit, is that what you mean? The tortoise and the hare? I can't believe my whole eternity depends on a silly pun!"

Behind me the glossy, grinning turtles stretched their glossy green necks and smelled the roses. The clerk nodded and smiled.

"Talk about banal!" I yelled. "'Tortoise and the hare'! 'Stop and smell the roses'!" Furious, I grabbed for his throat, but the clerk and the counter disappeared and I found myself at the tail end of a long snaking line. I was ranting at, grabbing for the ghostly customer in front of me.

Exhausted, I let my hand drop. It was too hot for such histrionics. Better I should see what this line was for.

"Take a number, please," the loudspeaker demanded.

I reached up to the dispenser beside me and pulled loose a 100. I was an expert on lines; I knew how to handle this. Now that I had my number I could relax and see what we were waiting for in this line. I jutted by head forward (like the damned turtles), but the sign was so far away I could barely see. The whole place was steamy hot. Already my "100" slip was getting damp in my hand. I stretched as far forward as I could and squinted. Now I could make out the sign: 99 FANS FOR SALE.

The Nieman Marcus Body

Lucretia Grindle

When Helena Moore was found upside down in a rain barrel, her impeccably booted legs sticking straight up to heaven, whither her soul may or may not have recently flown, there were quite a few people who were less than distraught about it. I am embarrassed to admit that I was one of them.

You see, Helena was really a rather difficult person—one of those types who put your back up without necessarily meaning to. I personally had a problem with her because of the riding breeches.

In addition to rearing my fifteen-year-old son, Ned, I run a small shop attached to the stables where Helena Moore kept her horse, and where the rain barrel that was destined to become her final resting place was located. So you might say that I was right in the thick of things. In any case, about a month before her untimely demise, Helena had ordered a pair of breeches from me. They were not expensive—more the sort of thing you'd slop around in from day to day than save for "best"—and they were a twenty-six long, which Helena said she had to have on account of her legs. You will gather from the sizing that Helena was tall and slender. All in all, in fact, she was in remarkably good nik for a woman of, shall we say, her second youth. I had never begrudged her this fact and had actually admired her for it. That is, I admired her for it when I happened to think of her, which was not often. At least, not until the matter of the breeches.

They duly arrived and I duly notified Helena—via a note on her tack trunk—and she duly appeared to collect them. A few days later, however, she reappeared in my shop, dumped the breeches unceremoniously on the counter, and announced that she could not wear them.

"Aren't they the right size?" I asked.

"Oh yes," she replied, fixing me with the blue gaze of her contact lenses. "It's not that. It's that I simply can't wear them."

"I see," I said, which I didn't. "Well, I'll return them." I started to write out a refund check. "Or perhaps," I said, "I'll simply keep them for myself." I'm certainly not a long, and only a twenty-six if I don't eat lunch, but for messing about on horses from day to day, which is all we ever do here, who cares?

"Can you wear them?" Helena asked, apparently amazed. I looked at the breeches, which appeared to have a hole at the top, a zipper, and two legs.

"I should think so," I said. "Why not?"

"Oh. Well, I can't." She began to look tragic, as if she was about to inform me of a disability or a crippling congenital disease. "People like you are so lucky," she said, shaking her head. "I just can't wear this cheap stuff. I've got a Nieman Marcus body."

Now we all stood in a semicircle around the rain barrel and observed the legs sticking straight up, the highly polished boots and silver spurs glinting in the sun.

"It is Helena?" someone asked.

"Of course it is," someone else replied. "Those are definitely Nieman Marcus legs."

The story had got around, thanks, I admit, to my big mouth. A titter ran through the assembled crowd, the way it does when something really awful has happened and you know you ought to feel worse about it than you do.

"Has anyone called the police?" Lorna Elmstrom asked.

"Yeah, Tom's doing it."

As if on cue, we all looked toward the office door in time to see Tom Perkins, who ran the barn, emerge from it and approach us.

"They're on their way," he said.

"Oh well," said Lorna, "at least she died with her spurs on."

The police arrived a few minutes later. There were several "uniforms" and a couple of plainclothes detectives. One of the latter, by the name of Todd, took over the case.

"Stand back! Stand back!" he commanded as he came toward the rain barrel. We stepped backward obediently.

"Now, what have we here?" asked the masterful Todd. And then he stopped and looked at the rain barrel.

"Oh," he said. And I was quite sure I heard someone giggling.

It took a couple of hours before the police actually got Helena out of the rain barrel. In the meantime they tried to shoo us away, a difficult task. The stable was officially closed and no one who had been present before the police arrived was allowed to leave. As always, the horses had to be fed and taken care of, which involved a good deal of to-ing and fro-ing. Given that the rain barrel was practically in the middle of the courtyard, right beside the mounting block, most of us saw pretty much everything that went on. Which was, to be honest, not much. It was established that Carolyn Stokes had been the first to arrive at the fatal barrel, at 7:30 A.M. Shortly thereafter Lorna arrived, then Tom, who called the police. A couple of other people arrived a few minutes later and I got in just under the wire, so to speak.

"I wonder," Lorna said dreamily as we sat in the doorway of my shop watching a policeman measure the height of the barrel, "if it was suicide?"

"Suicide?" I asked.

"Mm," said Lorna. "In a fit of despair and jealousy over her unrequited love for Tom. She shined up her boots and spurs, and when they failed to entice him, she climbed the mounting block and threw herself headfirst into the rain barrel."

"Well," I said, "it's certainly a theory." Indeed it was, but not, it turned out, a very good one. Because when, an hour later, they finally got around to getting Helena out of the rain barrel, it was fairly obvious, even to the untrained eye, that she had not died by drowning.

She wasn't looking her best, I have to admit. Apart from the fact that she was soaking wet, her hair had some pretty yucky things from the bottom of the rain barrel clinging to it. Her skin had gone a nasty gray-blue color. And her eyes and mouth were wide open in a look of startled surprise. But most unattractive of all, just above the collar of her United Colors of Benetton T-shirt were the marks on her neck. Even I, lacking a degree in forensic pathology as I do, could tell you what it was plain for all the world to see. Helena Moore had been well and truly garrotted.

In the course of the afternoon Helena's body was removed from the premises. Yellow plastic tape was slung around, giving the place the aura of a large impromptu parking lot. We were asked not to leave until we'd given Detective Todd, or one of his minions, a statement. At this point we were all suspects in a murder investigation, since everybody knows that 80 percent of the time the dirty deed is committed by whoever claims to have discovered the body, or some such rot. In a pinch, I suppose we all qualified. However, we were encouraged to behave as if it were a normal day.

And I was doing just that, behaving as normally as possible. That is to say that I was writing out a series of extremely confusing invoices—confusing because half of the time I write down what I've sold to whom on the back of envelopes, which I lose. The phone rang.

"Leatherwork," I said absently, wondering how many

grooming brushes I'd actually sold to Alan Taylor versus how many I could get away with charging him for.

"Claire, it's Anne."

Anne Harris is one of my favorite people—not that I know her all that well. And yes, I am aware that these two facts may be related. She keeps her horse at the stables and has lessons with Tom. To all appearances she's intelligent and not of an overly saccharine temperament. Like myself, she is thirty-seven and divorced—in her case from someone she disparagingly refers to as "The Willard."

"Claire," she was saying, "I'm just calling to see if that lead shank for Leander is ready yet?"

Leander is Anne's horse and the lead shank in question is one that I had made for her. It involved a four-foot piece of leather with a two-foot brass chain and clip at the end, to give Leander a yank with when he got above himself. I had also engraved a very nice nameplate with Leander's name on it that fit just below the chain. I was reflecting on all of this, and on the fact that I had no idea where I'd put the finished product, when I realized that Anne didn't know about Helena Moore. "Oh, Anne, you don't know."

"Don't know what?" she replied.

"Well," I said, "about Helena Moore."

There was a short silence.

"What about her?" Anne asked.

"Well, she's dead."

"Dead?"

"Quite dead," I replied, warming to the theme. "Someone strangled her and dumped her in the rain barrel."

"Oh my God," Anne whispered. "Oh, no!"

I admit that I was rather surprised at the vehemence of her reaction, which only served to highlight what callous toads the rest of us were.

"Anne," I said, "are you all right? Are you sitting down?"

"But, Claire," she said, "you don't understand. Are the police there? I've got to talk to them. You see, I saw Helena last night. At her house. When I left at nine thirty she was alive and kicking."

"Oh," I said. "Well, perhaps you had better talk to them then." And with that I forgot all about Leander's lead shank, which would make its own dramatic reappearance in the not-too-distant future.

Anne came along to the stable shortly afterward and was closeted with Detective Todd for a good half hour. The story leaked out in dribs and drabs, as stories do. And at first it didn't seem all that interesting. Anne, it transpired, had been at Helena's house from approximately eight fifteen to nine thirty. When she left Helena had definitely been alive. When Carolyn Stokes filled me in on this piece of intelligence, sometime in the midafternoon, I simply assumed that Helena and Anne had been having dinner together. Helena's husband, as everyone knew, was on an extended junket in Tokyo. So glutted with exotic goings on was I, it never occurred to me to question this assumption or to wonder why they might have been having a meal together since, as far as I knew, Helena Moore drove Anne Harris straight up the wall.

Another reason I failed to ponder the question was that I simply didn't have the time. Events were breaking hard and fast. No sooner had Carolyn finished telling me about the content of Anne's statement than we heard a horrific shrieking from outside, the familiar tones of which could only have issued from Melanie Perkins.

"Melly" as (à la *Gone with the Wind*) she prefers to be called, is Tom Perkins's wife. She's a tall, thin, hawklike lady with a signature screech to match. Lorna Elmstrom swears she eats mice for breakfast, but you can't believe everything you hear. In any case, the story is that back when he was young and rash and Melly may have weighed more than fifteen pounds and had not yet grown talons, Tom married her. There are those that say he may now regret the fact. But I suppose there are always unkind characters around, and just how many of these rumors stem from jealousy must be taken into account. You see, Tom has things quite nicely set up, being, as he is, virtually the only rooster in this particular henhouse.

However, Melly was not shrieking from the front seat of her Jaguar because Helena Moore was dead, but because the police were refusing to let her onto the property.

"I am the legal owner of this property!" she caterwauled. The uniform in charge of the situation was visibly flustered and after a few minutes Detective Todd was summoned. Melly was admitted. She drove her shiny sports car into the yard, stopped with neck-snapping precision just short of a wall, and disappeared around the back yowling for Tom. Carolyn and I watched this drama from the safe sanctuary of the shop doorway.

The admittance problem occurred again that afternoon when the vet arrived, just as I was thinking of trying to go home. The farrier had been turned away earlier, but the vet was a different matter. One of Tom's horses, a silly mare called Cora, had managed to collide with a barbed-wire fence the day before. Her wound simply had to be attended to. Detective Todd was summoned, the necessary permission was given, and Dr. Albany's truck rolled into the yard.

The next complication, it seemed, was that it was Alison's day off. Alison was the barn manager and, as such, was responsible for the feeding and supervision of the stables. I'd wondered earlier where she'd got to, since, as far as I knew, she lived at the barn. I recalled thinking vaguely that it was nice to know that she actually had a day off and that, having one, she took it. Tom Perkins had taught Alison everything she knew about horses. Now the stables, and by virtue of that the Perkinses, were, to all intents and purposes, her whole world. However, if I was glad to see Alison take a day off, I was in the minority. For it appeared that she alone usually dealt with Cora, who had a rather difficult temperament. It was pretty obvious that Cora was going to be less than thrilled with the idea of Dr. David Albany poking around at her stitches. In Alison's absence, no one was volunteering to help with the job. Being a brave soul, I said I'd do it.

Cora wasn't all that bad, and after some minor thrashing around David was able to get the old wound dressing off and put a new one on. When he was finished with his ministrations, he turned to me and held up two plastic packages of pills.

"Same as I told Alison yesterday," he said. "Two at four o'clock feeding and then two more at seven P.M. It's important not to miss the timing, since they work off each other." I nodded, taking the packages of pills, and went to put them in the feed room with a poster-sized note.

I was allowed to go home shortly afterward, having made my statement to one of the lesser detectives. I guess I wasn't much of a suspect, since I didn't even rate Detective Todd, but then again, it wasn't much of a statement. They took my address and telephone number anyway and asked me not to leave the area, so I didn't feel too left out.

My house felt large and empty, not so much because it was as because Ned, my fifteen-year-old son, had left the day before to spend a week with his father, who had gone back to nature somewhere off the coast of Maine. I applied myself diligently to concocting more invoices, but even so I was bored and restless and glad that Lorna had invited herself to dinner. At five P.M. I gave up and went out into the garden, where I weeded with greater enthusiasm than care for the next two hours.

I had just gone inside, fixed myself a gin and tonic, and thought about having a rapid go at tidying up my workshop, when I heard Lorna's car come careening up the driveway. Her husband, Lars Elmstrom, runs one of those agencies that represents professional athletes, and I don't think Lorna ever got over meeting Peter Revson.

Now she flung herself through the porch doors looking wild-eyed and clutching a bottle of chardonnay.

"Where have you been?" she cried. "I've been calling you all afternoon!" I relieved her of the bottle, which she was waving about in a dangerous manner.

"In the garden," I said. I glanced at the answering machine, which was indeed flashing insistently.

"Ignore that," Lorna said, "that's all me." She followed me into the kitchen, where I was making her a gin. "Listen," she went on, "you simply won't believe it."

"Try me." I dropped four ice cubes into a glass and then I

nearly dropped the glass altogether when Lorna said, "They've arrested Anne Harris."

We stood staring at each other for a minute, as if she were as startled by saying it as I was by hearing it.

"Yes," she said. "They've taken Anne in for questioning, and they're going to arrest her—she's sure of it."

"Lorna," I said, "who did you hear this from?"

"Anne herself. She called me at about five thirty and asked me to look after Leander for her."

"Leander?"

"Oh, she's paranoid about Alison—says she doesn't give him enough hay and forgets to water him, that sort of nonsense. Anyway, she told me, so it's true."

"I don't understand," I said.

"Well, there's more." Lorna was looking unpleasantly sly. "Make me a drink and I'll tell you."

When we were seated on the porch, each with a fresh drink in hand, Lorna embarked on the story. Apparently, late in the afternoon, after they had finished at the stables, the police had gone to Helena Moore's house and there, so to speak, they hit the mother lode. There were no signs of a break-in, but the front hall was a shambles. And in the middle of the shambles they found the murder weapon, a four-foot leather lead shank with a two-foot brass chain and a nice, new, shiny brass nameplate that said LEANDER.

If Lorna noticed the expression on my face, which, given the sinking of my stomach, must have been grim, it didn't deter her. Or even slow her down. She was in full flood.

"It gets better," she said. "You'll never guess."

"No," I muttered, "so you'd better tell me."

She settled herself deeper into her chair and took a sip of her drink. "It really started yesterday with the spurs. Anne and I were having a jumping lesson and I forgot my spurs. Helena was hanging around—you know, the way she does —and she insisted that I borrow hers. Spurs, I mean. So I did. And then, afterward, Anne and I went out for a hack and when we got back Helena'd gone and I still had the stupid spurs on.

"Well," Lorna said, "you know what she's like about her

things, how she has fits about them? And she'd already announced that these were German spurs, so I left them in the office, on the desk. And when I went home I called and left a message on her machine about where they were. It must have been, oh, about six thirty. So really, in a way, it was my fault."

"What was your fault?" I was having a problem making the connection here.

"That Helena found out and Anne killed her."

"Found out what? Lorna, you're not making any sense at all. Have another drink."

"I am and I will, thank you." She got up and followed me into the kitchen, where I was upside down in the refrigerator looking for another lime. "You just aren't paying attention," she insisted.

"I am." I found the lime and stood up. "I just don't understand what it was that Helena found out."

"Oh, Claire!" Lorna rolled her eyes. "That they've been having an affair, of course."

"Who?"

"Anne and Tom!" Lorna shouted. "Apparently it's been going on forever. They've just been incredibly discreet."

"You didn't tell me!" I said.

"I didn't know," she replied. "Until Anne told me to-night. I guess it's really serious. She says he says he's thinking about leaving Melly." I was beginning to understand.

"And in the middle of all this Helena walked in to collect her spurs?"

"That's right," Lorna said. "Anne's certain that she was hanging around outside listening to them before she made her entrance. Tom was just leaving and he was certain that Helena hadn't heard anything."

"So they weren't in flagrante whatever on the desk?"

"No, no," Lorna said, "nothing like that. They all said good night quite decently, as if nothing was going on, and Tom trotted off. Anne, however, wasn't so sure. She caught up with Helena on the way back to her car and apparently they had a real cat fight, right there in the middle of the yard."

"And then Anne killed her and dumped her in the rain barrel?"

"Oh no," Lorna said, dropping a lime into each glass. "That was later."

I trailed after her as she led the way back out to the porch.

"So," Lorna continued, flopping down into the same wicker chair that she'd staked out before, "Helena drove off in a fury. Apparently she swore to Anne that she was going to tell Melly, but she wouldn't say when. The guilty duo would just have to sweat it out and guess."

"That's just like Helena," I said, sipping my drink.

"Isn't it?" Lorna agreed. "In any case, Helena left and Anne left, and then Anne's temper began to cool down and she thought that maybe she ought to go and reason with Helena, talk to her about people's happiness and minding her own business and that sort of thing."

"Fat lot of good that would do."

Lorna ignored this observation and went on. "Well, she did. She got to Helena's at about eight fifteen and they talked and she said that she left at about nine thirty."

"And when she left Helena was still alive?"

"And relishing her position of power, yes. The police, of course, tell it a little differently."

"She followed Helena home, garroted her with the lead shank in the front hallway and then took her back and dumped her in the rain barrel?"

"Something like that."

I was thinking of Anne's phone call to me that morning. Had she lied when she asked me about Leander's lead shank?

"But she couldn't have," I muttered, more to myself than to Lorna.

"In the heat of passion anyone can do anything," Lorna said. "And, of course, her fingerprints are all over the place."

"What about Tom?" I asked.

"What about him?" Lorna shrugged and looked at me. "He went from the stables to Chip Carter's for a beer, where he was seen by half the world, and then he and Melly went to The Hogsback Tavern, where they were seen by the other half of the world."

"So you think Anne really killed her?"

"I don't know." Lorna shook her head. "I'll tell you one thing, though," she said. "Somebody really killed her."

Long after Lorna left I lay awake listening to the wind. I was thinking about Anne Harris and Tom Perkins and the heat of passion. I was thinking about Helena Moore's spurs. But most of all I was thinking about Leander's lead shank. Because there was no question, simply no question at all that I had had that lead shank. If it had not turned up in its now notorious role in Helena's front hall, I would be certain that I still had it. I would absolutely know that it was coiled safely in my workshop downstairs or sitting in a plastic bag under my counter in the shop waiting to be collected by Anne. But it was not in either of those places. At the moment, while it waited to be prosecution exhibit A, the murder weapon in the case of The State of Massachusetts vs. Anne Harris, I had no idea where it was. But I did know that some twenty-four hours earlier it had allegedly been used to garrote Helena Moore in her own front hall. And the fact bothered me mightily. Because, apart from anything else, I couldn't for the life of me figure out how it came to be there.

In the morning I spent a half hour rooting through my workshop like some kind of demented truffle pig. When I deliver repairs or finish work I do make an attempt to enter it in my record book. I am continually nagging at Ned for being lax on this account, although I admit that I don't have much of a leg to stand on when it comes to record keeping. Often, if I don't make it to the book, I write myself a note and stick it on the bulletin board. The book, needless to say, was a total strike—nor was there a note on the board informing me that Anne's package had been collected.

The more I thought about it, the more certain I was that I

hadn't taken the damn thing into the shop. I had left it, I could swear, coiled next to my workbench. Even so, as soon as I arrived at the stables I spent a good hour going through every old box, cupboard, or drawer in the shop, vainly hoping that I might find some clue as to how the wretched lead shank had left my possession. I came up empty and by noon I realized that I would have to go to Detective Todd and lay the problem before him.

The police were not in evidence at the stable, having nabbed their woman. Bits of plastic tape still hung about and the rain barrel had been taken away, presumably to be entered into evidence as prosecution exhibit B, the final resting place of Helena Moore. The story had made the front page of all the local papers and several sported a picture of Anne leaving her home in the company of Detective Todd and her lawyer. Another, in the spirit of enterprise, featured a muzzy shot of the rain barrel with Helena's bottom half sticking out of it. I stared at it for a while and figured that it must have been taken from quite high up in one of the large oaks that grew on the neighboring property.

I was spending my time dawdling with the newspapers because I did not want to go and make my report to the dreaded Todd. To be honest, I was loathing the idea. I could not help but feel that all I'd be doing was contributing to the mounting pile of evidence that was going to convict Anne Harris of murder. I was, however, granted a temporary stay by the state of chaos that the stable was in.

Alison had called in sick, a fact which had caused all manner of complications, not least of which being that when the vet appeared at eleven A.M. Tom was teaching and no one else dared to hold Cora. I did the honors again. The idea of being bitten by Cora was infinitely preferable to making a trip to the local police station. This occupied my time until noon, at which point Lorna appeared and announced that she had gone out for sandwiches and had brought me one. In every TV show I've ever seen cops always have lunch. So I figured that even if I went to find Todd I'd have to wait until he got back from stuffing himself with the lasagna special at

The Full Belly Deli. In which case, it seemed reasonable to dine with Lorna on the shop step, fortifying myself for the ordeal ahead so I did not become dizzy and weak. I would go to the police station at one, or perhaps two.

We were halfway through our chicken salad on rye when Ned called.

"Hey Ma," he exclaimed with all the gory relish of a fifteen-year-old, "I hear Helena Moore bought the farm?"

"She did indeed," I said. "And you missed it. How's your father?"

"Boring," he replied. "Is it true that she was upside down in the rain barrel?"

"Yes," I said.

"And that Anne Harris killed her?"

"I don't know," I said.

"Jesus, the one exciting thing that happens down there in a lifetime and I'm in shitty old Maine."

"Don't swear," I said automatically, wondering when, exactly, it was that I'd started sounding quite so much like somebody's mother.

Ned extracted what exciting details he could from me and was about to hang up when he added the words that have filled every parent with dread since the dawn of time.

"Hey Ma," he said, "I forgot to tell you—"

"Yes," I replied with caution.

"That stuff—"

"What stuff?"

"The repair stuff for the stable, the halters and stuff you had in the workshop—Alison came by a few days ago to collect it. I gave it to her but I forgot to write it in the book."

"Oh, Ned!"

"Chill, Ma," he replied. "At least I remembered to tell you."

After he hung up I stood staring at the phone for so long that Lorna came into the shop to ask if I was all right. I waved at her to indicate that I was thinking and that she was not to talk. She stood watching me for a few minutes and then she said. "If you're going to do an imitation of a deaf mute for the rest of the day, can I at least finish your sandwich?"

I shoved the waxed paper parcel toward her, pickle and all.

"Eat it in the car," I said, pushing her toward the door.

"What car?" she yelped, grabbing the sandwich as I shoved her.

"Mine," I said. "Hurry! I'll explain on the way."

It was one of those affairs built over the garage, what real-estate agents like to refer to as an "in-law apartment." I went up the rather rickety stairs two at a time, and when I pushed on the door, it gave under my hand. The curtains were drawn, and after the bright sunlight the room seemed nearly black inside. I was halfway across the living room and on my way to the bedroom before I saw Alison sitting on the couch.

She gave me quite a start. I was suddenly glad I'd had the presence of mind to make Lorna Elmstrom come with me. Alison was just sitting there in the same jeans and T-shirt and sneakers that she always wore. She didn't seem to be particularly aware of me. For all I could tell she'd been sitting there like that, ankles crossed, hands demurely folded in her lap for days. Possibly ever since she'd got home from killing Helena Moore.

"Alison?" I said quietly.

She turned and gave me an eerie little smile. "I wondered when somebody would come," she said. She looked down at her hands and then smiled at me again. "So how'd you figure it out?"

"The lead shank," I said. "Ned gave it to you by mistake when you picked up Tom's stuff."

"Why?" Lorna asked. She was standing in the doorway and Alison looked up as if she'd just noticed her.

"Because," she said, and a flash of bitterness shot through her voice, "that stupid bitch was going to ruin everything."

"You were there, weren't you? At the stable," I said. "You came back to give Cora her antibiotics."

"Yeah." Alison nodded.

"Do you want to talk about it?" Lorna asked.

Alison shrugged and stared at her feet. "I was just finishing up when I heard them," she said slowly. "Both of them screaming and yelling like you wouldn't believe. Jesus! Well, they were way too busy to notice me. Helena was screaming at Anne Harris, telling her that she was going to fix her good, that she'd tell Melly and then Anne would be thrown out on her ass with her fancy horse and all. And Anne screamed right back at her, just like an alley cat, told her that she could go right ahead and tell Melly 'cause he cared more about Anne than anyone else. And you know"— Alison paused, then smiled pathetically at me—"that just isn't true."

"So what happened?" Lorna asked, not moving from the doorway.

"Well, I sat there and I thought about it," Alison said. "And I thought about how, if he left, everything would be finished and he'd take the horses and go off with her and what would we all do? What would I do? And then I thought about Helena and her stupid shiny boots and her fancy horse and I thought, you know, she's got everything—a nice house, a husband, a horse—and now she wants to ruin this just 'cause she can't have Tom too. And you know, it just isn't right."

Neither Lorna nor I moved. After a few seconds Alison looked down at her hands and started talking again.

"It just isn't right," she said. "So I went over there. I drove over there on my way home."

"And you killed her?"

She nodded. "Uhh-huh. I stopped her. I parked down the street and waited until Anne left and then I just walked right up and rang the bell. I even remembered to put my work gloves on."

I was feeling slightly queasy. The air in the little room was stale with the smell of old cigarette smoke.

"Alison," I asked, "do you mind if I just open a window?"

"Oh no," she said. "Go right ahead."

I pulled back one of the curtains and pushed the window

open. Out of the corner of my eye I saw Lorna slip around the dividing wall and reach for the telephone on the kitchen counter.

"Did you mean to incriminate Anne?" I asked. "Or was that a mistake?"

"I thought of it while I was sitting in the truck," Alison said. "I had that stuff on the front seat and there was Leander's lead shank. So, you know, why not?"

Why not indeed? I thought. Two birds with one stone and all that stuff.

Suddenly it seemed important to keep Alison talking. I could hear Lorna hanging up the telephone in the kitchen and she came back and stood in the doorway again. Even so, Alison was no shrinking violet and the apartment's tiny fireplace was equipped with a perfectly good pair of andirons.

"I don't understand," I said, trying to keep my voice in an even and soothing tone. "Why the stable? Why the rain barrel? Why not just leave her where she was?"

Alison shrugged. "I didn't want to make too much of a mess leaving her lying there. I mean, it's summer and it gets pretty hot, right? So I thought it was better if she was found fast—you know, get it over with. I keep a tarp in the truck."

"Oh," I said. "Good thinking." Behind me I could feel Lorna starting to fidget.

"Yeah," Alison went on. "And she was always talking about how much she just loved the stables. So I thought, you know, let her stay there. I was gonna put her on the manure heap—I mean, that was my first thought—but then I saw the rain barrel." She looked at me and giggled.

Whatever Detective Todd was planning, I sincerely hoped that he was going to be quick about it. An eternity passed, with Alison rambling on while Lorna and I went calmly, desperately mad. At last I saw Lorna glance out the door and heard what I hoped was a police car pulling in.

"Ah, tell me, Alison," I said, "there's something that's been bothering me. The spurs. Why did she have her spurs on?"

"Well, when they were fightin' Helena dropped them on

the mounting block, and when she drove off she was so busy bein' mad that she left them there."

I heard footsteps on the stairs.

"Anyway," she went on, "I got her in there—she just plopped in real easy. It was a perfect fit—I didn't have to push or anything. And there were those legs and those boots stickin' straight up. She was so fussy about how she looked, you know? And I always think boots look so much better with spurs on them, don't you? So I just strapped them on for her—you know, kind of as a last favor. I mean, hell, if a job's worth doing, it's worth doing right."

And then, at the very moment that Detective Todd stepped through the doorway, Alison threw back her head and started to laugh.

Anna and the Snake People

Ed Gorman

Anna Tolan had just finished her rounds this sunny April morning—checking with merchants to see that their stores had suffered no vandalism during the night—when a man named Wydmore started shouting to her from the other side of the trolley tracks. He was pushing a sleek new bicycle.

Anna recognized the two horses pulling the tightly packed trolley by the patches of white across their foreheads. The duns were brothers and the slowest and most disagreeable animals in the trolley system. Next year all this would change. Next year Cedar Rapids was to have an electrical trolley system like the one in Chicago.

A few minutes later, Wydmore came panting up to her. "They did it, Anna, and now one of them's dead."

In 1890, Cedar Rapids, Iowa, was dominated by one family, the Wydmores, of whom thirty-year-old Trace was the only son. He ran the Visitors Bureau and loved rattling off the statistics that made the town seem even bigger than it was. Twenty thousand citizens. More than four hundred telephones. Electricity throughout the city. And an opera house that featured some of the world's biggest theatrical names. Last Thursday, Mark Twain had spoken to a full house.

One other thing about Trace Wydmore. He had this painful crush on Anna—painful for both of them. While he loved her sweet Irish face and slight Irish figure, which she kept modest inside the buff blue pinafore she washed and ironed twice a week, he did not approve of her being a police matron. He resented the nights she spent studying the works of Frenchman Marie François Goron, one of the creators of a new science called criminology. And he complained frequently that Police Chief Ryan unofficially let her take part in murder investigations. It was not seemly for a woman to investigate homicides.

"Slow down, Trace. I don't know what you're talking about."

He ruined his handsome if somewhat weak face by frowning. "This isn't the kind of publicity Cedar Rapids needs, Anna. Not if we want to be known as the Athens of the Midwest." That was another thing about Trace. He guarded the city's reputation with the same vigilance with which a father guarded his daughter's reputation.

"Trace, I'm sorry, but I still don't know who you're talking about."

"Those evangelists!" he said, straightening his black suit coat and adjusting his freshly laundered linen collar. "The ones Chief Ryan told to get rid of their rattlesnakes! You'd better come quick, Anna! One of them's dead now!"

Anna's first thought was to rush back to the police station and tell Chief Ryan, but since he was having a budgetary meeting with the city council—Ryan wanted to hire two additional officers—she decided not to bother him. She'd look into this herself.

"Let's go," she said, and then got up on the handlebars of Trace Wydmore's bicycle with the wooden tire rims and the slanted seat that Trace insisted helped him go faster.

By the time they reached the river bend where the evangelists held their meetings, more than a dozen people had rushed up to Anna to tell her that somebody had died. A few of the women, proper Lutherans and Presbyterians in

144

no way associated with the evangelicals, were crying. Even out on the river, people in rowboats were looking to shore to see what was going on.

From a hundred yards away, Anna saw a group of perhaps twenty people gathered near a gentle turn in the river. It was a day for a picnic, not death—bright April butterflies everywhere, and red and blue and yellow flowers blooming like fireworks against the soft blue sky.

Each member of the evangelical group held a Bible and sang an old fundamentalist hymn called "Amen, Amen, There's a Higher Power."

They looked like peaceful people until you got close to them and saw their faces. Rage and frenzy claimed every face. They did not love a benign God, rather they loved a terrible and vengeful God whom they believed had turned them into his own terrible and vengeful vessels. Even on the faces of the youngsters Anna saw anger and dark judgment and an almost frantic sorrow. The minds of these children had already been claimed by this sect and Anna felt great sadness for them.

They were dressed in faded work clothes—nothing fancy or ornamental because their God disapproved of frivolity in any form. They stood in a tight circle, so that from here Anna could not see what was on the ground between them.

But she did hear the terrifying noise of the rattlesnakes that had been snatched up and put in a burlap bag and used for the religious ceremony.

John Muldaur, the raw and angry giant who was the minister to these people, taught that if you were pure of soul, then you could hold one, even two angry rattlesnakes and they would not harm you. If you were not pure of soul, they would smite you.

A year ago Anna had accompanied Chief Ryan to a raid on such a ceremony. She had witnessed children as young as five and six standing at the head of the group, rattlers twisting in their white little hands. Ryan had taken out his six gun and pointed it directly at the head of John Muldaur and ordered him to take the rattlers from the hands of the children.

This morning, Anna stood a few feet from the group, letting them finish their song.

And then she stepped up to a woman wearing a much-patched calico dress and said, "Excuse me, ma'am, I need to step in here."

She put her hand on the woman's shoulder and eased her away from the crowd.

Anna then got her first look at what lay on the ground inside the circle.

A very pretty young woman lay on the ground, hands folded on her stomach the way they would be in a coffin. This was Rachael, Reverend Muldaur's wife. She lay unmoving and obviously dead, though no sign of blood or wound showed anywhere. The only sign of anything untoward was a ragged crust of vomit on her chest.

The burlap sack was next to her. It had a life of its own, the rattlesnakes inside enraged at imprisonment and striking out every few moments. Their rattles occasionally sounded like castanets in a Mexican band.

Anna made sure to stay away from the sack. Snakes horrified her.

Standing in front of Muldaur, in his protective grasp, was his twelve-year-old daughter Stephanie, a slender girl with tumbling chestnut hair and her mother's sad, dignified beauty. Her dress was of gingham and except for a faint green stain near the knee looked surprisingly good on her.

Stephanie's eyes were fixed on the form of her mother there at her feet.

Anna went up to Muldaur and said, "How did your wife die?"

He scowled at her. "I don't honor your law and therefore I don't honor your questions."

"She's dead," Anna said. "You should respect her enough to treat her properly."

Stephanie looked up at her father with dark and sorrowful eyes. "Please, Papa. I don't want Mama to just lie here."

"How did she die?" This time Anna addressed her question to Stephanie, who wiped her hands on her gingham dress.

"Don't answer her," Muldaur said. He pushed his daughter aside, stepping close to Anna. He stood at least six feet three and always wore the same attire—white shirt, black vest, green corduroy trousers. He was bald except for a fringe of white hair. He had the kind of eyes Anna had seen on a trip to Mt. Pleasant, where the insane, particularly the violently insane, were kept.

"What happened here is none of your business," Muldaur said. He looked at the small badge she wore on the breast of her pinafore. "You defile God's law—doing a man's work this way. You'll be punished for it, too."

Just then there was a clatter of hooves and the rattling of a wagon, both familiar to Anna's ears. Bjornsen the undertaker was here, no doubt acting on a tip that there was a dead woman somewhere within the confines of the city limits. Chief Ryan always joked that Bjornsen could sniff out a corpse the way a hound could sniff out a rabbit.

The wagon was unadorned, a battered farm wagon pulled by a dusty old mare blind in the left eye. Bjornsen saved the fancy carriage for later, after he was sure that the relatives were going to pay him.

Stephanie chose just then to step up to Anna and say, "The snakes did it. Ma brought them down here for the ceremony and one of them must have bitten her through the sack."

Anna looked down at the dead woman. Snakebite would explain why there was no sign of violence on the woman.

"Did your mother handle the snakes very often?"

Stephanie glanced at her father. Though he scowled, he didn't stop her from speaking. "All the time. She was real good at it, too. Till today." She nodded to a plump man that Anna recognized immediately as a town drunk named Jake Foster. "Brother Foster was going to handle the rattlers today and prove to us that his heart was pure now and then we were going to baptize him in the river, but—" She shook her head. Though she was young, she spoke with real authority.

Muldaur took his daughter by the shoulder and turned her back toward the silent crowd of evangelicals.

Anna looked at them. They seemed to belong to some
other species. Here was a dead woman on the ground, yet
none of them expressed the least grief or sorrow—except for
a handsome young man who walked with a limp and carried
a black Bible in his right hand. Every few moments he would
look down at Rachael Muldaur and tears would fill his eyes.
Anna wondered what his name was.

"We're going now," Muldaur said. "You can do whatever
you want with the body. It's the soul that's our concern—
and Rachael is with her maker now."

And with that the entire group of evangelicals turned and
started up the dusty road to the tiny, closed two-block
neighborhood where they lived.

Anna was happy to see Muldaur bend down and pick up
the sack of rattlesnakes. She hadn't looked forward to its
disposal.

Just before dinner Anna went into the backyard of Mrs.
Susan Goldman's rooming house and played basketball for
twenty minutes. Anna herself had erected both pole and
basket. In the autumn Anna played on the Cedar Rapids
women's team, wearing an uncomfortable but modest uniform of long black hose, full-length sleeves, and full bloom-
ers of woolen material. Anna preferred her costume
tonight—a pair of corduroy pants and one of the work
shirts her father had worn until his death two years ago.

As dusk settled in, Anna could smell what Mrs. Goldman
was making for dinner—pot roast with vegetables and
potatoes stewing in the beef juices. Mrs. Goldman was a
widow who had turned her nice white sturdy home into a
boardinghouse for farm girls who came to the city to work.

A year ago a man had hanged himself and Anna had been
the first police officer on the scene. She was afraid to let the
other officers see how upset she was. They'd use it as proof
that women weren't meant for this job. After work that day,
she'd come back to Mrs. Goldman's, had gone up to her
room, had thrown herself across the bed, had said endless
Hail Marys, and had wept. Mrs. Goldman had brought in
tea and sweet cakes and stayed up all night with Anna as she

described again and again the man's face and how the flesh had turned ashen. And Mrs. Goldman had held her. Anna's own mother having died years ago, Anna desperately needing a mother at that moment. In the morning, Mrs. Goldman had made Anna eat a bowl of homemade bean soup, which she insisted was good for your bowels. Mrs. Goldman seemed to rank all foods by what they did for your bowels, a trait Anna found both amusing and endearing.

Now Mrs. Goldman called through the window, "Dinner's ready, Anna. Take six more shots and then come in."

Anna smiled as she dribbled the ball over the new spring grass. Mrs. Goldman was precise about everything. Take six shots—not five; not seven. Six. And then come in. In a very real way, Mrs. Goldman, who was in her late fifties, had indeed become Anna's mother.

After dinner Anna went into the parlor and put a match to the wick on Mrs. Goldman's beautiful new banquet lamp and then sat in a comfortable chair, reading through a new article by Allan Pinkerton on the impact of "electrical science" on the capturing of criminals. As always in any Pinkerton piece, good old Allan managed to brag about himself incessantly while seeming to write about something else entirely.

She was just finishing the Pinkerton article when Mrs. Goldman, tall and slender and regal in her gingham dress, came in and handed her a copy of *Arthur's Home Magazine*.

"Your friend Trace Wydmore dropped this off for you today." She smiled. "He's still trying to convince you that you're not a proper lady."

Anna took the magazine, opened to the page Trace had marked, then exploded into laughter.

"Listen to this," she said, smiling. "The title is 'The Art of Tidying.' Here goes, Mrs. Goldman.

"'One of the few anecdotes intended to prove a warning to my heedless youth, which I can now remember, related to the homely subject of tidying up. It was to this effect, and was short and sour. Miss Smith had long been engaged to be married to Mr. Jones. That gentleman was invited to sleep a night at Mr. Smith's house, and coming down to breakfast he passed his intended wife's bed-room, from which she had gone down, leaving the door wide open. There he saw such a scene of confusion that he felt sure his home would not be a comfortable one under Miss Smith's management, and so he broke off the match.'"

By now Mrs. Goldman was laughing, too. Once or twice a week Trace Wydmore dropped off some magazine or pamphlet aimed at convincing Anna that she was a most peculiar woman—one who wanted a full-time job, one who wanted a job that properly belonged to a man, one who believed that women were right in wanting the vote, and one who felt no sympathy for the upper classes when their workers asked for better pay. "Being rich isn't as easy as it seems," Trace Wydmore always said plaintively. "Yes," Anna always laughed, "it does sound like a terrible burden, doesn't it?"

"I'm going up early tonight," Mrs. Goldman said now. "I think I'm coming down with my annual spring cold."

She nodded and left, leaving Anna to sit there and close her eyes and think again of Stephanie Muldaur's sweet aggrieved face. Unless she soon escaped her father's clutches, the girl's life would become just as mean and narrow as those of the evangelicals surrounding her. She wished there were something she could do for the girl.

And then Stephanie's face faded, replaced by that of the handsome young crippled man who had looked shocked and grief-stricken as he stole a glance at Rachael Muldaur's corpse every few moments.

Who was he? And why was he more distraught-looking than either Muldaur or Stephanie? And, come to think of it, why hadn't Muldaur and Stephanie seemed more heartbroken than they had? And if Anna hadn't been mistaken, hadn't she seen vomit all over Rachael's dress?

The body had been carted away, Anna had given Chief Ryan a complete report on the death, and then the police had waited for the county coroner to return by train from Green Bay, Wisconsin, where he had attended a wedding.

She was thinking of all these things when the phone rang

in the kitchen. Telephones, with all their wires and bells, still intimidated her. She lifted the receiver and recognized Chief Ryan's voice immediately. "Just thought I'd tell you, Anna. Doc McWilliams got back tonight and had a look at Rachael Muldaur. He said he found vomit all over her so he's wondering if a snakebite killed her after all."

So Anna had been right about the vomit. But what did it mean?

They talked a few minutes more, and then hung up.

Almost without realizing it, Anna went to the hall closet, took down her denim jacket, and went out the front door.

It was time to pay John Muldaur a visit.

The people of Cedar Rapids took pride in how well lit the city was. They wanted to keep the crime rate low. At dusk lamplighters set about putting their matches to more than three hundred streetlamps. In the morning the same lamplighters set about turning the lamps off.

Anna's destination was the southwest side of town, near where the large Czechoslovakian population had settled. Last year this stretch along the river would have been raucous with player piano music and the drunken laughter of men who should have been home with their families. A group of temperance women had tried in vain to shut down the two most egregious taverns. Then two elderly sisters named Tomlin devised the idea of going into the taverns themselves to do all their knitting and darning. The owners objected, of course, but the women were careful to buy one small glass of beer each hour and to hide themselves at a corner table. The women intimidated the men. The drunkards felt they couldn't swear or fight or tell dirty stories. And so they soon sought other places to drink in. The owners demanded that the city council force the women to leave—but ultimately it was the owners who left, sixty miles east to Dubuque, where they opened taverns on the more hospitable Mississippi River.

As she thought about all this, Anna moved through an alley that moonlight cast in deep shadow. She could smell the clean, chill river a hundred yards away. The windows in

Muldaur's shacklike little house showed flickering kerosene light. On the road behind her, a hansom cab rolled on toward the city. The spring night smelled of apple blossoms.

Muldaur appeared suddenly in his doorway. He turned back and said, "You get to bed now, Stephanie, you hear me?" As usual, there was a threat in his voice.

He slammed the door behind him, walked upslope from the river, and then started moving quickly along the main road.

Anna followed, staying one hundred feet behind him at all times and never once stepping into the road. She moved from tree to tree, the way Indians always did in the yellowback novels her older brother had always read.

Muldaur walked for fifteen minutes and then stopped in front of a cabin.

No lights shone. No sound carried from the darkness inside.

Muldaur strode up to the front door of the cabin. He raised a mighty foot and kicked the door in clean. Then he half dove into the shadows inside. A man's scream could be heard—not Muldaur's—and then the sounds of punches being thrown and landing.

Suddenly, a small man was thrown out of the cabin and onto the grass. He tried to scramble to his feet, but even from here his crippled leg was obvious.

Before the crippled man could quite find his balance, Muldaur raced out and kicked him in the stomach.

The man folded in half, collapsed to the ground. Muldaur kicked him three more times. The man screamed twice.

Lights came on in a nearby house. In moments a woman in a nightgown and robe appeared, carrying a formidable shotgun.

Muldaur got in one more savage kick and then ran away, lost in the midnight moon and the train whistle up in the bluffs surrounding the city.

Anna did not sleep well that night. She lay abed wondering why Muldaur had kicked the crippled man. Surely it had something to do with his wife's murder.

* * *

"You're determined to go and get me in trouble, aren't you, Anna?" Chief Ryan said. But he smiled as he said it.

"Well, you can always say that since I was the one who saw the body first, you think it's only right that I follow up on it."

The chief's smile vanished. With his white hair and big Irish face he would have been grandfatherly except for the scar that stretched from his cheekbone to his jawline. Chief Ryan hadn't been a very exemplary cop in his younger days. It was said that he'd occasionally lock himself in a cell with a criminal who had done something particularly onerous and give the man a chance to defend himself in a fistfight. It was safe to assume that Ryan had won most of those fights.

The chief shook his head. "Anna, I've got two detectives in there who're just waiting for you to make a mistake so they can go running to the mayor. Those two can make all the mistakes they want and nobody'll bother 'em. But if you make a mistake—I won't have any choice, Anna. The mayor, the sonofabitch—and please excuse my French— the mayor'll make me fire you."

"I won't make any mistakes, Chief. I promise."

He smiled again and, despite the scar, looked just the way grandfathers should always look.

Stephanie Muldaur answered on the fourth knock. Instead of a dress, today she wore a man's work shirt and corduroys.

"Is your father home?"

Stephanie shook her pretty head. "No."

"Do you know where I could find him?"

"He's at the quarry today, I expect."

Muldaur's religion did not believe that white men should have anything to do with any other race. This included work. There was a quarry on the edge of town run by a man of Muldaur's faith. Muldaur worked there whenever the owner needed an extra hand.

Anna looked past Stephanie into the jumble of the shack. "Mind if I come in and we talk for a minute?"

"About what?"

"About your mother and father."

"My dad said you're violating God's law by bein' a policewoman."

Anna smiled. "I expect I'll leave that for God to decide."

The girl frowned. "That's blasphemy, talkin' like that."

Anna went inside.

The main room consisted of a potbellied stove; a sad, cheap three-piece parlor suite of upholstered sofa, rocker, and armchair; and enough pictures of a brooding Jesus to cover a dozen walls. But the smell was what held Anna—the high, sour odor of vomit.

Anna again felt sorry for the girl. She lived like an animal here, with no idle pleasures in her young life, just the dark, harsh world of a malevolent God.

Anna sat on the edge of the armchair. "When did the snake bite your mom?"

"How come you're askin' the same questions Chief Ryan did yesterday?"

"We just need to make sure of things."

The girl looked down at her hands. "It bit her yesterday when she was out back."

"Out back?"

"Snake pit. Dad keeps 'em down there and brings 'em when we need 'em."

"How many snakes?" Anna said. She wanted to shudder.

"A dozen or so, I guess."

"Would you show it to me?"

The girl looked up. "The snake pit?"

"Yes. Please."

So Stephanie took her out to the snake pit.

The backyard was just as cluttered and dirty as the main room, a junkyard in the making.

Stephanie led Anna to the pit, which was covered with a grate and anchored with bricks. The river ran past less than ten feet away.

Even before she saw them, Anna heard them, the rattlesnakes with their sleek, sickening skin and their murderous noises.

She peered down through the grate and saw them entangled, heads darting upward as they shot fangs at her. The smell was unclean. Their eyes seemed to glow and glare.

"How did your mother get the snakes out of there?"

Stephanie shrugged. "Used a stick. They'll wrap around it."

"When did she take them out?"

"Real early. Then she let 'em set in the sack so they'd get good and mean. That's the way God wants 'em to be."

"How many snakes did she take out?"

"Three, I guess."

"And took them to where the baptism was being held?"

"Uh-huh."

"Did you see her get bit?"

Stephanie stared at her a long time. "You don't think she got bit?"

"Stephanie, I'm just asking you a question. No need for you to get mad."

Stephanie sighed. "You're gonna get me whipped, I hope you know that. My dad, if he finds out I talked to you—" She looked down at the snakes. "I guess I didn't actually see her get bit."

"But you're sure it was a snakebite that killed her?"

Stephanie raised her eyes and stared hard at Anna. "What else would it have been?"

She waited for him on the corner, the handsome young crippled man she'd seen John Muldaur beat last night.

In the afternoon light his face looked grim, bruised and puffy. He had the kind of gentle good looks that bring out the maternal in some women.

He worked at an awning company—the day shift—and was just now getting off work. He had a clubfoot and every time he stepped down on his right leg, his whole body jerked a little.

"Mr. Ames?"

"Yes."

He did not seem happy about seeing her.

"Mind if I walk home with you?"

"What if I did mind? Would you leave me alone?"

She smiled. "No, I guess I wouldn't."

He glared at her. "You're a sinner, lady. I hope you know that."

"We're all sinners, Mr. Ames. Even you."

They walked half a block. Downtown Cedar Rapids was busy, almost festive on this warm, early spring afternoon. Ladies in big picture hats and formidable bustles strolled the sidewalks. Young couples in fancy bicycle costumes rode by on tandem bikes. And horses of every description trotted by.

"I saw him beat you up last night."

"What're you talkin' about?"

"You know what I'm talking about, Mr. Ames. John Muldaur came to your place and beat you up. I want to know why."

Ames shrugged. "I owed him some money and didn't pay him back."

She thought of how Ames had been the only one with tears in his eyes as Rachael Muldaur lay dead yesterday. She made an assumption. "He beat you up because you made love to his wife."

"He tell you that?"

"No, Mr. Ames, but you just did."

He didn't say anything, though he did look as if he were going to cry again. *Trust your instincts,* the great criminologist Marie François Goron always said. And so she had. Reasonable to assume that a woman would be involved with the kind of violence she'd seen last night between Muldaur and this man.

"I didn't want it to happen and neither did she. It just . . . happened is all."

"And Muldaur found out?"

He shook his head. "No, Stephanie found out. There was a spot where her mother used to take her out in the woods. That's where Rachael and I always went when we . . . you know. Anyway, Stephanie went walking out there by herself a couple of weeks ago and stumbled on us."

"What did she say?"

"Nothing."

"Nothing at all?"

He shook his head. "Rachael got dressed and ran after her, but Stephanie wouldn't say anything to her at all."

"But she told her father?"

"Not for a week or so. It was terrible—us just waitin' for her to let him know about it and all. But we knew soon as he found out because he came in the house one day and picked Rachael up and threw her against the stove—knocked the whole thing down—and then he started kickin' her the way he kicked me last night."

"Did she come to you?"

"She tried. But he followed her. He kicked her around some more and then dragged her back home." He paused, looking mad for the first time. "I went out and got drunk that night. I couldn't stand the thought of what he was doin' to her. Then I came home and found out that he was plannin' on payin' me back, too."

"Paying you back?"

"Like I said, I was drunk, so I wasn't too swift that night. I got inside and laid down without lightin' a lantern and then I heard them."

"Them?"

"Rattlesnakes. He'd dumped half a dozen of them in my place."

"You didn't get bit?"

"No. But it took me till dawn to find every one of 'em."

"You think he really wanted to kill you?"

Ames snorted. "Sure he did. Half a dozen rattlers? Sure he did."

"When was the last time you saw Rachael alive?"

"Yesterday, just as she was goin' to the river. I decided to go to the baptism. He couldn't keep me from that. But I went early so I could speak to Rachael."

"And did you?"

"I tried but she was sick. Couldn't swallow right or something. Kept kind've grabbin' her throat."

"She'd already been bitten, probably."

"I never saw no snake-bit person act like that. She kept throwin' up. I had to hold the snakes for her while she got sick."

"Did she tell you a snake had bitten her?"

"No. She just kept sayin' she was sick and didn't know why."

They had reached Ames's cabin.

By now tears stood clearly in Ames's eyes.

"I don't think it was no snakebite. I think he killed her some other way."

"What other way?"

"I don't know. You're supposed to be the high and mighty policewoman. Why don't you figure it out?"

And with that Ames took his limp and his tears and his petulant anger and went into his cabin.

"No marks?"

"None whatsoever," Doc McWilliams said.

"Are they usually easy to spot?"

"Oh, sure. They get infected. You can't miss 'em."

"Does that mean she wasn't bitten by a snake, then?"

"Not absolutely. I mean, I suppose there's a way to get bitten without it showing. But after you telling me what that feller Ames said, I'm more doubtful than ever."

"Then how did she die?"

"Well, if she was throwing up and having trouble swallowing, that sounds like she might have been fed some strychnine."

"Isn't that what they use for rat poison?"

"Uh-huh."

Doc McWilliams's office smelled of his pipe and the peppermint candy he was always giving youngsters. McWilliams was a sixty-year-old widower who could be seen in his fez leading the Shriner parade every year.

"How many places in town sell rat poison?"

McWilliams thought a moment. "Oh, probably two, three at most."

Anna stood up, straightening her pinafore and inhaling the peppermints. "They always smell so good."

Doc McWilliams laughed. "You always manage to get one of these, don't you?"

Anna smiled and accepted the peppermint. "Yes, and I appreciate it every time, too."

She had just left Doc McWilliams's office when John Muldaur appeared before her on the sidewalk.

"You stay away from my daughter!" he shouted.

Several people standing in front of the Greene Opera House turned to watch the two.

"I was only investigating your wife's death."

"There's nothing to investigate. She died of a snakebite and you can't prove otherwise."

By now Anna was almost as angry as Muldaur. "Maybe I can, Mr. Muldaur. Maybe I can."

And with that she turned and headed toward Second Street, where the two stores she wanted were located.

Muldaur did some more shouting but she hurried on, blocking out his rage. She kept thinking about what he'd just said: "You can't prove otherwise."

That was something a guilty man might say.

Fifteen minutes later, she left the second store, clutching a small dark box in her right hand.

Dusk was just starting to fall. The lamplighters were already at work. Mothers called children in for supper.

She walked briskly to the cabin where Ames lived and knocked.

He came to the door disheveled and sad-looking.

"I have one more question for you, Mr. Ames."

"I'm sick of seein' your face."

"This won't take long."

He sighed. "Go ahead. You will anyway."

"Do you know what I mean when I say a convulsion?"

"Like epilepsy?"

"Yes. Like that."

"What about it?"

"When you were walking with Rachael Muldaur yesterday, did she go into convulsions?"

"I—Yes, I think she did. Right after she vomited the second time, her whole body started shaking. I had to set the snake sack down and hold her tight."

"That's all I wanted to know, Mr. Ames. I won't bother you anymore."

Ten minutes later, as she drew near the Muldaur shack, Anna could hear the soft lapping of the river. In the summer months she wished to have a suitor who wore a straw boater and played a banjo as they drifted downriver in a canoe past the glowing Chinese lanterns of the Ellis Pavillion. She'd seen this in a vaudeville skit last winter and hoped it would happen to her.

Just as she was about to knock, she heard an unwelcome sound. A rattlesnake angry at something. At first she assumed the rattle was coming from the snakepit out back. But then she realized that the sound was coming from inside the shack.

She knocked.

Stephanie answered the door. She wore the same dress she'd had on at the river the other day. Around her slender left forearm was wound a diamondback rattlesnake.

Seeing who it was, Stephanie smiled. "You're a-scared of him, aren't you?"

"Yes."

"If you was good instead of evil then you wouldn't have no cause to be a-scared of him."

"I'd like to come in and talk to you about your father."

"I won't put him back in the pit."

"That's all right. I'll come in anyway."

Stephanie glared at her a long moment and then stepped back and let Anna enter.

Anna took the same edge of the same chair she'd sat in earlier.

Stephanie went over and sat on the couch. The rattlesnake coiled and uncoiled, hissed and hissed. Anna tried not to notice it.

"Do you know what this is?"

Anna held up the small box she'd bought a while ago.

"No."

"It's rat poison. Your father bought a box of it the day before yesterday."

"We got rats, so close to the river and all. When we catch 'em, we put 'em in the snakepit. The snakes go crazy."

"Your mother was killed by rat poison. Somebody put it in something she ate or drank."

"You mean my dad?"

Anna nodded. "Yes. Your father."

Just then, as if he'd been summoned, John Muldaur came through the door and said, "I told you to leave my little daughter alone." He turned to Stephanie. "How come you let her in here anyway?"

Stephanie was cowering. Even with the rattlesnake twined around her arm, she was afraid her father would strike her.

He stood in the middle of the floor, crazed and frightening as an asylum escapee.

Anna stood up and showed him the box of rat poison pellets.

"Where'd you get those?" he said.

"The same place you did. Baxter's Drug Company. You murdered your wife with them."

"That's what you think?"

"That's what I think."

"Well, I'd like to see you prove it." His growing anger made the room seem smaller, escape impossible.

"I think I can. Ames told me how she threw up and had trouble swallowing and how she went into convulsions. You don't do any of that when you've been bit by a snake. But you do that when you've been fed strychnine."

Muldaur looked at his daughter and then he looked back to Anna.

"I want you out of here. You defile this room with your presence. Do you understand me?"

As if in harmony with the master of the house, the rattlesnake started hissing again.

But Anna had to press, goad him into a confession.

"I can prove you bought these, Muldaur, and intentionally gave them to your wife."

She started to say more but then, without any warning, Muldaur brought his hand around and slapped the box from her fingers to the floor.

The small pellets were hurled across the floor, noisy as dice.

"I want you off my property right now!" Muldaur said.

He grabbed Anna's shoulder and started to push her to the door, but just then Anna got her first good look at the pellets in lantern light.

She hadn't examined the pellets before. She hadn't even thought about what color they might be.

They were green.

And that was when she remembered Stephanie at the river the other day and the faint green stain on her gingham dress. Some kind of green dye?

She stared at Stephanie now. Wearing the same dress. With the same faint green stain.

"I've made a mistake, Mr. Muldaur," Anna said. "A terrible mistake."

Muldaur saw where she was looking and said quickly, in a voice almost gentle with grief, "I'm the one who made a mistake. I shouldn't have poisoned my wife."

For the first time Anna felt some respect for the man. He would take the blame for the murder his daughter had committed.

She spoke softly. "You killed your mother, didn't you, Stephanie?"

"Say nothing! Say nothing!" her father said, his voice booming again.

But Stephanie waited until it was quiet again and said, "She was a sinner and had to be punished. And I knew my father loved her too much to ever punish her the way he should." She stroked the snake coiled around her arm. "She asked me to make her some lunch—it was her time of month and she was feelin' peaked—and so I didn't have no trouble puttin' it in her food—except I spilled a glass of water when I had one of them pellets in my hand and it stained my dress."

"Child," John Muldaur said, tears making his eyes shiny

162

and his voice almost terrible to hear. "Child, I would've told them that I killed your mother. That's my duty as your father, to protect you that way."

Just as he was starting toward his daughter, it happened.

Stephanie took the rattlesnake in both hands and turned its head toward her face. Then she squeezed it very hard, so that it became enraged. Its rattling sounds filled the room. The snake's head lashed out at her, its fangs sinking deep into her neck.

Even before it was through imparting its poison, John Muldaur had the snake in his hand and was killing it by smashing it against the doorframe.

As for Stephanie Muldaur, she had leaned her head against the back of the shabby sofa and was crying softly.

"She was a sinner and I had to kill her; I had to."

Her father sank to one knee and put his head in her lap, where he, too, began to cry.

That was how Anna left them, sorrowful and crazed in their dark religion, as she set off to get Doc McWilliams to purge the poison from Stephanie before it killed her.

". . . That Married Dear Old Dad"

Margaret Maron

"I didn't know old-fashioned girls like Jessica still existed," Florence Weston had said when her only son abruptly eloped seven months ago and cheated her out of the fun of a big splashy wedding.

Of course, it's the bride's mother who always gets to run things, she reminded herself. The groom's mother has to stand where she's told, tell the bride's mother how lovely everything is, and buy a beige dress. Mrs. Weston hated what beige did to her skin, so maybe an elopement was just as well. Besides, if James had been made to wait through engagement party, showers, teas, tuxedo fittings, and all the other formalities connected with a big wedding to a *good* girl—

No mother wants to think that her only child is that strongly influenced by his . . . um, libido; but when she considered that string of really unsuitable young ladies— *Ladies?* Strumpets, more like it—that James seemed to attract—well! Forgoing "O Promise Me" and being escorted down the aisle (in a beige dress, don't forget!) seemed a small price to pay if James's hastiness brought her dear little Jessica as a daughter-in-law.

James had inherited the family real estate firm when he was only twenty, and surely it showed an underlying strength of character that he *did* work as hard as he played? Nevertheless, when he first started talking about settling down and taking his rightful place in the community, Mrs. Weston had been afraid he meant to try and housebreak that flashy (trashy) Sherri Conrad—so afraid, in fact, that she'd insisted upon attending one of Miss Conrad's performances.

And performance was certainly the right term for what she did with that cordless microphone right there in the Holiday Inn's cocktail lounge. Mrs. Weston conceded a certain earthy charm to her smoky voice, but those vulgar lyrics! Mrs. Weston might be a lady, but she was shrewd enough to see that the golden spotlight lent the young woman pseudosophistication and glamour; and judging by what the creature was willing to do in public, James probably wasn't strong enough to resist what she was no doubt willing to do in private.

Like father like son, Mrs. Weston worried. (A good man, but too prone to the weaknesses of the flesh. Had he controlled his appetites, he might have avoided that acute ptomaine—or was it botulism one got from indulging in oysters out of season?)

She invited the young woman to Sunday morning brunch; and, just as she'd expected, bright morning sunlight was less kind than subdued spotlights. The singer's makeup looked tawdry, her nail polish garish, and she could certainly stand to scrub her neck and elbows.

Mrs. Weston liked to think it was that brunch that opened James's eyes to Miss Conrad's unsuitability. In truth, Miss Conrad turned out to be as indiscreet as a Harvey Wallbanger.

She'd been booked to sing for a week at the Blue Star Lounge down in Wilmington, and when James went down to surprise her, he caught her in bed with the Blue Star Lounge's piano player. He'd stormed off to a party at someone's beach house, found Jessica in the kitchen slicing brown bread, and, entranced by her quiet wholesome beauty, swept her off to the nearest preacher.

With his pick of the town's houses, he had installed her in a Victorian cottage that suited her old-fashioned charm.

A *perfect* daughter-in-law, thought Mrs. Weston, watching Jessica knead bread dough in her sunny kitchen. No need for *her* to shrink from sunlight. Everything about the child radiated well-scrubbed cleanliness. "I do hope James appreciates you," she said.

"He does." Jessica smiled. "You know he does. But he's so worried about the business. Even with the lowered interest rates, if this recession keeps up . . . I really ought to look for work myself."

"Surely not *now!*" said Mrs. Weston, and was absolutely delighted to see her suspicions confirmed by Jessica's rosy blush. Impulsively, she jumped up and hugged the girl. "My dear! I'm so pleased. Have you told him yet?"

"No, not while he's under so much pressure." She blushed again. "Besides, it's been such a lovely secret. I'm glad you've guessed though. With my own mother dead . . ."

Teary-eyed, they hugged again.

"I always envied my friends who had daughters," Mrs. Weston said shakily. "And now I finally have a daughter of my very own."

Contentment wreathed the kitchen as Jessica returned to her kneading. She broke off a lump of dough and shaped it into a miniature ring.

"What's that for?" asked Mrs. Weston.

"Dessert. James is crazy about sweet rolls with my special honey-nut topping."

"You spoil him," said Mrs. Weston, beaming.

But that's what a wife *should* do, thought Jessica as she tidied the kitchen after Mother Weston left. Marriage was a partnership, wasn't it? If the husband wanted to spoil the wife by going out to earn their living single-handedly, then why shouldn't the wife spoil him back with a perfectly ordered house and delicious little treats?

Dreamily, she pictured James's reaction to her news. He claimed not to want children, but she knew exactly what he'd say. He'd be tender again, solicitous, anxious for her well-being. She would smile indulgently, assure him she felt fine, that the doctor had said . . .

Jessica stopped daydreaming and considered doctors. Perhaps an up-to-date obstetrician?

No.

Old Dr. Mills was a GP who'd been the Weston physician for almost forty years, and Jessica believed in family traditions. He'd brought James into the world and he could certainly deliver James's son, too. Besides, Dr. Mills was such a sweetie and so considerate of her fears—had even scolded James for taking too many barbiturates when the real estate business worsened.

"Less alcohol and more exercise!" he'd ordered.

She should probably start exercising, too. That afternoon she wrote a note to her sister about the baby. The post office was twelve long blocks away, but the walk would be good for her.

"For both of us," she emended happily as she rummaged through James's desk in the den for a stamp.

Outdoors it was a glorious spring day. She walked briskly past yellow forsythias and purple hyacinths, past drifts of daffodils and flowering dogwoods, thinking positive and beautiful thoughts. Inside that secret recess of the mind never touched by intellect, Jessica superstitiously believed one could prenatally mark one's baby for good or ill; so she dwelt on butterflies and blossoming crabapples and blue skies overhead.

At eight-thirty, when James let himself in through the garage door, the house was redolent of freshly baked rolls and a perfect coq au vin. Because he often had to show houses at odd hours, Jessica never knew when he'd get home, so she'd learned to cook things that were all the better for being reheated.

She threw aside her apron and rushed to kiss him. James

gave her a squeeze, sniffed the air, and asked, "When's dinner?"

"You have time for one gin and tonic," she said, handing him a tall chilled glass with a slice of lime perched on the rim, just as he liked it.

But by the time she brought in their plates to the candlelit dining table, he was gulping down the last of a second drink. While they ate, Jessica noticed puffy bags under his eyes. "You're working too hard," she said. "You look tired."

He gave another of those impatient sighs. "Would you stop being the perfect attentive wife for just once? Quit babying me, okay?"

"Maybe I'm getting into practice," she said demurely.

"In practice for what? Oh, my God!"

Jessica saw his dismay, and tears flooded her eyes.

James laid aside his fork and patted her hand. "Look, I'm sorry, Jess, but dammit! I thought we agreed. I mean, with business so rotten— Don't cry. It complicates the hell out of things, but I'll manage. Somehow."

"You mean *we'll* manage, right, darling?" she asked, trying to smile through her tears.

"Yeah, yeah, sure." He patted her hand again. "Got any more of this chicken stew left?"

He mixed himself another drink as she refilled his plate and then put dessert in the oven.

It took twenty minutes for the yeasty confection to bake, for the viscous mixture of honey, walnuts, and spices to seep down the edges and permeate sweetly through the soft crust.

James greedily eyed the second portion. "Aren't you having any?"

"I have to watch my diet now," she said. For the first time she really looked at his faint double chin, saw how self-indulgent his mouth looked as he chewed.

James was sipping his fourth drink as she cleared away the dishes, which was probably why his mind seemed to wander from his favorite program. Much earlier than usual, he rose, yawned, and said, "I've got a couple coming to see that house over in Dobbs after they get off from work, so I'll probably be late again tomorrow night. Guess I'd better turn in early."

"Me, too," said Jessica.

She was in bed before him and had almost drifted off to sleep when she heard James fumbling with the sleeping pills in the bathroom. Another, she thought dreamily, and wondered if that many would seem credible? Still, Dr. Mills *had* warned him how easy it was to overdose while drinking.

In memory, she read again the letter she'd found in James's desk and that now lay strewn like confetti along her walk to the post office:

James luv—
  The earrings are gorgeous!!!! Of course, I'll forgive you for thinking a two-bit piano player could ever— But I won't talk about him if you won't talk about that man-stealer who tricked you into marriage just so she can stiff you with a big divorce settlement. Surprise! I'll be singing at the Dobbs Tavern all this week and I'm just dying to have my sweet baby show me some more houses. I won't wear anything but my new gold earrings!!!!

                                        Love and kisses forever,
                                        Sherri

James stumbled clumsily into bed and turned out the light as Jessica reviewed her neat kitchen. She'd thoroughly scrubbed all the dinner dishes, especially the dessert pan. Not that anyone would even think of checking. Not after Dr. Mills confirmed how freely James mixed barbiturates and alcohol. There'd be no more suspicions about James's accidental death than when James's father had died.

Of ptomaine, was it?

("And a good thing, too, if you ask me," Mrs. Weston's sister had confided shortly after she and James were married. "Florence would have just *died* if she'd known that he and Mable Byrd's oversexed teenage daughter bzz-bzz-bzz.")

An absurd speculation leaped to mind, but she dismissed it firmly, closed her eyes again, and, as James slept himself to death beside her, Jessica folded her hands protectively over her still-flat stomach and began to think beautiful, positive thoughts.

Parris Green

Carole Nelson Douglas

London: November 1886

I find no Sunday morning task more satisfying than that of
rousing the slothful. Doubtless this is due to my upbringing
as a parson's daughter, but it was aggravated by my days as a
governess.

In this case the object of my dutiful disturbance had more
reason than most to lie abed. Nonetheless, I crossed the
threshold of her bedchamber with a certain smug rectitude.
I, after all, had already been to church that morning, and she
had not been to church in all of our acquaintance, unless it
was to sing a solo.

The room lay beneath the drawn-curtain pall of half
shadow that speaks of the sick chamber or the place of ill
repute. A figure in the corner lurked motionless; luckily, I
knew it for a dressmaker's form called "Jersey Lillie." I
moved slowly to avoid stubbing a boot toe against the maze
of trunks and hatboxes that lay scattered through the dim
room. In due time I arrived safe and silent at the window,
where I wrenched open the heavy brocade panels on their
rods so swiftly that the curtain rings . . . well, rang.

"Agh!"

The bedclothes rose like a disturbed spirit as daylight

scalded the coverlet, then a head emerged from under the linens. My friend and chambermate Irene Adler sat blinking in the sudden brightness.

"What on earth is it, Nell? Flood? Fire? The Apocalypse?"

"It is nearly noon on Sunday, Irene," I replied. "And that awful man has called again."

She pushed tumbling locks of russet hair from her face, her eyes still wincing at the light. Irene would never go to bed braided like a sensible woman. "Awful man—oh, you mean that Norton creature who stormed our lodgings a few weeks ago. Well, send him away!"

She swiftly grasped her coverlet—an oceanic expanse of emerald-green brocade that had begun as draperies—and coiled into an indiscernible lump under the covers.

I went over to address this interesting cocoon.

"It is not that Norton creature. It is that odious self-appointed poet. He is wearing brown velveteen breeches with yellow hose, an orange vest, and a soft hat the color of rust. On the Sabbath," I finished with indignation, if not relevancy.

"Oh." The buried form flailed to the surface again, finally flinging away a tidal wave of green. "You mean Oscar Wilde. I believe that he has Roman Catholic leanings. Perhaps that explains his gaudy Sunday attire. What does he want?"

"You."

"He said nothing more than that?"

"He said a great deal more, but none of it made much sense."

"What time is it?" she asked with a frown.

I consulted the watch on my lapel. "Eleven."

"Eleven? How ghastly." Amid a froth of nightgown, Irene squirmed to the bed's edge and swung a bare foot over the erratically carpeted floor. She yawned. "He must have been at the theater last evening, too. What urgent matter—imagined or real—could drag Oscar Wilde from his bed at such an inopportune hour? Oh, very well. I'll come see for myself as soon as I'm presentable. In the meantime, entertain him, Nell."

"How?"

"Make conversation."

"I cannot talk to the man! He is so full of elaborate nonsense that he quite makes my head ache and my tongue tie."

"Of course you can talk to him. Oscar Wilde could make conversation with a cockroach."

"Perhaps I should provide an audience of such, which will better appreciate his company."

"The longer you dawdle here, the longer it shall be before I can emerge to relieve you," Irene pointed out sweetly.

I sighed and returned to our parlor, where a very large and colorful spider awaited his sacrificial fly.

"Ah, the fair and faithful Penelope," he greeted me, presuming to employ my Christian name. "Four seductive syllables that end with o-p-e. Add the *H* from Huxleigh and you have all men's hope. Ope the door to my soul, my Psyche with a crochet hook."

I refused to rise to his ludicrous bait. Soon Mr. Wilde was safely discoursing on his favorite subject, himself, and quoting Mr. Whistler's cruel letter about him in *The World:* "'He dines at our tables and picks from our platters the plums for the pudding he peddles in the provinces.' An outp-p-p-ouring of p-p-pathetically p-p-poor alliteration," Mr. Wilde stuttered mockingly in complaint. I never knew a man to thrive so on insult.

At last came the soft click of Irene's bedchamber door. This subtle sound was followed by the crackle of what I recognized as her crimson Oriental wrapper, hardly the proper garb in which to receive a gentleman caller on any day of the week, but the theatrical temperament will not be denied.

I saw our guest's long, slightly melancholy face brighten as if dashed with a dose of daylight, and turned to watch her arrival myself. At least she had put her hair up into a brunette satin arrangement of tendrils and chignon that glinted red and gold in the daylight.

"You must forgive me for calling at so inopportune a time, my dear Irene," the abominable Oscar began. "You have sung late at the theater and deserve to slumber undisturbed until twilight. I have given you scarce time to attire yourself, but one can never catch you *en déshabillé*, I suspect. You look splendid—like a savage empress from the court of Xanadu."

"Thank you," she said simply, sitting on the old armchair with its embroidered shawl hiding the wear. She crossed a leg over the other with a crackle of elderly silk sharper than paper rustling. A dainty foot just visible in its purple satin slipper swung in measured pendulum time. "Why am I so honored to have Oscar Wilde serving as my personal Chanticleer?"

"An ugly hour," he admitted with a sigh. "But an uglier event unfolds only miles away," he declaimed. That is another thing I have never liked about the man, his endless bent for self-dramatization. "A tragedy in the making, even as we speak."

Irene laughed. "My dear Oscar, at least half a million tragedies are in the making of a Sunday morning in London town. What is so special about yours?"

He sat on the fringed ottoman by the fireplace—an unfortunate choice, for the low seat jackknifed his long awkward legs like a stork's—and pushed the spaniel's ears of silky brown hair from his face. "It is perplexing. And scandalous."

"Ah." Irene's idle foot tapped the floor smartly. "You are consulting me about another . . . case." She had recently and successfully inquired into the whereabouts of a gold cross he had given to Florence Stoker when she was still Florence Balcombe.

He nodded soberly. "Have you heard of the artist Lysander Parris?" When Irene shook her head, he waved a languid hand. "No matter. He is not very successful—one of these dedicated souls who lived in Chelsea before it became fashionable, a neighbor of mine. He could earn more from selling his house than from his entire collection of works."

"An impecunious artist—a redundant description if I ever heard one. Are not all artists impecunious?" Irene asked ruefully. "What difficulty faces this Lysander Parris that makes him of any interest beyond a passing charitable instinct?"

"He has gone mad."

Irene waited. Mad artists, she might have pointed out, were no more notable than poor ones.

"Quite mad," Mr. Wilde repeated, rising to pace on the worn runner before the fireplace. When a man of more than six feet paces before two seated women, the effect commands their attention, if not their admiration. "He has barricaded himself in the attic studio with his latest model and will not cease painting her. He will answer no knock, take no food or drink, say nothing to his distraught wife and children. He will not even talk to me," Mr. Wilde added with utter disbelief.

"I cannot imagine that," Irene commented. "Can you, Nell?"

I murmured something indecipherable.

"Artists," she added loftily, "are given to such obsessive spates of work. No doubt he will emerge when his latest painting is done, or he is hungry and thirsty enough. Or when the exhausted model demands to leave."

"No." Oscar Wilde paused before our hearth, one hand thrust into the breast of his velveteen jacket. His momentary stillness and silence were ever so much more impressive than his chatter and clatter. "The exhausted model will not demand to leave. From all I can determine, she is dead."

Within the half hour, our mismatched trio was jolting along in a four-wheeler toward Chelsea. Irene had dressed in a striking bronze satin gown bordered with rose moiré, and she donned long, tan-colored gloves in the carriage.

"Tell me of the household," she instructed even as she thrust the final pins into her rose moiré bonnet. Its pink and white plumes trembled in protest of such treatment.

Mr. Wilde complied with far more grace than he had managed in whistling for the vehicle minutes before. He folded his hands atop his cane—his gloves at least were conventional, the color of spoiled clotted cream—and began with an odd smile.

"The household. What can one say of any painter's household? It is as irregular as his compositions may be symmetrical. I should begin with Parris himself. He is a man of late middle age, of no distinguishing social graces, who has achieved fame in only one arena: for the lovely, decadent, lush, languid, gorgeous, gilded, intricate greens that signal his work. He is a master of the color green. I cannot look at an acanthus leaf or meet the eye on a peacock's tail, or view the emerald on the forehead of the goddess Kali, but that I think of it as Parris green."

"I presume that Mr. Parris is not Irish?" I asked somewhat tartly.

The poet's supercilious eye rested upon me with content. "I fear not, but you mistake my passion for green, dear Miss Huxleigh. I adore green not as a patriotic symbol but as the lost shadow of Eden in our world today; as the occult flame of jealousy; as the velvety unseen mosses that clothe and conquer the stone; as the ageless power in the very pinpoint of a cat's eye."

I could not help shuddering. "I do not care for cats. Or green."

"Of course not," Mr. Wilde said with something of pity in his voice. He turned to Irene. "Has my description been of assistance?"

"Of course not," she echoed him, "that is why your descriptions are always so enchanting. Mere usefulness would destroy their effect. Tell me, if you can, of the other inhabitants of the house, including the model who is now an apparent epitome of the still life."

I shuddered again, but was not much noticed. Irene had an unfortunate talent for matching gloomy poetic maunderings macabre stroke for macabre stroke. No doubt it came of too long study of excessively mordant opera librettos—all blood and betrayal and death. In fact, her eyes sparkled with mischief behind the clouds of her veiling as she watched the poet struggle to report mere fact instead of fancy.

"As well compose a sonnet from a laundry list," he said, sniffing. "Very well, the dramatis personae as recited by

Bottom: We have the artist in question. We have his latest model, a pale and interesting girl employed as a housemaid, whom he has elevated from her knees on the kitchen stones to similar poses on a studio couch."

"A kitchen maid? How long has Mr. Parris been so taken with her?"

"For months, say the gossips along Tite Street."

"What of the artist's family?"

"His wife is an industrious little woman, much given to worrying, as any artist's spouse must."

"Speaking of which," Irene interjected, "I understand that I am to congratulate you upon the birth of a second son."

Our fellow passenger sighed, a slight smile on his strong-bowed lips. "Vyvyan."

"A lovely name," Irene said.

"Lovelier for a daughter, perhaps. I had hopes, but—"

"How commendable," I put in, "for a father to desire a daughter rather than an endless parade of sons."

"Praise, Miss Huxleigh?" Mr. Wilde's eyes were wickedly amused, as if he well understood how much he scandalized me. "I fear I had nothing to do with it. A higher power than mere hope determined the matter."

"And how is Constance?" Irene inquired.

"Well," he said of his wife, flicking a spot of lint from his velvet knee. "Better than Amelia Parris, poor woman. Her husband's mania for the new model has been the talk of Chelsea, but Mrs. Parris is a simple soul who cares more for the price of eggs than the bankruptcy of reputation."

"What other family members inhabit the house?"

"The usual parade of offspring, most young enough for the schoolroom, except for Lawrence."

"The eldest son?"

Mr. Wilde nodded, then leaned his slouch-hatted head out of the carriage window. For such gestures his unorthodox headgear was more suitable than the conventional top hat. "We near Cheyne Place. I will let you see young Lawrence for yourself."

Once the carriage had jolted to a stop, he stepped out to

assist us. I hated to take the creature's hand, but there was no help for it. Nor could I forgo murmuring my thanks. I cannot say why I had taken such a dislike to Mr. Wilde; there was no more reason for it than for his taking such a mad fancy to me. Perhaps, like the clever puss, he made a point of loving those who hated him. I suppose that could be considered a kind of Christian charity, but in Mr. Wilde's case I felt that the impulse was far more perverse.

We stood for a moment on the cobblestones, surveying the house. Unlike many in fashionable Tite Street, where even I knew that such artists as Whistler and Sargent kept studios, this house had not been revived with fresh, stylish colors. A smoky patina fumed its dull brick facade, and the door was painted a sober but chipping black, as if in tawdry mourning.

Faded damask draped the windows, all in sinister shades of green.

"Why do you think Mr. Parris became so obsessed with his model?" Irene asked the poet.

"She was young and from outside this depressing house. He thought her beautiful, no doubt. Perhaps he had tired of failure and growing older, and painted a more appetizing future on his canvases."

"If you have been unable to enter the studio, why are you convinced that she is dead?"

"It is possible to view a section of the room through a . . . er, keyhole. Yes, Miss Huxleigh, to such vulgar snooping even I was forced to stoop." Mr. Wilde eyed Irene again. "Parris had a strong lock put on the inside of the door years ago. He has always disliked being interrupted while painting. I can only attest to what little I saw with my own eyes: the lady in question not only is supernaturally motionless, but her pallor is beyond the ordinary pale of fashionable rice powder. Her lips have turned blue."

I made an involuntary cry at this macabre detail, but Irene merely narrowed her eyes as if to better visualize the grisly scene. "And what do you think has killed her? Or who?"

"That I am afraid to speculate upon," the poet admitted.

"Poor Parris must be made to forsake his studio so that the lady's body can be carried away before the neighbors and the police scent a scandal."

"My dear Oscar, when the young woman's body is carried away, there is certain to be a scandal if her death was not natural."

"No death is natural," he declared, launching another high-flown speech. "A death should always be witnessed by a great poet, so that proper note may be taken of it."

"I really do not see what you expect me to do in this instance," Irene said, ignoring his egocentric prescription for death scenes.

"Pry the madman loose from his easel! Although they do not know the depth of my suspicion, his wife and son cannot do it, despite all their beyond-the-door pleadings; that is why I was sent for. I know Parris well, and in fact had obtained him some meager employment for illustrations in the literary magazines," he added. "Not my most eloquent words nor gilded syllables could wrest the man from his feverish painting. I count upon your woman's wit, my dear Irene. Besides, few men can resist you."

She smiled ruefully. "I encountered one of that rare breed only weeks ago."

"No!" Mr. Wilde drew back, clutching his breast. "What manner of depraved creature is he?"

"A barrister," Irene answered dryly.

"Oh." The poet recovered his aplomb and dropped his theatrics. "One cannot expect intelligence or sense from a barrister. My faith in your powers remains undiminished."

"We shall see," Irene answered. "Meanwhile—" She gestured to the rather grimy stoop that awaited our footfalls.

The house was as I expected: dark and narrow, with a battered spine of stairway and that stale wet odor of domiciles built near the supposed advantage of a river.

A woman admitted us, a stern figure in black bombazine who might have been a widow. She identified herself as "Mrs. McCorkle, the housekeeper" in a voice like a hacksaw and regarded Mr. Wilde with visible skepticism. Mrs. Parris, we were told, lay prostrate in her bedchamber; the children visited the homes of assorted acquaintances, who had been told only that their father had fallen suddenly ill; Mr. Parris still kept to his studio.

"These ladies," said Mr. Wilde, gesturing to us both with one sweep of a plump hand, "these lovely sibyls of Saffron Hill, will lend wisdom and succor to a sad situation. Miss Adler, Miss Huxleigh, and I will need no guidance to the upper stories."

"As you wish, sir," the woman answered sourly. "No one is here to gainsay you." She eyed Irene and myself as if we were dingy laundry, then retreated into the dismal drawing room on our left.

We climbed the dark, uncarpeted stairs, a landing window offering a glimpse of neglected back garden gone to weed and wildness. Up we went, for what seemed endless turns of the ungracious stairs but was only four stories.

At last the stairs ended at a broad wooden door.

"Much of the top floor has been made into a studio," Mr. Wilde informed us in a whisper.

I saw why it had been so convenient to view the room. With the steps leading up to the door, one could stand two or three risers down, lean forward, and be eye level with the peephole.

Mr. Wilde demonstrated by backing down four steps and doing precisely that. Irene and I flattened ourselves against the yellowing walls, while I contemplated a larger and more intimate view of the poet's velvet breeches than I wished.

He finally unbent with an almost satisfied sigh. "Nothing has changed. Not the model, nor the sounds of paint slap-dashing on canvas. Parris works on quite assiduously."

"Allow me." Irene assumed the same undignified posture with much more grace and squinted through the brass keyhole. She straightened a moment later, looking less optimistic than the poet. "The long plait of hair that entwines her throat," she asked him, "was it there before?"

"It entwines her throat?" He blinked like a cogitating owl. "I confess I was more impressed by her pallor than the disposition of her tresses. I have never been partial to that unimaginative shade of chestnut. You believe that Parris strangled her with her own hair? A most artistic conceit. I would not have thought it of him."

"Or a most conceited artist, to think that a model would care to die for a painting. The question is how she was posed before she died. Mr. Parris may have planned another of these languishing ladies mimicking death so popular in the salons—Ophelia floating amid her waterlilies, or Desdemona adrift on her bed linens. The woman's pallor could be merely cosmetic; she could keep so still simply because she is an accomplished model."

I clasped my hands. "Oh, Irene, of course! This is all a silly misunderstanding. We need not have come here at all." I gave Mr. Wilde a pointed look.

She regarded me fondly. "However, I must confess in turn that she looks quite convincingly dead. Mr. Parris will not open the door?"

The poet shook his head until his doleful locks rippled.

Irene lifted a fist and knocked briskly.

"Go away!" a voice thundered promptly. "I told you meddling fools to go away. I am not finished yet."

"Mr. Parris, sir," she replied, "your family is most concerned, and no doubt your model is . . . exhausted."

"Go away, damn, impertinent disrupters! I must put it on canvas. I must capture that look—"

"And we all are impatient to see the results of your labors. Even Oscar Wilde is here, waiting to tell a wider world about your work."

"That fulminating fop! He tells no one about anything other than himself! I told him to leave my house, and you may go, too, madam, whoever the devil you are."

Irene drew back, then lowered her gloved fist.

"Well?" Mr. Wilde asked breathlessly.

"We retreat," she ordered. With great difficulty, and much unwelcome jostling, we turned in the cramped stairway and made our sorry progress below.

At the first landing Irene drew Mr. Wilde to a stop. "Are Mr. Parris's paintings kept anywhere besides the studio?"

"I saw a number of canvases in a second-floor room."

"Then I would like to see them."

"Why?" I asked. "Surely there is nothing we can do here. The man's door is bolted from within and he will not open it. It is a matter for the authorities."

"Perhaps," Irene conceded. "Ultimately. Until then, if the artist refuses to speak with me, I will make do with the next best thing: I will commune with his work."

Mr. Wilde lifted his eyebrows, but led us without comment to the room in question.

Within minutes Irene and Mr. Wilde had pulled the stacked canvases from the wall and had propped them against the furniture. Most of the canvases were narrow, and as tall as people.

Oscar Wilde made a face, which was not difficult for him to do under any circumstances. "Not to my taste."

"What is your taste?" Irene asked.

"San Sebastian by Guido Reni," he retorted with authority. "A sublime subject."

"Ah." Irene tilted her head with a Mona Lisa smile. "The swooning, half-naked young man pierced by arrows. How . . . interesting, Oscar."

"The martyrdom of St. Stephen!" I exclaimed, happy to have understood what they were talking about for once. "I know it. A most inspirational subject, though sad."

His smile was as mysterious as Irene's. "More inspiring than these modern, insipidly lethal belladonna madonnas cloaked in green, whose suffering is so much more commonplace."

I studied the array. We stood amid a company of the dead model's likeness in every guise, her long dark hair caught up in a jeweled snood while she strolled in classical garb with a peacock—"Jealous *Juno,*" Irene pronounced; or she hung suspended in weed-swirled water clothed in mermaid's scales, a drowned sailor caught in the toils of her seaweed-dressed locks—*The Siren of the Rhine,* according to Irene; or she floated in diaphanous veils of lurid green from a bottle bearing a French label.

Irene nodded at the last work. "*La Fée Verte*—the seductive green fairy of absinthe, the liquor that entoils men and drives them mad. Does Mr. Parris drink it?"

Mr. Wilde shrugged. "Perhaps. All these . . . fancies feature the green pigments for which he is famous."

She nodded. "Parris green. Most effective. Most decadent. Is not arsenic a component of such green pigments?"

"Arsenic? I have heard—" Mr. Wilde's pasty complexion showed a more verdant cast. "You think that . . . ? I cannot see how."

"Nor can I. I merely comment on the fact that Mr. Parris's addiction to green has a deadly undertone. Of course, one would expect a pigment-based poison to affect the artist, not his model."

Irene strolled around the assembled pictures, contemplating their heavy-lidded subject face-to-face. "Mr. Parris's mania seems fixed upon the femme fatale, the kind of ruinous woman who preys upon men. One seldom sees the ruiners of women glamorized, perhaps because so few women paint, or are encouraged to. Yet the legions of ruined women must far outnumber the few men who stumble at the feet of a Delilah. At least my art—the opera—offers equal roles in villainy and heroics to men and women."

"Your art," the poet put in, "has an edge."

"So," said I, "does Irene. "And if she wishes a perfect model of an *homme fatale,* she need look no further than that Mephistopheles in miniature, the American artist, James Whistler."

Oscar Wilde laughed. "My neighbor, my mentor, my enemy, but then Jimmy is everybody's enemy, and his own most of all. A pity that he so seldom does self-portraits."

"Wicked women are too common these days to be intriguing," Irene put in. "It's Mr. Parris's heroines who intrigue me. Such unusual choices."

I studied the canvas she tilted into the light of the gasolier. Gone was the turgid hair; the figure's cropped head and rough masculine dress proclaimed Joan of Arc, if the copious fleurs-de-lis in the background had not already given away the subject.

Irene examined the brush marks. "From the looser strokes, a recent work, I would suggest. And this. What do you think, Nell?"

She indicated a female figure in long Renaissance robes, again the fleurs-de-lis figuring her gown, but a stern, almost fanatical expression on her gaunt, impassioned face.

"Can you guess, Oscar? No? Is this not a Daniel come to judgment? The female Torquemada of Mr. Shakespeare's plays?"

"Portia!" said I. "The artist marches to a grimmer tune of late."

"Indeed." Irene let the canvas lean back against the table and turned to a humble assembly near the window. "But what are these? They look intriguing."

"Hatboxes! Truly, Irene, you have a great quantity more than you need at home."

"But not so charmingly covered—with wallpaper—and some cut so the design of one lays against the pattern of another. Oh, I must have one—or several!"

"Easily done." Oscar Wilde exhibited the amused tolerance a man expends on a woman taken by something trivial. "Amelia's fancywork. She sells them to the ladies hereabout. I don't doubt that it shoes the children's feet. With Parris devoted to his mania for the servant girl model, he can't have sold much work of late."

"Well." Irene turned from the hatboxes. "To work. I must interview the vital members of the household. Mrs. Parris, her eldest son, and perhaps the so charming lady who answered the door. The children, I think, can be left to their ignorance. Bring me Mrs. Parris first. Tell her that I am interested in hatboxes."

The poet took no offense at being commissioned as a messenger. He withdrew to be replaced some few minutes later by a compact woman with fading brown hair. Her navy serge skirt's telltale box pleats and draped bustle indicated that it had been purchased several years before. Her face was as well worn as her gown, the eyes a wan blue set in dark circles of skin, but there was no sign of recent tears or hysterics.

"My dear Mrs. Parris!" Irene's voice warmed with welcome, as if she were the householder and Amelia Parris the visitor. "How good of you to meet with us. Oscar has hopes that I can persuade your husband to abandon his studio."

"Why should he listen to you?" Mrs. Parris inquired a trifle sharply. "I have never heard of an Irene Adler."

"Because Oscar has decided that he must. I am a singer, you see, and poor Oscar is convinced that my voice can soothe the savage breast."

"Lysander is not particularly savage." Mrs. Parris sighed and tucked a dull lock of hair behind one ear. "Or at least he was not known to be. Before . . ."

"Before?"

"Before he developed a mania for one particular model."

"He has not had such a single-minded fancy previously?" Mrs. Parris's features puckered listlessly. "There were models, of course, often the subjects of a series of paintings. That is why he put a lock on the inside of the studio door. He did not wish anyone to see his work in progress."

"When was the lock installed?"

She shrugged as listlessly as her face changed expressions. "Some years ago, perhaps six."

"Six," Irene repeated for no apparent reason, spinning away from the paintings. "What I am simply mad about are these enchanting hatboxes of yours, Mrs. Parris. You use— pardon the pun—Paris papers, do you not?"

A flush warmed the woman's drawn cheeks. "Why, yes. Thank you. However did you know?"

Irene dropped into a graceful crouch that only an actress could manage without seeming in imminent danger of toppling. She studied the piled round boxes with the intensity of a happy child.

"Why, by the patterns. None but the French show such whimsy, such joie de vivre—or use so many Napoleonic bees." Her gloved forefinger tapped an example of the latter. "But I do not see a single fleur-de-lis."

"I suppose not," Mrs. Parris admitted, "although I find the flower designs . . . cheerful."

"And you appliqué one paper atop the ground of another, like lace," Irene went on admiringly. "How utterly clever."

Again the sullen cheeks burnished with pleasure at praise rubbed on so warmly. "I am not considered a clever person ordinarily," Mrs. Parris said, "but the ladies of Chelsea find my small efforts appealing."

Irene rose, her bronze silk skirts falling into folds around her, like a theatrical curtain descending after a performance. "I must have at least one—and one for my dear friend Miss Huxleigh."

"Oh, no—" I began to object.

"Nonsense, Nell." Irene's stage-trained voice drowned out my demurs without sounding rude. "You have been longing for the right hatbox; I am certain of it. Which one do you want?"

"I don't know," I began, meaning to say that I didn't even know the price of such a frivolity.

"Impossible to decide on just one." Irene turned again to the now openly pleased woman. "How do you choose which pattern to use? They are all so enchanting."

Mrs. Parris ducked her head in an odd combination of shyness and shame. "Many houses hereabouts are being redecorated in the new aesthetic manner. Some are old papers taken down; others remnants of the replacements. The ladies of the house see that I get them; I am awash in wallpapers."

"Wonderful," marveled Irene, adding in a kindly tone, "No doubt the sales of these lovely things come in handy in an artistic household."

The poor woman was so flushed by now that she could blush no more. Her answer flowed like paint from a brush. "Oh, yes. An artist's lot is hand to mouth, and so also for his family. Lawrence can only spare so much from his position."

"Your son. With a position. How proud you must be."

"He is only a clerk in the City. His father calls such employment 'tattooing with a goose quill for an association of geese,' but it brings in a regular salary."

Irene smiled. "I fear I share the artistic suspicion of matters mathematical, like accounting."

"You are utterly charming, Miss Adler," Mrs. Parris said

suddenly, her face saddening again. "If anyone can coax Lysander from his . . . mania, you can."

"Thank you," Irene said. "I will try, and try again, until I succeed. And then I will reward myself and Miss Huxleigh by purchasing two of your little masterpieces."

"No—a gift."

"We will debate that when I have earned the privilege," Irene insisted. "And now, I wonder, is your hardworking son at home?"

Mrs. Parris blinked at the sudden change in topic. "I believe he is below stairs. I will send him up, if you wish."

Irene beamed. "I do."

The moment the woman's skirts had hissed into the uncarpeted hall I broke my commendable silence with a stage whisper. "Irene! I do not require a hatbox."

"Are they not charming and original?"

"Yes! But my funds—our funds—are unoriginally meager."

She waved an airy hand. "Money can always be found for small necessities."

"Hatboxes?"

"Hush. I hear a firm tread on the stair."

In a moment a young man's form followed the sound of his approach into the room. He saw first us, then the array of propped-up paintings, and stopped at the threshold, frowning. "My mother said you wished to see me. Miss Adler, is it?"

"Mr. Wilde and I are concerned about your father," Irene said calmly.

He concealed sudden fists in his pants pockets, a graceless gesture that I should never have allowed in any charge of mine during my governess days.

"Father can go to hell, if he hasn't already," young Lawrence announced through his teeth.

I drew in my breath, but Irene remained unshaken. "You disapprove of your father's obsession with his model. Yet often such artistic obsessions produce many canvases and much money."

"Father's paintings are the fancy of a failing mind. That

'famous' Parris green you see there has eaten him away like some festering mental moss. An old fool has no right to be forcing himself on servant girls and elevating them to heights where they cannot keep their heads. Who does she think *she* is?" His broad gesture dismissed the model's many guises. "Who does he think *he* is—an old man whose fancy flies in the face of his family honor. Nobody. He should sign his damned puddles of putrid green 'Nobody.'"

"I take it that you do not approve of your father's calling when it becomes obsession."

"I do not approve of calling it art when it is something much more obvious. He has a mania for *her*, not for his paintings of her. He has painted her half to death, until she has exhausted herself into a shadow, and now he rushes to finish painting her before the sun sinks and even a shadow is too weak to be seen. May I go now? I do not like to see so many shadows spun through the poisonous web of his paintbrush."

He had turned on his heel before Irene could finish saying, "Leave if you must."

Again we were alone in the room, and I was mystified. "The young man disapproves of his father's mania, and rightly so. His mother is slighted by such obsessions, even if there's no harm in it."

"Oh, there's harm in it." Irene's face hardened to alabaster, as if often did when she confronted something dangerous. "Deep poison. Parris green poison."

"In the paints?" I asked, confused.

She turned to me. "In the paints, and in the persons who share the roof of this unhappy domicile."

"What poison is there beyond the arsenic pigment you mentioned?"

"Jealousy," she said obliquely. "And on that note, it is time to interview the key figure in this domestic tragedy."

She went to the door, where I was surprised to find that Oscar Wilde stood modest guard, and whispered something to our conductor into this den of death and deception. He vanished with a clatter of boots down the stairs. I found my stare passing numbly from the many paintings of a possibly murdered girl in shades of green to the gay towers of hatboxes awaiting owners. I saw all, but I saw nothing.

A more discreet set of steps announced a surprising person: the sour servant who had admitted us to the house.

Irene began without frills. "You are aware that your master has locked himself in the studio."

"'Tis nothing new," the woman replied.

I had seen her sort before in the houses in which I was a governess: hardened by service into sullen semicooperation, slow to say anything yet quick to see all. She would give only what she had to, and that grudgingly.

"What is the situation here?" Irene asked.

"I thought you knew."

"I meant your own."

A rough shrug, one a world away from the timid gesture of Mrs. Parris. "I cook, clean if I have to, which I have to when the cleaning girl is lounging on a scarlet shawl under the eaves for the pleasure of the master's paintbrush."

"Where do you sleep?"

Irene's question surprised the woman. "Under the eaves. Not all of the fourth story is given over to art. I have a room off the little landing just below there."

"And she?"

"She?"

"Your sister servant."

"Huh! She's no sister of mine, Phoebe Miller." The woman brushed the back of her hand across her nose. "She's got a cubbyhole, too, though she's not been in it lately."

"Some would suspect a man, a painter with a passion for depicting women, of harboring a passion for his model as well as his art. Do you?"

"Gossip is not my job, miss."

"I am not asking about gossip. I am asking what you saw and heard."

"Saw and heard?" Mrs. McCorkle's face showed wary confusion.

"In your room. Under the eaves. Did the master ever visit the maid?"

The woman's feet shuffled uneasily on the floor, but Irene

was implacable—a force that must be answered. A mistress interrogating a servant. Mrs. McCorkle finally spoke, her plain voice curdled with a thin scum of contempt.

"I heard noises. Footsteps. At night. The servant's stairs are narrow and dark. A light would slither along the crack under my door like a yellow snake. Footsteps from the bottom to the top. Sometimes they didn't go all the way up. Sometimes they stopped halfway." She frowned. "And sometimes they went all the way up, and came down soft so I couldn't hear, and went up halfway again. Did the master visit the maid, miss? Do snakes slither?"

Irene took a leisurely turn around the room, holding our attention as a strolling actor does. "What do you think of the young woman who models for Mr. Parris?"

"What I think doesn't matter."

"To me it does."

"Oh, you're nice, aren't you? Asking so sweet and sharp. Never wrinkling a brow or your petticoats. Well, I'll tell you, Miss Who Wants to Know! I'll tell you what it's like to be scrubbing the stoop and washing the stairs and the kettles and some so-called 'girl' is taking her ease behind locked doors and turning up with her face leering out for everyone to see—even his wife and son and little children."

Irene nodded, undisturbed. "What do you think of her?" she repeated softly.

"Isn't much to look at. Not really, especially now she's so thin and pale. Master must be losing more than his mind of late; eyesight more likely. Quiet, Phoebe is. Never looks at you straight—always cringing on the back stairs when we meet, like she expects me to hit her. I suppose she was steady enough at her work before the master brought her up to the studio." The woman frowned. "But she was always the favorite. There was the kitten, you see."

"Kitten?" Irene asked alertly.

"Starved wisp of a thing Phoebe found by the embankment. We're not allowed kittens in servants' quarters, though there be mice enough for 'em. This one was too young for mice—all fuzz and bone. Phoebe would feed it scraps from below. Not allowed, that. But no one took it from her."

"Perhaps no one knew," I put in, breaking the long silence I had kept as I watched Irene pull answers from this woman as a dental surgeon pulls rotten molars from diseased gums.

Mrs. McCorkle's harsh gaze turned on me. "Oh, someone knew, all right. The creature would mew something fierce when she left it alone all day. On and on. *He'd* have heard it, on the other side of the wall, working at his quiet painting. But he never said nothing; his favorite could have certain favors, you see."

"And Mrs. Parris was unaware of the kitten?"

"How would she know? Now there's a real lady, for all she has to hawk her hatboxes to her very own neighbors to pay for food on the table and the few pence servants cost. A sweet, honest soul. She didn't ignore me like I was a doormat to see only in coming and going. She even took some of them fancy papers she got from the likes of Mr. Whistler and Mrs. Wilde and put 'em up herself in my room—a real pretty pattern of these yellow birds and flowers, twining like. Brightened up the place. She even papered Phoebe's cubbyhole. I'll give that to Mrs. Parris. She's a charitable soul who sees past evil to do good."

"You mean that Mr. Parris's obsession with Phoebe was already evident when his wife papered the servants' quarters?"

"To all but the blind."

"Then Mrs. Parris must have seen the kitten," Irene suggested, "and said nothing."

Mrs. McCorkle shook her head. "No. It was dead by then."

"Dead!" I exclaimed weakly. I had been touched by the tale of a kitten that had found a home with the servants under the eaves.

Mrs. McCorkle nodded with weary callousness. "Too young, too ill-used. It stopped eating and retched its little insides out. They seldom survive when they're taken too young from the mother. Phoebe was a fool to try to save it."

"You may go," Irene said suddenly, as if disgusted.

Mrs. McCorkle caught her tone and flushed a bit, but turned without comment.

"You must be overrun with mice now," Irene added as suddenly.

"Mice?" Mrs. McCorkle stopped without turning. "No, don't hear them anymore. Maybe that silly kitten did some good before it died. I could use some quiet in the servants' quarters." She walked through the door. Shortly after we heard her discreet step on the stairs.

"The treads do creak in these old houses," Irene observed. "Imagine how they scream in the servants' stairway. What a story there is in a flight of stairs!"

Oscar Wilde's unwelcome face popped around the door-jamb like a puppet's at a Punch and Judy show. "I am aquiver with curiosity, dear Irene, and could barely remain away, save that I know an artist needs solitude to work. What have you learned, and how are we to release Parris from his lair and prevent a scandal?"

"I'm afraid that there is no way to prevent a scandal," Irene declared.

The poet fully entered the chamber. "That is the wonder you needed to work."

"I am not a wonder worker. As for Mr. Parris, I know of only one way to extract him."

"How?" Oscar Wilde demanded.

"Come and see." She swept from the room and I heard her firm, quick step on the front stairs as she ascended once again to the locked door.

We followed her mutely, the great lumbering poet and I, each drumming our own rhythm upon the stairs—his a heavy, regular tread as he took steps two at a time, mine a faint staccato as I followed him.

Irene was straightening from inspecting the keyhole when we arrived.

"Nothing has changed, and everything has changed," she announced.

"Then how are we to enter?"

She eyed him up and down. *"You* are to enter, dear Oscar. You are a brawny man. You and Bram Stoker make me wonder if blarney breeds giants, you are both such towering Irishmen. I understand that you excelled in sport as well as scholarship at Oxford." She stepped back against the wall, drawing her bronze silk skirts as close to her as forty yards of fabric would permit. "Break down the door at your leisure."

"Break it?" His homely face broke into an angelic smile. "I will be the talk the Chelsea. Of course. I must break down the door."

With this he clattered down a few steps, turned sideways, then went charging upward like a velveteen bull and hit the door shoulder first. There came a great groan of wood and wounded poet, but Mr. Wilde gamely drew back and hurled himself again at the barrier. Splinters flew as the door bowed inward. An enraged male voice thundered from within, then fell silent. Oscar and Irene braved the breach as one.

I was the last to broach that threshold, last to see the sight that had stilled and silenced my fellow intruders and even the man who had painted it.

She lay dead—of that there could be no question—her face a hollow death mask of palest ivory. Against her deathly pallor, the emerald silk of her gown lapped like a vast, poisonous sea. The uncompleted painting on the artist's easel shone wet, a ghastly reflection in an opaque mirror of green paint.

The artist himself had slumped onto a pigment-spattered stool. Light spilled from a skylight above, drawing in every cruel detail, including the lines in Lysander Parris's haggard features, the coarse, thick clots of white hair streaking his natural brown color, the shaking arm that loosely supported a predominantly green palette.

"My masterpiece," he said in a raw voice.

Irene approached the dead woman, drew the plait of long dark hair from across her throat. Mr. Wilde gasped at her gesture, but the braid merely rested there. No marks marred the slender neck.

Lysander Parris started up from his stool as if waking into a nightmare. "Do not disturb the pose! I am almost done."

The stairs creaked.

We turned.

Mother and son stood in the doorway, the wife's eyes upon her husband, the son's upon the dead model.

"We heard—" Mrs. Parris began, moving toward her husband, drawing the palette from his grasp to set it aside.

The son took two steps into the room, then stopped as if dumbfounded, staring sightlessly at the dead woman. "She's . . . not alive."

"No," Irene said gently. "She's gone. We should leave as well."

"But—" Young Lawrence looked up, his gaze afire with fury, then saw the wreck that was his father as his mother led him from the room like a sleepwalking child. "I don't understand . . ."

Irene took his arm, then led him to me. Only an hour ago he had been storming in the room below; now he was the dead eye of the storm. I guided him down the stairs, my own adoptive child in tow, behind the artist and his wife.

I could hear the voices of Oscar Wilde and Irene Adler in consultation behind me.

Mrs. Parris bore her prize down to the drawing room, seating him on a settee covered in worn tapestry. At the door hovered Mrs. McCorkle.

"Tea," Mrs. Parris ordered as I guided her stunned son to a Morris chair crouching in a corner.

The men sat in common shock, while women bustled around them. I couldn't help thinking that Mrs. Parris was in her element—that her role and her rule came through mastering domestic crises; that the servant, Mrs. McCorkle, also took a certain pride in being of use; that some intimate mechanism had been rebalanced and a terrible tension eased.

Tea was steaming from four cups when Irene's figure darkened the doorway.

I started.

"Nell, could you come with me for a moment?"

I murmured my excuses and left that dour drawing room with its silent population of victims and survivors.

"Where is Mr. Wilde?" I asked in the hall.

Irene was amused. "Surely you do not miss him."

"No, but—"

She took my arm in her most confiding, yet commanding way. "He has gone for the doctor, who will declare the poor girl dead and see to her removal. Nothing will be left of that macabre scene but the painting of it, and I wonder if that will survive."

"Why should it not? It is his 'masterpiece,' despite its price."

"What is its price, Nell?"

"Dishonor. Dishonesty. A family stricken."

She nodded, pleased. "You put it well. A family stricken, as virulently as if by poison. If they are fortunate, no one will suspect the murder."

"Murd—"

Irene's fingers clamped quite effectively over my mouth. "Hush, Nell! One can only invoke such words in ringing tones in a Shakespearian play, and this is merely a domestic tragedy by Webster."

She led me down the staircase to the kitchens below the ground floor. I sensed a cramped, dingy space and the shining bulk of a tea kettle on a hearth. Irene led me to a small door and opened it.

"What is this place?" I asked.

"The servants' stair."

"Oh. We're not going up there?"

"We most certainly are; otherwise I'll never know if my theory is correct."

"Theory?"

"Of how the murder was accomplished."

"Irene, I do not wish to climb any more stairs in this ghastly house. I do not wish to know how or why, or even if. Can we not go home to Saffron Hill and pretend that you slept undisturbed till curtain time and Mr. Wilde never came and—"

"And that you never enjoyed waking me up?"

"I did not! Enjoy it, I mean. Not too much."

She was leading me inexorably up the narrow stairs. Each step moaned at our passage like a ghost trod upon.

"Not so much that I must pay penance," I added as the stair turned and grew darker. The walls felt damp as I brushed them, and were rough enough to snag Irene's silken skirts. I tried not to think how it must feel to mount such stairs every night, to be a forgotten housemaid, to be brought from such a place to a silk-draped sofa. Might not any poor wretch choose the studio over the garret, no matter the price?

At a tiny landing, Irene paused, then half disappeared into the wall. I cried out despite myself.

"Mrs. McCorkle's bedchamber," Irene explained. A match struck, then smoke assaulted my nostrils. Light grew beyond Irene and she walked into it, out of my sight.

"Come in, Nell. There's nothing to fear here."

I followed to find her shadow thrown so large upon the room's cramped walls that it seemed all in shade. "Are you saying that Mrs. McCorkle is a murderer?"

Irene's hatted head shook on her shoulders and on her shadow. She seemed one of those monstrous pagan gods, horned and terrible. "Observe the wallpaper, Nell."

"There is too much shadow to see . . . yes, a print of yellow and ivory and blue. I see it in the corner. Wallpaper, Irene?"

Irene sighed, her shadow's shoulders heaving with her. "Few bother to paper servants' quarters, even such dreary holes as this."

"Mrs. Parris is indeed a thoughtful woman. I wonder that she can nurse her husband after what he has done."

Irene turned on me, her voice cold as steel. "What has he done?"

"Why—abandoned his family for a servant girl; pursued his art at the cost of every person around him. Look at the man! He is half mad and wholly deteriorated."

She brushed by me, a silhouette holding a burning coal of lamplight. I heard the stairs cry out as she mounted the last flight.

I did not want to go farther. I did not wish to know more. But I could not stop myself.

When I reached the very apex of the house, Irene blocked the last doorway. She crouched suddenly, in that graceful way she had, and I saw the miserable hole that served as home for the dead girl. It made me cringe, the barren meanness of it, the equation of cot and shelf and chamber pot. How hard to blame the one who lived here for anything. In the silence I thought I heard the faint scratch of kittenish paws, a phantom mewling added to the groans of the lost souls on the stairs below, and my eyes filled with tears.

"The wallpaper, Nell," Irene said in deep, sad, angry tones. "The wallpaper."

I could not see wallpaper. I could only see dark, and light, and more dark. But my eyes finally cleared and little figures danced into focus before me—blue butterflies on an ivory ground, gay, hovering creatures at the top of the house. Not butterflies, but fleurs-de-lis.

"Artists are not usually prone to puns," Irene's voice came ponderously. "Lysander Parris was an exception. That's why he called his trademark color 'Parris green.'"

"I don't understand, Irene."

"There is an actual, original 'Paris green,' named for that city of art and gaiety and fashion. That Paris green is a preparation used to keep certain colors—such as blue, paradoxically—from running in wallpapers. It is made from an arsenic compound and can never, ever lose its lethal properties. It will never die, Nell, and therefore it will deal death forever."

"What are you saying?"

"The kitten, Nell. Remember the kitten."

"It died."

"Precisely."

"But if it was poisoned, surely the food from the kitchen, meant for Phoebe—"

"Not food. And the mice."

"There are no mice now."

"Precisely."

"Irene." I clutched her bronze silk sleeve. "Are we—"

"I would not linger," she said wryly, rising and lifting the lamp, so her silhouette blotted out the artful blue French wallpaper imbued with death and Paris green.

Four months later Oscar Wilde forwarded an invitation to a showing of Lysander Parris works at a small gallery near the British Museum.

"I am amazed the man still has a taste to paint," I said.

"He is an artist," Irene retorted. "The artistic temperament thrives on suffering. Look at me."

I did so. She was lounging on our sofa, sipping hot chocolate illegally brewed upon the fireplace fender, wrapped in another of her sunset-colored Oriental gowns.

"Indeed," I said dryly. "I do not care to see another Parris painting."

"The affair might be instructive. After all, no scandal resulted; no charges were brought. The word *murder* was heard only in the far reaches of the servants' quarters."

"If you are right, it was an unimaginably dreadful murder. That sweet woman so consumed with jealousy. And that poor girl, sleeping each night, her own chamber a death trap. No wonder she looked so properly pale and wan in those awful paintings—she was slowly dying."

"And the artist was in love with death, as artists so often are these days, whether it be with the green fairy of absinthe or some imagined temptress who may be only a housemaid at heart. But it is remarkable that Mr. Parris has lived to paint another day. *He* was being slowly poisoned as well. That is why he became so irrational and locked himself in with the dead woman. He never even noticed her condition."

"He was in jeopardy? How?"

"Need I point out the incident of the footsteps in the night?"

"Oh." I blushed for my innocence. "You mean that if he, when he . . . visited Phoebe, he also was exposed to the Paris green."

"Exactly. As he succumbed to the poison, he began putting the fleurs-de-lis—truly *fleurs de mal,* 'flowers of evil'—in his paintings. And the more often he visited, the more poison he absorbed through his very pores. An ingenious scheme—he would pay to the extent he abused his wife's honor. He would, in fact, dispense the dosage of his own death. If he was innocent of infidelity, only she would die."

"Irene, that's diabolical!"

"Is it any more diabolical than the propensity of artists to introduce the models with whom they are obsessed into the bosom of their families, expecting them to be accepted? And, in this case, the son *would* be foolish enough to rival the father."

"The son? He was involved in this folly as well?"

"Whose were the second footsteps that halted halfway up? Lawrence, too, had become enamoured of the girl. He knew what was going on and raged inwardly, but he was not as clever as his mother—who had been secretly seething over her husband's indiscretions for years, else why did Mr. Parris bar his studio door?—and Lawrence did not find a way to murder."

"Why was there no scandal, Irene? Did the authorities never question the death?"

"Never."

"Why not?"

"She was an artist's model, a poor servant. People of her sort and class die young all the time—of drink, of debauchery, of neglect. No one cared enough to note her passing."

"I have been very wrong."

"You certainly have not anticipated the turns of the case."

"Not that, Irene. I have judged that poor dead girl harshly. I have condemned her as a fallen woman, but the wronged wife in this case was willing to kill an innocent girl on mere suspicion. That poor Phoebe was not innocent does not lessen the wife's wrong."

Irene reached to the sidetable and selected one of her annoying cigarettes. I had to endure the perfume of sulfur before she would go on.

"She *was* innocent," Irene declared on a misty blue breath. "Perfectly innocent."

"How can you say that for certain?"

"Because I went to the morgue to identify the body."

"Irene! How could you do that?"

"Easily. I donned rusty black and a county accent and said I was the deceased girl's long-lost sister and, please, sir, could anyone say, did she die a ruined woman? And they talked and thought and hemmed and hawed and finally decided to relieve my sisterly mind and said no, she did not."

"How can they tell?"

"That is another bedtime story, Nell, and I am sick of telling this one."

"But the footsteps—"

"He went there often, but he did not succeed, despite all his pleadings. He captured her only in paint."

"So it was all for nothing."

"Murder usually is."

"And we will not go to the exhibition."

"We will see."

"We" did nothing of the sort. Irene decided to go, and I could not resist glimpsing the end of the story, even if it meant another encounter with Oscar Wilde.

The gallery was crowded, a long, narrow space glittering with gaslight and glasses of sherry and festively garbed people. Parris green leered from the walls. The gaslight gave Phoebe's plaintive features a sad beauty that even I could detect now.

Naturally, Oscar Wilde captured Irene the instant she swept in the door (at public events, Irene always swept).

"Parris says you are to have any one of his green period paintings you wish," he announced.

Her eyebrows arched at this generosity.

Oscar Wilde leaned down over the rim of his glass to speak in confidence. "His wife is confined in a remote establishment in Sussex. The room under the eaves has been walled off."

"Couldn't the paper have been stripped?" I demanded.

Irene shook her head. "The compound would have already seeped into the wood beneath. At least they will have no mice."

"Which will you choose?" Mr. Wilde wondered aloud, trailing us through the gallery. Irene passed Joan of Arc, Portia, the mermaid, and a dozen other representations of the woman we only knew secondhand.

Finally she stopped at a small, square frame of lacy gilt. "This one."

She had chosen no femme fatale in her green and lethal glory, only a sketch of Phoebe playing with the kitten condemned to succumb first to Paris green. If only someone had noticed! Tiger-striped, I saw with a lump in my throat. I was glad that Phoebe had found one friend in that house of horrors, even if only briefly.

Mr. Wilde shrugged. "None of them will ever be worth anything, but the ignorant would have been more impressed by the larger paintings."

"I am not interested in impressing the ignorant," Irene said blithely.

"Ah, but you shall, despite yourself!" Oscar Wilde trumpeted, pouncing. "Let me lead you, my dear Irene and my dear Miss Huxleigh, to an example of the radical new turn in Lysander Parris's work. It is a pity he did not feel up to being here tonight, for he has found a dazzling new model who has revolutionized his monomaniacal palette. But see for yourselves."

He led us through the crowd and around a corner.

A blazing full-length portrait greeted us like a sudden sunset. I recognized the subject matter instantly, though I suspect Irene was at a loss. Surely this gorgeously stern figure clothed in gossamer red-orange and holding a flaming sword against the green of forgotten forest represented the angel at the gates of Eden. The figure was the broad-shouldered, small-breasted one often done of heroic women, but the face floating above it in serene, haughty justice was unmistakably Irene's.

After a stunned moment, Irene laughed. She bent to read the bottom plaque bearing the title. *"Excalibur in Eden,"* she declaimed. "He has a flair for titles, if not for models."

Oscar Wilde smiled slyly. "I could better picture the indomitable Penelope as the angel with the flaming sword."

"I would not presume to portray an angel," I answered stoutly.

Irene laughed again. "I am no angel, either—nor do I ever care to be. Earth and the present tense is my medium—not the would-be of the promised Empyrean or the has-been of ancient Edens."

"And not, I trust," Oscar Wilde suggested limpidly, "Paris green."

Kim's Game

M. D. Lake

"Nora, are you sure you wouldn't like to play Kim's Game with us?" Miss Bowers called to her from over by the great stone fireplace.

"I'm sure, thank you," Nora replied politely, glancing up and then dropping her nose back into her book. Outside, she could hear the rain falling on the sloping roof of the lodge. It had rained steadily ever since they arrived at camp.

She was at the far end of the room, curled up on a sofa, her feet tucked under her, as far away from the other girls as she could get. It wasn't that she didn't like them exactly; it was just that, after being cooped up with them for three days, they didn't interest her very much. None of them liked to read and they all seemed to have seen the same television shows and movies. As a result, she couldn't understand half of what they were talking about or, if she could, why they got so excited about it.

"Nora's not very good at Kim's Game," she heard one of the girls say, in a high, clear voice that was meant to carry.

"She beat us all yesterday," another one pointed out.

"Twice. The first two times. Beginner's luck. She lost the third game and then she quit."

Nora smiled to herself. She'd never played Kim's Game, never even heard of it, until she got to summer camp and the counselors were forced to come up with indoor activities because of the cold weather and rain. But after she'd won the first two games, she discovered it was too easy for her, and so she decided to have fun with the third game. She put down on her list things that weren't there—silly things, but the other girls didn't notice that—and left out obvious things that were—the tea kettle, the butcher knife—and so of course she lost. Even then she didn't lose by much, because the other girls weren't very observant.

They didn't have to be, Nora supposed, in their lives. That thought went through her like a sharp knife and she realized she was suddenly close to tears. She straightened her back and put her feet firmly down on the floor and told herself she was glad she was so observant. It was a lot more important to notice things with your eyes than to cry with them.

She hadn't wanted to come to summer camp. She'd wanted to stay home, where she could keep an eye on her parents. She knew that something was wrong between them—worse than usual, a lot worse—and she thought that if she were there, she'd at least be able to figure out the meaning of all the little things she'd noticed and heard: her father's coming home late at night and going to work on the weekends, something he never used to do; his slurred, angry speech sometimes; the tears she'd seen in her mother's eyes; the abrupt changes of subject when she came into the room when her mother was entertaining friends; and the quarrels between her parents that got more and more frequent, when they thought she was in bed and asleep.

Usually they didn't insist that she do anything except homework and chores, but this year they'd insisted that she go to camp. She wondered what she'd find when she returned home. She wondered if both of her parents would still be living in the house and, if not, which one of them would be gone.

The main door of the lodge opened and a wet figure in a raincoat and hat came in. It was Miss Schaefer.

She hung her coat and hat on a peg and stepped into the

room, looked around, and saw the girls standing in a circle over by the fireplace. They were staring with great concentration down at objects scattered on a blanket, with Cathy Bowers standing behind them, timing them with her watch.

Kim's Game! Lydia Schaefer had never liked it, thought it was stupid. She didn't have the kind of memory you need to be good at games like that either.

She nodded to Cathy Bowers and crossed the room to the far corner, with its comfortable overstuffed chairs and a sofa and a coffee table littered with books and old magazines. She sat down in one of the chairs and picked up a magazine. She took her reading glasses out of a case and put the case back in her shirt pocket. As she did, she noticed a girl on the sofa opposite her, sitting up straight, her pointy nose buried in a book. She looked as though she'd been crying, or wanted to cry. Lydia Schaefer smiled and said: "I was always rotten at Kim's Game, too, when I was your age. Don't let it bother you."

Nora glanced up, as if surprised she was no longer alone. Her eyes met Miss Schaefer's without expression. She didn't like Miss Schaefer because she knew Miss Schaefer didn't like her—and not just her either: Miss Schaefer didn't like children period. Nora wondered why she was a camp counselor. Then she shrugged, decided it didn't matter. She had enough adults to try to figure out without adding another one to the list.

"What's your name?" Miss Schaefer persisted, somewhat uneasy under the child's stare. She also didn't like getting a shrug for a response. Hadn't she tried to console the child for being no good at a game?

"Nora." It wasn't just objects on a blanket Miss Schaefer wasn't able to remember.

"I'd probably be rotten at Kim's Game now, too," Miss Schaefer went on. "Oh, well, I'm sure you and I have inner lives that are much more interesting than theirs. Don't we?"

"I guess so," Nora said, wanting to get back to her book.

"It's probably why we wear glasses," Miss Schaefer went on, as if determined to make friends with Nora. "We don't need outer reality as much as other people, so our eyes—"

Before she could finish what Nora already knew was going to be a dumb sentence, a voice interrupted. "Could I see you in my office, Lydia?" Miss Schaefer turned quickly and looked over her shoulder, startled at the officious tone of voice. It was Ruth Terrill, the head counselor.

"Sure, Ruth," she said, trying to keep her voice normal. "Now?"

"Please," Ruth said.

Nora watched the two women disappear into the hallway. She'd known they hadn't liked each other for most of the three days she'd been at camp, but until that moment she hadn't known Miss Schaefer was afraid of Miss Terrill. She wondered why, then shrugged again. These adults, and the things going on between them, weren't her problem. Quickly she dipped her nose back into her book.

Over by the fireplace, the other girls were playing another round of Kim's Game. You'd think they'd have just about every small object in the lodge memorized by now, Nora thought.

She would have.

That night, when she first heard the voices, she thought she was at home and in her own bed, because they sounded the way her parents did when they thought she was asleep and wouldn't be able to hear them discussing whatever it was that was wrong between them that they were keeping from her. Then, seeing the log beams in the darkness above her, and hearing the rain dripping from the eaves, she remembered where she was. She could hear the quiet sounds the girls around her made in their sleep, and the sound of the wind in the forest outside. She hated the wind this summer, a sickly, menacing noise that never seemed to stop.

The voices were those of the camp counselors in the main room of the lodge. Just as she did at home when her parents' voices woke her up, she slipped out of bed and went to listen. She tiptoed down the row of sleeping girls, then down the dark hall to the door to the main room. It wasn't closed all the way, which was why she'd been able to hear the voices.

Lydia Schaefer was describing how, just a little while ago, she'd been hurrying up to the lodge from her cabin. She'd heard a sudden rustling in the forest next to the path, and then a man had grabbed her from behind. He had a knife, she said, and he threatened her with it, but she managed to tear herself away from him and run back to the lodge. She was still out of breath. Nora could hear that.

One of the other counselors asked Miss Schaefer why she hadn't shouted for help. She said she was too frightened at first and then, when she saw the lights of the lodge and knew the man wasn't going to catch up to her, she didn't want to scare the girls by making a lot of noise. The head counselor, Ruth Terrill, asked her if she could describe the man. It was so dark, Miss Schaefer answered, and it happened so fast that she didn't get a good look at him. But she thought he was tall—and he was wearing glasses, she was certain of that.

Miss Terrill said that she was going to call the sheriff, and they all agreed not to worry the girls with it.

That's what adults were always trying to do, Nora thought, as she tiptoed back down the hall to bed. There's a rapist or even worse out in the forest, but they don't want to worry the girls with it! My mom and dad are breaking up, but they don't want me to know about it!

Adults are a lot more childish than children in a lot of ways, she thought.

She was just barely awake, trying to identify every creaking noise the old building made in the night, when she heard a car driving up the dirt road to the lodge. A car door shut quietly and, as she fell asleep, she could hear the voices again in the main room, a man's voice among them now. She dreamt of the forest and of a man waiting in it for her among the trees.

The next morning, Nora looked up from her book and saw, through the big front window, a police car pull up in front of the lodge and a large man in a brown uniform climb out. Miss Terrill and Miss Schaefer must have been watching for him too, for they met him before he could come inside. They stood on the wide porch, out of the rain, talking in voices too low for Nora to hear.

She wondered if it was the same man who'd come when Miss Terrill called the police the night before. The other girls probably wouldn't have paid any attention to him even if he'd come in, Nora thought. They were all sitting at the dining room table, writing letters home, probably complaining about the lack of television and shopping malls and anything fun to do. Nora wasn't going to give her parents the satisfaction of complaining about anything. Besides, she didn't know which of them would be there to read whatever she wrote.

The weather was clearing up and they were supposed to go horseback riding the next day. Maybe, on account of the man in the forest, they'd stay indoors. She hoped so.

After the other girls were asleep that night, she lay in bed and thought about the man in the forest with the knife. She had a good imagination and could see the knife blade and the lenses of his glasses glittering in the moonlight as he watched the lodge from the darkness, watched and waited for somebody to come down the path alone. What would Miss Terrill do, she wondered, if he tried to come into the lodge, tried to kidnap one of the girls? Miss Terrill always slept in the lodge with them. The other counselors had small cabins of their own, two to a cabin except for Miss Schaefer, who had a cabin all to herself, farthest down the path. Apparently none of the other counselors wanted to share a cabin with Miss Schaefer, or else she didn't like any of them. Nora was glad she didn't have to sleep in one of those cabins, alone in the forest with the darkness and the sick wind in the pines that never stopped—and the man in the trees.

Then she heard a noise—it sounded like the start of a shout—coming from the lodge's main room, and then the sound of something falling. She sat up and strained to hear more, but there wasn't anything more—only the quiet breathing of the sleeping girls in the room with her and the wind. She stared at the door to the main room, waited for it to open and for a tall man wearing glasses to come through, but nothing happened.

Maybe she'd been asleep and dreaming. Maybe it had been her imagination. But she couldn't stand it, here any more than at home. She had to know.

She slipped out of bed and crept silently down the dark hall on her bare feet. She opened the door a crack, very slowly, and peered into the room. At first she thought it was empty, except for the moonlight, but then she saw something on the floor by the fireplace, a huddled figure. She forgot the man in the forest with the knife. She forgot to be scared. She went across the room to see who it was.

It was Miss Terrill. She was lying on her back, staring up at the ceiling, the wooden handle of a knife protruding from her throat.

Nora stared for a long moment, seeing everything there was to see—Miss Terrill's brown leather bag on the floor by her hand and the things that had spilled from it, some of them in the slowly spreading blood and some where the blood didn't reach.

A sound, a flicker of movement, made her look up. Miss Schaefer was coming through the front door.

"What are you doing out of bed, child? You get—Ruth!" She rushed over to Miss Terrill and knelt by her, saw what Nora had seen, and scrambled back to her feet.

"Did you see what happened?" she asked.

"No. I just heard something, so I—"

"You can't stay here," Miss Schaefer said. "Come with me." She took Nora by the hand and, instead of taking her back to the dormitory, almost dragged her across the room and down the hall to the kitchen.

"What's your name again?"

"Nora."

"Oh, yes, Nora," Miss Schaefer said. "The little girl who likes to read. You stay here until I come back. You'll be all right. Whoever did that to poor Ruth is gone now." She pushed Nora down onto a chair. "I'm going to call the police. Don't go back to the dorm—you might wake the other girls, and we don't want to scare them. Do we? Promise?"

Nora promised and Miss Schaefer turned and went quickly back down the hall.

Nora didn't like it in the kitchen. The clock on the wall made an ominous humming noise, like the wind outside. It was almost one A.M. There were knives on the drying board by the sink that the cook used to cut meat and vegetables, sharp and glittery in the moonlight pouring through the window, with handles like the one on the knife in Miss Terrill's throat. The man from the forest might have been in here, might be in here now, hiding in the pantry or the closet or in the darkness over by the stove.

A sudden noise behind her made her jump up and spin around, but nothing moved in the kitchen's shadows. It was probably a mouse. Nora didn't like that thought either, because she wasn't wearing shoes.

She didn't care what she'd promised Miss Schaefer. She ran back to the main room. She meant to cross to the door next to the fireplace, run to the room where the telephone was and Miss Schaefer, but when she got to Miss Terrill's body, she couldn't help it—she stopped to look again.

What she saw this time terrified her.

"I told you to stay in the kitchen," Miss Schaefer said, so close that Nora jumped and almost screamed. Her voice was soft and cold with anger—the worst kind—and she took Nora in her hard grip.

"I got scared," Nora said, trying not to tremble. They were alone with the body, the two of them, and the hallway door was closed. The other children slept soundly, the other counselors were far away.

"Scared? Of what?"

Then Nora blurted out, so suddenly it surprised her, "Of *him!*"

"Who?" In spite of herself, Miss Schaefer straightened up and looked quickly around the room.

"A man," Nora said. "He was looking at me through the kitchen window!"

"What did he look like?" Miss Schaefer sounded as surprised as Nora.

"He was big," Nora told her. "Tall—and he had dark hair. Miss Schaefer, what if he comes back?"

"I locked the door," Miss Schaefer said. "He can't get in now, nobody can." And then she asked, "How could you see him through the window, Nora? It's dark outside."

"Because," Nora said, and hesitated, trying desperately to think of an explanation, feeling Miss Schaefer's cold eyes on her and remembering the knives in the kitchen that glittered in the moonlight. "Because the *moon* was so bright, I could see it glittering in his glasses!"

Miss Schaefer thought about that for a moment and then she exhaled and relaxed her grip on Nora's arm. She almost smiled. "I called the police," she said. "They'll be here soon. I don't think you have anything to be afraid of now."

Nora didn't think so either.

The police arrived, and the sheriff, the man she'd seen talking to Miss Terrill and Miss Schaefer that morning. The other counselors came too, staring down in horror at Ruth Terrill. One of them took Nora by the arm and led her over to the couch by the front windows, away from the body. She said that wasn't anything for a girl her age to see, but since she'd found the body, she'd have to talk to the policemen. Nora almost laughed at how dumb that sounded. She could see the heads of some of the other girls, crowded in the entryway to the dorm, their eyes big. A counselor was standing in front of them, to keep them from seeing too much.

Miss Schaefer explained to the other counselors that she'd been afraid to go outside and down the path to tell them what had happened—not with a killer on the loose—and of course she hadn't wanted to leave Nora and the rest of the children alone either. After all, he'd attacked her too, out there in the forest, but she'd been lucky—luckier than Ruth Terrill—she'd managed to get away from him.

The sheriff asked her why she'd come up to the lodge in the first place. She told him she'd left her book there, the one she wanted to read in bed before going to sleep. "I had my flashlight," she said, "and I ran all the way." Then she called over to Nora, as if anxious to turn attention away from herself, "Tell the sheriff about the man you saw at the window in the kitchen, Nora."

"I didn't see anybody," Nora answered. "But I saw something else—over by Miss Terrill's body."

"What did you see?" the sheriff asked. "Come over here and tell me."

"No. You go over by Miss Terrill's body."

"Go—" The sheriff hesitated, gave her a puzzled look, and then he did as she asked. Something in her voice made him do that.

"What's this all about?" Miss Schaefer wanted to know. "You told me, Nora—"

Nora didn't pay any attention to her, only looked to make sure one of the policemen was standing between her and Miss Schaefer. "You just tell me if I'm right about the things scattered around Miss Terrill," she called to the sheriff.

"Nora," Miss Schaefer said, and tried hard to laugh, "we're not playing Kim's Game now."

"What's Kim's Game?" the sheriff asked.

"It's a game we play sometimes," Nora told him, "when we have to be indoors on account of the weather. Miss Bowers gives us about fifteen seconds to look at a lot of things she's put on a blanket on the floor and then we have to go to another part of the room and write down everything we remember. Whoever remembers the most things wins."

"Nora's just like me, sheriff," Miss Schaefer said. "She's not very good at it." Her laugh had the same sickly sound as the wind had in the forest, but the forest was quiet now.

Nora looked back at the sheriff and said, "There's a pen and a little tube of sun cream and a pocketknife with a red handle. There's a change purse too. It's brown."

"That's right," the sheriff said, glancing across the room at her. She was staring straight ahead, with her eyes wide open. The sheriff had a daughter too, but when she tried hard to remember things, she screwed her eyes tight shut.

"There're some keys on a ring," Nora went on, "in the

middle of the blood, and there's a box of Band-Aids and a comb next to them. There's money too. Two quarters and some dimes—three dimes, I think."

"Is that all?" the sheriff asked.

"That's all there is *now,*" Nora said. "But when I found Miss Terrill, there was a glasses case, and the glasses were still in it. It was blue and red—plaid—and part of it was in the blood. You can still see where it was, if you look—I could, anyway, when I came back in here, after Miss Schaefer took me to the kitchen and left me there alone. There's a kind of notch in the blood where the glasses case was. The blood must have run up against it and then had to go around."

The sheriff looked and said, "The notch is still there, Nora, in the blood. Do you know where the case is now?"

"No," she said.

"Do you know who has a glasses case like that?"

"Yes," she said, in a very small voice, but forcing herself to look at Miss Schaefer.

"You have a plaid glasses case, Lydia," Miss Bowers said to Miss Schaefer.

Miss Schaefer ran out of the lodge, but she didn't get far. Maybe she didn't try very hard, maybe she didn't want to be alone in the forest.

"I should have cut your little throat when I had the chance," she said to Nora when one of the policemen brought her back into the lodge. She was smiling when she said it, but it wasn't the nicest smile Nora had ever seen.

The glasses case had fallen out of Miss Schaefer's jacket pocket as she killed Miss Terrill. She didn't notice it was gone until she started down the path to her cabin, but when she came back to get it, Nora was there. After she took Nora to the kitchen, she went back and got the case, wiped off the blood, and then put it back in her pocket before she called the sheriff.

Why had she killed Miss Terrill? Nora never found out, and she didn't care anyway. It had to do with something that happened between the two women a long time ago— probably before Nora was even born—the kind of thing adults fight over, not really caring who gets hurt. It was the kind of thing kids aren't supposed to know about, so Nora only got bits and pieces of the story.

When they heard about the murder, some of the parents drove up the mountain and took their daughters home. For a while there was a regular parade of cars arriving and departing with little girls. Some of the cars had one parent in them, and some had both.

The sun was shining and Nora was getting ready to go horseback riding with the girls who were left when Miss Bowers came out and told her that her mother was on the phone and wanted to know if she wanted to go home.

Her horse had huge eyes, like brown marbles with curiosity in them. Nora wondered what it would be like to ride a horse like that.

"Tell Mom I'm fine," she said to Miss Bowers, "and that I'm having a good time. Tell her to say hello to Dad for me too, and give him a big kiss if she can."

The man in charge of the horses showed the girls how to mount them, and when they were all ready, they rode into the forest together.

Arsenic and Old Ideas

Jan Grape

Robbie Dunlap had a feeling she should stay home, miss her writers' meeting, but she couldn't put her finger on exactly why. It wasn't a premonition. It was only a vague uneasiness and had more to do with the fact her husband, Damon, the sheriff of Adobe County, was going on a raid with some Austin law officers than anything else. She always felt tense when Damon had to be out in the boonies, kicking doors open to search for bad guys.

Frontier City, the county seat of Adobe County, was small and crime usually ran to misdemeanors. But the county's rugged limestone and granite hills and small canyons made good hiding places for criminals and their activities. Located one mile off Interstate 35, the town was forty minutes northwest of Austin, Texas, and a mere one hundred thirty miles southwest of the Ft. Worth-Dallas metroplex, making it highly accessible to the bad guys. Tonight's raid was to round up a gang suspected of truck hijacking.

Robbie didn't worry much about Damon; at four inches above six feet tall and two hundred thirty-eight pounds, he was capable of taking care of himself. It was just—well, she didn't know exactly what it was. She pushed her uneasy thoughts aside and continued loading the dishwasher.

Robbie Dunlap was fifty-five years old—in her prime, she thought on her better days. Their two children were grown and on their own.

Robbie was glad to have the mother things over with so she could do what she had always wanted to—write mystery books. She had worked at the Adobe County hospital for twenty years as an X-ray technologist and now she wanted to fulfill her dreams.

Her KP duty was completed when Damon walked into the kitchen and asked, "Honey, where's my new belt?"

"I hung it in your closet on your belt rack."

"Well, I can't find it."

"I'll swear you can't find your behind with both hands, Damon." After twenty-nine and a half years, they shared the easygoing banter of longtime companions. "If you don't get your eyes checked, I'm buying you a seeing-eye dog for Christmas."

"I'd be happy to get my eyes checked if you'll tell me where I'm getting the money to pay for it." The Adobe County sheriff's pay wasn't the greatest and without her income they often had to struggle.

Damon groped for her backside as she walked past him. "I can still find *your* behind even if I can't see."

She laughingly pushed at his hand. "And being half blind makes it harder for you to see my wrinkles and gray hair."

"Wallowing in self-pity because you're menopausal?"

"Don't mess with me. Besides, I have more important things on my mind than my body changes."

"Like your writers' meeting tonight? Worried about your chapter?" Damon was pleased Robbie was writing and encouraged her. Their only conflict came when she wanted to nose around on his cases for "research." Damon felt "police business was police business" and a civilian—especially a wife—should stay out of it.

"Yes, maybe a little, but I'm . . ." She bit her lip, not wanting to tell him of her uneasiness. Instead she got the new belt and handed it to Damon, who was standing just inside the bedroom door. "If it had been a snake, Damon, it would have bit you. It was right there on the belt rack, like I told you."

"But then I wouldn't have got you into the bedroom, would I?" He threw the belt across the bed and took her in his arms. "I know, we're both in a hurry, but don't we have time for one little kiss?"

"You'd better have, old man," she said, kissing him, "or I might look around for a young stud to keep company with—one who can see."

"What would you do with him? Spend all your time training him?" Damon released her, picked up the belt, slid it through the loops on his Levi's, and attached his holster and gun.

"Don't worry about me, hon," Damon said. "I'll let those city boys pop that door and I'll wait until they've secured the house before I go in. About all a blind man can do, anyway."

"Ha. I know you, Sheriff Dunlap. You'll be right there up front. Besides, you don't want those city slickers thinking you're a cowardly old lion. Just remember your flak jacket."

They walked back to the living room, arms around each other, and Damon asked, "What time is your meeting over?"

"Nine thirty to ten, as usual."

"Meeting at Mary Lou's office—right?"

"Ummm," she said, and handed him a thermos of coffee.

"I'll be back whenever," he said, and gave him another quick kiss before walking out the back door.

Ten minutes later, Robbie drove the six blocks into downtown Frontier City. As in many Texas county seats built around the turn of the century, the county courthouse sat in the center of town. Businesses ringed the courthouse square; a flower shop, two restaurants, an insurance office, a dry cleaner's, a drugstore, a card and gift shop, two dress shops, a jewelry store, a movie theater, and a Sears catalog store were on three sides, a hotel with a coffee shop and a bank made up the fourth side.

Economic times had hit hard in the late 1980s, but

because of the natural lake west of town, excellent schools, and a lower tax rate, new growth had begun. People from Austin were lured in record numbers as they scurried from the stress-filled city to the ease of small-town life.

Robbie drove one block south of the courthouse square and parked next door to the one-story building that housed MacLean's Real Estate office and where their meetings were held every other Thursday. It was six forty-five P.M. and everyone tried to be on time and start promptly at seven.

Lilabeth Watson, the group's youngest member at age thirty—painfully shy, with a fragile ego Robbie tried to mother along—began reading. "Caladonia Jones gave the nod to her lead guitarist to begin the final song of the evening, opened her mouth, and her band kicked in, right on cue.

"Ah-maz-zing Gra-ace, how swee-eet the sound . . .
That saved a wretch li-ike me-e . . ."

Robbie said, "Wait. Are you going to include the whole first stanza of the song?"

"Well, yes . . ." said Lilabeth. "I think so."

"That might slow it too much there. How about just the first line."

"I agree," said Winona Baldwin, her voice barely concealing her impatience. Winona had wanted to read first, but Lilabeth said she had to because little Adam was running a slight fever and Bob always got so nervous. Winona gave in, but had rolled her eyes.

Winona Baldwin was even more shy about her work than Lilabeth, especially when it came to reading out loud. She'd just recently gained some confidence, but only when her sister-in-law wasn't around.

There were four regulars in the Thursday night writing group, but sometimes a fifth member came, Arlene Saunders. Arlene and Winona were sisters-in-law. Winona's husband, Eric, and Arlene were brother and sister.

Tonight everyone planned to read her first chapter to

ensure their openings were intriguing and fast paced, to double check that everyone had a hook—that sometimes elusive, unputdownable magic that keeps readers and editors turning pages.

Robbie was secretly glad Arlene Saunders had not showed up tonight. Arlene didn't want to write as much as she wanted to talk about writing. The woman also had a way of giving a scathing critique without knowing what she was talking about that was devastating. Especially for Winona and Lilabeth.

The five women planned to enter their manuscripts in the River City Mystery Association's First Novel Contest and the deadline was January 1st, only thirteen weeks away. The winner would win a $15,000 advance and publication of her book.

Lilabeth was writing a romantic suspense featuring a country-and-western singer; Winona, a psychological thriller; and Mary Lou's was a cozy. Robbie's own entry featured a husband and wife who owned a detective agency. The absent Arlene's was about a woman in jeopardy, although no one had ever seen anything in writing.

Robbie was the only one in the group who'd ever been published and paid for it—two mystery short stories in *Ellery Queen* magazine. She wanted to win the first prize and be published. She also wanted that prize money.

When Lilabeth finished reading, Winona Baldwin got up for her turn. After clearing her throat excessively, Winona read. Nothing was said as she finished, but in a moment Lilabeth stammered, "I—I like it. Your characters are excellent and everything works well, but . . ." She paused and looked at the others. Lilabeth didn't like to give an opinion entirely on her own.

"The opening was definitely boring," said Mary Lou. When Lilabeth and Robbie agreed with her, Winona's face twisted and tears came into her eyes.

Mary Lou said, "Winona, don't get upset. You've got it. That second chapter you read last week is the beginning. That's where your story really starts."

Winona's tears were threatening to spill. "Oh, great." She

gathered up the pages and held them in one hand while she slapped on them with her other hand. "I've rewritten this until I'm blue in the face. Now y'all say I have to do another stupid rewrite."

Robbie tried to placate Winona. "No, you don't have to change a word or sentence. Just start with chapter two and feed the narrative from chapter one into the second and third chapters."

Lilabeth said, "It's all on computer—it'll only take an hour or so."

"Easy for you to say." Winona's voice got argumentative. "Do you know what I have to go through to use Eric's computer?" She threw the manuscript across the room and the pages scattered all over the floor.

"Winona, getting angry doesn't help," Robbie said, although she'd rather see a little anger than Pitiful Patty tears.

"Eric's feeling bad—vomiting—some kind of intestinal flu, and that means he'll be home all week, griping and complaining. Especially about me touching his precious computer.

"If he's home he won't let me use his computer because he needs it, he says. And if I use it when he's gone, he bitches and says I always mess up his stuff somehow. I might as well give up writing. It's just not worth it."

Robbie knew Eric resented Winona's writing. "So copy everything onto a floppy. Next week, when he's gone again, you can come to my house and work."

"You mean it?"

Robbie nodded and got up to help Winona pick up the papers.

When they finished, Winona said, "I'd better get on home now. Eric will be mad if I'm late." Winona stuffed her manuscript into a grocery sack and, without waiting for the others to read, walked out the back door.

"Gosh," said Lilabeth. "Is she just touchy tonight or what?"

"She gets uptight when Eric's in town, and if he's sick, I'm sure things are worse," said Robbie.

Mary Lou snorted. "I doubt Eric's sick. He's probably on dope."

"Really?" asked Lilabeth, her eyes growing big and round with the news. For a thirty-year-old she was still quite naive.

Mary Lou said, "He's abused alcohol for years. Drug abuse wouldn't surprise me."

Mary Lou glanced at her watch, took her own manuscript out of her briefcase, and set it on the desktop. "We'll just have to forget about the trials and tribulations of Eric and Winona Baldwin. Else we'll never get through." She glanced at Robbie and raised an eyebrow. "Do you want to read next?"

Robbie was glad Mary Lou had changed the subject back to their writing. She didn't want to get into idle gossip about the Baldwins. It made her too angry. She had seen Winona's bruises and knew the real story behind the cracked ribs and broken arm. But what made her even more angry was that Winona stayed and put up with Eric's brutality.

"You go ahead," said Robbie. "My first chapter is only five pages."

Mary Lou said, "Good. Maybe we'll get home early tonight." She read her title: *"A Pforensics Pfable Pfrom Pflugerville* by Mary Lou MacLean."

Robbie had to cough and fake a sneeze to hide her dismay at the cutesy title. She did, however, understand Mary Lou's brand of madness. The woman had grown up in the town of Pflugerville, where her father was still an undertaker, and Mary Lou was an unabashed fan of Charlotte MacLeod. Anytime she could emulate Ms. MacLeod she didn't hesitate.

Mary Lou continued: "Victoria Gladstone had just finished wiping the blood up from her previously spotless kitchen floor, washed her hands, and fluffed her hair when the doorbell rang."

Someone began a loud knocking on the door of the real estate office. Mary Lou stopped. "Lilabeth, you're closest . . ."

Robbie spoke up. "Ask who it is first, okay?"

Lilabeth went to the door. "Who is it?"

"Damon Dunlap. Is my wife there?"

Lilabeth unlocked the door and Damon stepped into the doorway and greeted them with a grim-faced hello.

Robbie walked over to the door. "Are the kids all okay?" and followed when he indicated he wanted her to step outside.

"The kids are fine. Is Winona Baldwin here? I didn't see her car."

"She left a few minutes ago." Robbie felt her stomach lurch and her uneasiness returned. "What's wrong?"

"Eric Baldwin is dead."

"Eric is wha . . . ? My Lord, what happened?"

"We don't know yet. His sister, Arlene, went by the house. Said she'd talked to him a little earlier and he said he was sick—really bad sick. When she drove out there, the garage door was open and a light was on inside. Arlene found his body on the ground next to his car."

"How horrible. Oh, heavens, Winona's going home to . . ."

"My deputies are out there, but I'd hoped to break the news myself. How long did you say she's been gone?"

"I didn't, but probably not more than fifteen to twenty minutes."

"What time did she get here?"

"She and Lilabeth were last. They came one behind the other. About three minutes to seven. Why do you want to know?"

"And exactly when did she leave?"

Robbie saw it was now nine thirty. "Probably a little after nine. She'd mentioned Eric was sick. How did he . . . ?"

"I can't tell you what it is, but there is strong evidence of foul play."

"Why are you asking all this about Winona?"

"You know the old cop's adage about checking out the spouse."

"Oh, Damon, surely you don't think Winona could have . . . I can't believe Winona . . ." Robbie's voice trailed off as she remembered Eric's harsh treatment of his wife.

"It's just routine to establish an alibi," said Damon. "Not that she's given me one yet. I'd better get back to their farm."

Robbie went back inside and told the others Eric Baldwin had died, but that she didn't have any details.

"Poor Winona," said Lilabeth.

"Poor Winona, my foot," said Mary Lou. "It's the best thing that ever happened to her."

"Mary Lou, don't. I know you don't mean it." Robbie stopped her friend. She had been thinking the same thoughts, but her worry that somehow Winona was involved made her want to keep Mary Lou from starting gossip.

"I'm only being truthful. Eric Baldwin was not a pleasant man. It's no secret he made Winona's life miserable. I wouldn't be surprised . . ."

How had Mary Lou come up with the idea? All she'd told them was what she knew—that Eric Baldwin was dead. She had to get Mary Lou's mind sidetracked. "Look, we'd better call it a night. I can't concentrate now, and besides, Winona will need help tomorrow. By the time the families get here there'll be lots of mouths to feed."

The others agreed and they all went home.

Robbie tried to stay awake until Damon returned, but had dozed. Damon didn't know much more. They'd have to wait until an autopsy was done to determine the exact cause of death. He took a quick shower and climbed into bed beside Robbie.

She was nearly asleep again, but roused up to ask him what happened on the Austin police raid.

"It was postponed."

"Why?" Robbie asked, and stifled a yawn.

"The feds' informant called and said if we waited until Sunday night, the barn would be full of stolen merchandise."

"Oh." Robbie yawned again.

"I'm sorry—you have three more days to worry."

"Worry?" she mumbled, "'bout old blind man?"

"Maybe only because you love this old man?" Damon asked.

But Robbie didn't answer. She'd fallen asleep.

"Arlene Saunders says Winona told her more than once she'd get even with Eric someday," Damon said. "Get even for all those beatings."

Damon would carefully edit his answers, omitting police evidence, but he'd answer most questions when she asked for details. She thought talking to her helped him to clarify his thinking. "I'm sure she was just mouthing off, like anyone would. Winona didn't kill him. I feel it in my bones."

"Well, somebody sure did. Doc Timmons says Eric Baldwin has traces of arsenic in his digestive tract. He'll know for sure when he gets the lab results, but he's ninety percent sure it was rat poison." Damon took another bite of his luncheon salad. "Winona admitted last night how afraid she was of Eric."

"I'm sure she was. I don't think anyone who knew her would doubt it, but if she was so afraid, how could she have the nerve to kill him?"

"It doesn't take much nerve to put rat poison in somebody's food, and I'm afraid the method puts Winona at the top of the list. Women have a history of using poison . . ."

Robbie sighed in exasperation. "Oh, you chauvinist, you only remember *Arsenic and Old Lace*. I remember doing some library research for one of my stories and reading about poison. Historically more men than women have used poison to kill. They've been doing it for hundreds of years."

"Well, if you have a better suspect, why don't you tell me. Winona had motive, opportunity, and means. The arsenic was conveniently in Eric's garage."

"Where almost anyone else had access to it." Robbie got up to refill their iced tea glasses.

"But who else had a motive?"

"I don't know. Let me think about it."

"Robbie, you'd better stay out of this. This involves one

of your friends and she just might turn out guilty. This is real life, honey, not mystery fiction."

Damon smiled to show her he wasn't mad, but she also knew the question time was over. "I'm going to be late if I don't leave now." He did stay long enough to drink half of his iced tea and kiss the top of Robbie's head before he left.

Robbie cleared the table and rinsed the dishes. Her writing group—Winona, Mary Lou, Lilabeth, and herself—shared a kinship, a sisterhood even. None of them was capable of killing except on paper. She somehow had to steer Damon to another motive or suspect.

Before noon Robbie had made a potato casserole to take to the Baldwins' house, and when the kitchen was clean from lunch, she got out the ingredients to make pecan pies. She wanted to have everything ready to deliver by three.

Robbie rolled the piecrust and thought about murder. If Winona wasn't guilty, then who? Only two other people—Arlene and J. T. Saunders—were close to Eric and Winona. Robbie didn't care for Arlene, but the woman hero-worshiped her brother and probably wouldn't kill him. That left her husband, J.T., or someone unknown.

She didn't know if J.T. was capable of murder—she barely knew him. But what motive could he have? Robbie couldn't think of anything.

A business associate or coworker of Eric's maybe? Could someone there have a reason to want Eric dead? She knew practically nothing about his work.

Eric Baldwin had traveled the southwest selling farm equipment for years, but had been laid off two years ago. Winona said he'd found another sales job, and he went out of town regularly, but Robbie didn't know what he sold these days. She'd ask Winona about Eric's work when she made her bereavement call with the food. A real motive was what Damon needed.

Robbie dreaded seeing Winona; the death of a husband—even a brute—wouldn't be easy. And the Baldwin children's grief would be heart-wrenching.

To Robbie's knowledge, Eric had never abused his children, but she had worried it would happen one day. Now he would never have the chance to harm them and she couldn't help being relieved about that.

Most of all she dreaded talking to Arlene, the quasi-member, of their writing group. Her jealousy had caused her to become bitter and vituperous. But Arlene had only herself to blame. They wrote and she didn't.

The Baldwin farm was five miles south of Frontier City. Robbie drove out and turned into a long gravel driveway that led to a garage and continued on to a huge barn in the back. Up next to the house, the driveway had been paved and widened enough to accommodate several cars. An old Plymouth, an RV, and two pickup trucks were parked there today. Robbie pulled up next to the pickup she recognized as belonging to Arlene's husband, J. T. Saunders. She noticed the yellow crime-scene tape across the garage door as she got out and looked around. She was surprised at the signs of neglect she saw.

She remembered when Winona and Eric had bought the old two-story house ten years ago. It had originally been built and owned by one of Eric's ancestors. A huge front porch wrapped around to one side—good for catching an evening breeze in the days before air-conditioning. Winona had once been excited about restoring it.

Now paint peeled from the wood and a streak—the color of old blood—ran down from a corner rain gutter. Portions of the weather-beaten porch sagged. The refurbishing dreams crumbling along with the job and the marriage, Robbie thought.

Five or six children of indeterminate ages were throwing a volleyball around on the sparse front lawn. As Robbie waved to Winona's two, she noticed Arlene standing at the side entrance holding open a screen door.

Arlene helped bring in the food and Robbie asked about Winona. Arlene said Winona was lying down, that the doctor had given her some sleeping pills. Once inside, the two women walked down a short hallway to the kitchen. Several people wandered in and out of the kitchen and

Arlene introduced them. Some were Eric's relatives and some were Winona's.

"How are you holding up, Arlene?"

Arlene was putting the casserole Robbie brought into the icebox. She turned and Robbie could see her eyes were red rimmed. "I'm doing okay. It was hard this morning when I went with Winona to make funeral arrangements." She sniffed. "How about some coffee or iced tea?" Robbie said tea would be fine and they sat at the kitchen table.

J. T. Saunders suddenly came in through the back door. "Arlene? Where's the Lava soap? Damn old truck engine was filthy." His hands were covered with black grease and his sweaty face had two smudges. He was dressed in tattered overalls and no shirt. His surprise at seeing Robbie sitting there with his wife was unmistakable.

"Howdy, Robbie," J.T. said, recovering quickly. "Didn't know you were here." He had what Robbie always thought of as a beer belly and it was the only thing that detracted from his overall appearance as an attractive man. He was in his late thirties, with blue eyes and blond hair. His classic lantern jaw and full lips were softened by a reddish blond moustache.

Robbie didn't know him well and she'd never felt the urge to change that fact. "I brought some food," she said. "It was the least I could do."

Arlene had looked under the sink and silently handed J.T. the requested soap.

"Well, right kind of you, Robbie." J.T. turned on the faucet and began washing his hands and arms. He turned as he dried off. "Got an old engine out there in the barn I've been meaning to work on. Thought today might be a good time." He finished drying, nodded to Robbie, and headed to the front room of the house.

Robbie thought the idea of his working on a truck engine the day after his brother-in-law's death was a little odd—kind of disrespectful or something. She also idly wondered why he was working here at Eric's barn. He had a perfectly good garage over at his place. Maybe it was some project he and Eric had begun.

Robbie asked about Winona's children and Arlene said they were too young to realize exactly what was going on about their daddy.

"I'm thankful it was me that found him and not Chip or Tammy," Arlene said.

And Robbie agreed that would have been a tragedy.

Arlene continued, "It's going to be powerful hard for me to forget finding Eric's body. I can still see him lying there on the garage floor. I'll dream about it for months. The only good thing is I won't have to carry around all that guilt like Winona."

"What guilt?"

"Winona knew Eric was sick and yet she went off to her stupid writers' meeting anyway."

"Arlene, it's only natural. As I understand it, Eric wasn't that sick. Winona said she thought he had a stomach virus."

"If you ask me, she should have taken him to a doctor three days ago."

"Arlene, I knew Eric. Not well, I'll admit, but I did know him well enough to know that unless he was flat on his back there was no way anyone could get him to go to a doctor."

Arlene sniffed. "Maybe so, but all I can think about is if that heifer had taken my brother to the doctor, he would still be alive." Her voice dripped venom.

Robbie was shocked to her toes. Surely Arlene didn't mean what she was saying. She had to have known what a horse's patootie Eric was. "Arlene Saunders, I can't believe you're blaming Winona. You know Eric ruled this house. Winona couldn't even go to the toilet without his permission. If he decided he wasn't going to the doctor, then that was the end of it. She couldn't bodily drag him."

Arlene had the decency to blush. "Maybe you're right. I probably don't even know *what* I'm saying. I haven't slept since night before last."

"Oh, I'm sorry. I should go," Robbie said, and stood. "You try and get some rest. Did the doctor give *you* a sedative?"

"Yes, but I don't like pills, so I didn't take any."

"Maybe you should this time."

They walked down the hallway to the side door and outside. Robbie remembered she had wanted to ask what Eric did. "Without sounding like a 'nosy-rosy,' are Winona and the kids going to be okay financially? I mean, did Eric have life insurance at work or something?"

"I'm sure I don't know," Arlene mumbled.

"I guess I've forgotten," said Robbie. "Who did he work for?"

"For himself." Arlene wouldn't look Robbie in the eye. She turned, stepped to the screen door, and opened it, keeping her back to Robbie.

"Oh, I didn't realize," said Robbie. Arlene was acting uncomfortable about the questions and she couldn't imagine why. It made her determined to find out what she could about Eric's work. "But he was still in sales, wasn't he?"

"Yeah, sales. Look, Robbie, I have to get back inside. They'll be wanting to eat soon."

"Oh, Arlene, I could stay and help if you want to rest." Robbie felt guilty because she hadn't offered to serve.

"No, no, that won't be necessary. There are enough aunts and in-laws to handle it. I'll just have to show them where things are." Arlene stepped inside the door and latched the hook on the screen with a snap.

Robbie could take a hint, but asked anyway, "Well, if you're sure?"

Arlene nodded her head.

"Tell Winona to call if she needs me. I can baby-sit the kids or whatever."

Arlene turned abruptly away from the door and Robbie walked to her car wondering why Arlene had suddenly gotten so upset.

She opened the station wagon door and heard the screen door when it slammed behind her. She turned around and J.T. was striding toward her.

"Robbie, darlin'," he said, "can we talk a minute?"

"Of course, J.T."

"Whew." He smiled and gestured toward the front yard. "Let's get out of this hot sun and into that shade."

Robbie closed her car door and J.T. hooked his arm

through hers as if they were best buddies and steered them over to a magnolia tree.

J.T. released her arm and turned to face her. "Robbie, I don't want you to get the wrong idea."

"Wrong idea about what?"

"Arlene's overwrought. That stuff she said about Winona and Eric. She was just mouthing off." J.T. had showered and shaved. His Western shirt was open at the neck and his aftershave had a woodsy scent. His blue eyes looked deeply into Robbie's brown ones as if she were the only woman in the world. "I never noticed before what beautiful eyes you have, Robbie."

Robbie was startled to realize J.T. was flirting with her. Did he think she would be susceptible to his charm because she was an older woman? Some women might be, but not me, thought Robbie. Besides, being totally secure in her relationship with Damon made her impervious to his conceited charm. Anyone else, and she might have been a tiny bit flattered, but J.T. had some ulterior motive and that made her curious. "I can understand about Arlene," she said, ignoring his remark about her eyes. "She's still in shock and I'm sure she doesn't realize what she's saying."

"That's right," said J.T. "Arlene looked up to her older brother. It was awful to find him like that. She's angry and wants to blame someone. Winona just happens to be it, at the moment. Tomorrow it will be someone else—maybe even me." He flashed the big smile at her once more.

"It's no big deal, J.T. I don't think badly about her."

"Good, I feel better. Let me walk you back to your car." He lay his arm across her shoulder. "How's the sheriffing business? Damon staying busy?"

"Oh yes, he's busy, but he enjoys his work."

J.T. opened the car door. "By the way, Robbie. You musta thought it was funny, me working on that truck engine while the rest of the family is in there holding a wake for Eric. Truth is, I have to go out of town tonight to finish a job and get back for the funeral on Sunday."

Robbie lied through her teeth. "Pshaw, I didn't think

nothing of it." She climbed into the car and started the engine. "You take care of Arlene and Winona, you hear? They're going to need your strong shoulders for a while." When Robbie backed and turned her car, J.T. waved goodbye. She waved back and headed toward Frontier City.

Robbie kept thinking about the encounter with J.T. Why did he think she needed an explanation about things? And what about that flirting? He was obviously using his sexual magnetism to try to distract her, but from what exactly? He was up to something and he didn't want her prying.

But as she kept thinking about him, up popped a very weird thought. Winona was an attractive woman in a vulnerable position in her unhappy marriage. Her husband was gone much of the time. And when Eric was home, he *was* a brute. So along comes this sexy brother-in-law. Thinking about lovers' triangles and jealousies between Eric, Winona, Arlene, and J.T. occupied her mind as she straightened the house.

Robbie felt a headache coming on—the countryside was full of ragweed and that caused her allergies to react. So when Mary Lou called to complain about Arlene and not getting to see Winona, she wasn't too sympathetic.

"It's nothing to do with *you,* Mary Lou," said Robbie. "I didn't get to see Winona either."

Mary Lou complained only a bit more before she changed the subject to her writing project. She'd just received a new reference book on poisons and planned to spend the entire evening reading it. Robbie's head pounded and she was relieved when Mary Lou had to hang up and feed her cat.

Robbie took an antihistamine and a nap. By the time Damon came in, her headache was down to a minor dull ache.

"Did you talk to Winona today?" he wanted to know. "I drove out there before coming home and Arlene said Winona was asleep."

"No, I was there this afternoon, but Arlene said Winona was sedated," said Robbie. "And Mary Lou called right after I got back. She was mad because she had gone out there around noon and Arlene wouldn't let her see Winona."

"Isn't that odd? Her sleeping all day?"

"Well, some people get knocked on their cans from ever one tranquilizer. I'm sure that's what happened to Winona Sleep is probably the best thing for her right now."

"You look like you're not feeling too well yourself."

"Ragweed season."

"Why don't I get a pizza for dinner and you won't have to cook. Pepperoni okay?"

"Sounds great. When you get back I'll tell you all about my encounter with a sexy young man today."

"I sure don't want to miss that." Damon took off for the pizza parlor.

Robbie was putting out paper plates when the telephone rang. This time it was Lilabeth complaining about Arlene and how she had not been able to see Winona.

"Arlene did the same with me and with Mary Lou," said Robbie. "She admitted she hasn't slept for two days. She doesn't know what she's doing or saying."

"All those relatives must be driving her nuts. I offered to stay, but she insisted I leave."

"And J.T. isn't any help."

"No way. In fact, when I was leaving, he came barreling out from the barn in this huge eighteen-wheeler. Nearly ran over me."

"He was coming into town?"

"No, he turned off, heading north for Dallas," said Lilabeth. "Oh, I gotta hang up, Robbie, the baby's crying."

When Damon came back with the pizza, Robbie told him what Lilabeth had said about Winona and Arlene.

"Are you worried, hon?"

"Maybe. Just a little. I keep thinking Winona must be wondering why none of us has been around to see her."

"We could go out after we eat, but only if you feel up to it."

"I'm not sure we should. Maybe tomorrow."

"Well, I've got a few more questions for her, but they can

wait until tomorrow," Damon said. "If she's been sedated all day, she won't be able to give coherent answers. You want to call?"

"I don't think so. I imagine their phone has been ringing off the wall and I would just add to the confusion."

As they got ready for bed, she told Damon how J.T. had flirted with her and about her suspicions of him and Winona having an affair. "Maybe Arlene found out and told her brother," said Robbie. "And Eric had such a volatile temper he would have confronted J.T."

"Sure, and Eric would have killed J.T. on the spot."

"What if they just had an argument then, and later on J.T. somehow got Eric to take the rat poison. Gave it to him in food or something to drink."

"Or maybe J.T. told Winona to get rid of Eric," said Damon, "so they could be together."

"Winona is my friend, and I just don't think she's capable of murder." Robbie crawled into bed.

"Anyone is capable of murder given enough provocation."

"I don't really believe that. I think some people would argue, fight, throw tantrums, do anything else, but never, ever commit murder."

"I can't see you ever killing someone."

"I could kill in an instant if anyone hurt you or one of our kids."

"I'm not so sure you could. Just how would you do it, anyway? Shoot them or poison them?" He got into bed beside her.

"I'd hack them up with an axe."

Damon was silent a moment before he laughed. "Okay, Miss Lizzie of Frontier City, you've made a believer out of me. Now we'd better get some sleep—tomorrow will be a busy day."

"Do we have to?"

"You have a better idea?"

She told him and it was a while before they went to sleep.

* * *

Saturday was the only day Robbie and Damon Dunlap allowed themselves to lollygag, and they slept a good hour past their usual awakening time. Robbie hadn't slept well. She'd dreamt about Winona all night—bad dreams—but couldn't remember them. She told Damon she wanted to go see her friend.

Damon said, "If Arlene refuses to let me see Winona, I'll use my legal authority as sheriff to override her objections."

After breakfast they drove out in his county vehicle, a four-wheel-drive Ford Explorer. A cold front had moved down from the panhandle overnight and the day was crisp and hinted of autumn. High, wispy clouds raced southward toward the Gulf of Mexico. The Baldwin farm looked deserted when they arrived—no cars or sign of life.

"Looks like no one's here," said Damon as they got out and walked to the side door. He knocked, but got no answer.

"That's strange," said Robbie, and walked to the front to peek into the windows. When no one responded to her knocking at that door, she walked to meet Damon, who had gone around to the back. "I guess everyone's in town at the funeral home or over at Arlene's."

"Could be. I'll call Dispatch and have them check at the funeral home."

Damon looked out at the barn and Robbie looked too, shading her eyes with her hands.

"Damon, it looks like the barn's been remodeled. Why would they do that and let the house practically fall down?"

"I don't know." He stood there a moment thinking and then walked a couple of steps in the barn's direction before he stopped. "What was it you told me about J.T. working on an engine?"

Robbie had been getting ready to ask if he'd also send a deputy to Arlene's house and it took her a second to comprehend his question. "Uh . . . he said he was working on this truck engine, getting ready to go out of town on business. He wanted to be back in time for the funeral tomorrow."

"And he was out in the barn? Not in the garage?"

"That funny yellow tape was still across the garage doors." Suddenly Robbie remembered something else. "Last night Lilabeth said J.T. came barreling out of here in a big eighteen-wheeler. Almost ran her down."

"Hmmm," Damon said, and began walking toward the barn.

"Damon?" He didn't stop. "Damon, where are you going? I think we ought to get back to town. I want to talk to Winona."

Damon ignored her. She started to follow, but he heard her and stopped long enough to say in a firm tone, "Wait for me in the car."

Robbie, torn between wanting to follow and wanting to do as he asked, stopped. She watched as he reached the barn and went inside. When he didn't come right back out, she slowly began walking toward the barn. Before she reached the door, Damon came out, grim-faced, carrying Winona Baldwin in his arms. Her small frame looked like that of a child in his big arms.

"Oh, my heavens," said Robbie. "Is she uh . . . ?"

"She's alive. Run! Call Dispatch! Tell them to send an ambulance." Damon walked steadily toward the house. "I think she's been drugged. I'm going to break in, try to revive her."

Robbie ran for the Explorer and the police radio.

Damon had just broken into the side door, picked Winona up again, and stepped inside, when Robbie came bursting in. "We'll have to take her. EMS had to respond to a car wreck over on I-35."

Robbie sat in back—holding Winona, talking to her, trying to wake her up. An emergency room team met them at the door with a hospital gurney, rushing Winona inside and out of sight.

An hour went by before a nurse came out and said they'd pumped Winona's stomach and they thought she'd be okay.

Damon told Robbie that he had to go back out to the Baldwin barn with a search warrant.

"What is going on, Damon?"

"Looks like this is all involved with those truck hijackings. That's all I can say."

The cold front intensified and the next evening Damon and Robbie were snuggled on the sofa, in front of the fireplace. "Strange, isn't it?" Robbie mused as she sipped hot chocolate topped with marshmallows.

"How's that?"

"How you'd never have solved this case with your skewed ideas about poison. You thought it just *had* to be Winona who'd given Eric the arsenic. I was right about men being the chief poisoners historically. According to Mary Lou's poison book . . ."

"Okay, I've admitted I was wrong—don't rub my nose in it."

"Sorry." She snuggled closer to his side, pulling his arm tighter around her shoulder to let him know she was only teasing.

Damon started telling her what he'd found at the barn. "Eric and J.T. were hijacking trucks. The barn was full of stolen merchandise. Arlene says Eric got mad about something, maybe a fight over the profits. And Eric was going to talk to me—expose the whole operation."

"Was something going on between J.T. and Winona?"

"Arlene says not, but what else could she say? We'll probably never know for sure because J.T. isn't talking. Winona says she found out J.T. gave Eric the rat poison and she thinks he somehow got her to take the tranquilizers. Put them in her coffee probably. After the first ones," Damon said, "things got pretty hazy."

"Did Arlene know anything about the pills?"

"She's admitted she didn't try to stop it."

"What will happen to her?"

"She'll get immunity if she testifies."

Robbie pulled away from Damon's arm and sat upright.

"What's wrong, hon?"

"Nothing. I just thought of a great subplot for my

book—how wife steers husband in the right direction to catch murderer. I want to write it down . . ."

Damon pulled her back down and gave her a kiss. "Okay, little helper, but not tonight. I've got a subplot of my own here we need to act out."

"Uhh . . . huh," said Robbie. "In that case I'll write tomorrow, dear."

Cold and Deep

Frances Fyfield

———————

The ice formed over eighteen hours. Sarah could feel the
sharp edges hardening around her. It was too cold to snow.
Snow would only trap her for longer and she was trapped
enough already. What a fool she was, what a silly cow to
agree to help out her sister, as if she even *liked* children. In a
split second, on stepping out of the train, Sarah examined
her reasons for being where she was and found them lacking.
She was so successful at being single, she had nowhere else
to go. Mary had asked and Christmas was a nightmare
anywhere.

There would be quite a crovd. Sarah struggled to remember how many. Mary, of course, with her husband, Jonathan, plus two daughters, aged six and eight, plus a baby.
Then there was Fiona, the devoted fiancée of Jonathan's
brother, who had been on site three days in advance to
organize provisions and prepare the house. Richard would
follow her lovingly. By comparison, the prospect of the
elderly father was almost appealing in Sarah's estimation.
He and she could celebrate their single status, with herself in
the role of the hard-bitten aunty and him as a hard-drinking

granddad. They could survive the season with the aid of a liter of gin.

The station was ugly and chilly—not a place to linger. Sarah remembered her instructions to call the invincible Fiona but somehow balked at the idea when she saw the queue for the phone. A taxi plus a walk would do better to postpone the claustrophobic wretchedness of it all, and at least at the other end, in a house graphically described by her sister, there would be a dog for company. A bitch, with puppies, Sarah recalled, and in the remembering she was suddenly, violently sick while standing in the rank. On that account, it took a while to get a taxi.

In a slow-moving car approaching the Midlands from the north, weary bickering had trailed into dreary pauses. "I don't know why we have to do this," Mary was saying for the last time. Jonathan was above yelling and banging the wheel by now: All that had come earlier.

"You know for why. Because it's good for us. The girls get to run around, Dad's still suffering from that stroke and can't come to us, and," he added cunningly, "with Fiona there, *you* don't have to do anything, except sleep. Surely Sarah will help."

Oh, clever, very clever, Mary thought. The prospect of sleep was unbearably appealing. The car was a cocoon without comfort, padded with resentment. Beth and Sylvie, six and eight years respectively, preserved temporary silence, otherwise programmed to create chaos whenever the damp twelve-week-old baby tried to slumber in his mother's lap.

Jonathan looked at Mary's face in the rearview mirror, saw a pinched, exhausted look beyond his income or his curing. He envied the insouciance of his younger brother and the careless decade that came between them. He envied not only Richard's life, but his car and his delicious, competent, caring Fiona.

"We got Granddad's dog! With puppies this time!" Beth

shrieked, sick of the silence. "And I can go swimming in the lake!" Mary winced.

"I don't think so, darling."

"Can I tell you som'ink, Daddy? Can I, can I, can I?" Beth continued, always inclined to change the subject. There was never a child so ready with words. Mary's eyes closed.

"Go on, since you will anyway."

"I don't like Fiona, not after summer holidays. Not much."

Mary's eyes opened and her voice rose in desperation. "Don't be silly. Fiona's lovely. Everyone loves her."

"Granddad's dog doesn't. Granddad doesn't. I doesn't."

Mary lost control. "Rubbish! You must be mad! Without Fiona, we don't eat or sleep for two whole days. So shut up. . . . Just *shut up!*"

Silence fell, Beth's eyes closing as she sulked, Sylvie defiantly awake. Another mile passed sluggishly, the road ablaze with lights. Another small voice rose from the back, full of smugness for evading the rebuke this time.

"How very long till we get there, Daddy? How long? How long? How long?"

It became a chant. He sighed.

"Soon. If you're good, you can play with Granddad's dog."

A yellow bitch, mostly Labrador, and still Richard's pet. Maybe it would snow this Christmas, but since the ugly house of his father was the place Richard best loved in the world, the prospect of snow wasn't so bad.

"Such a sweet little house," Fiona was saying to him on the car phone. "We're going to be a bit crowded, darling," was the gist of it, "what with Mary and the babies."

And her sister. Why'd she have to bring her sister? "We'll have to be very quiet. Never mind," he said.

"We aren't so quiet in bed," Fiona giggled. Richard smiled like an idiot.

"Was Dad pleased to see you?"

"Oh yes, but not as much as the home helpers and the night nurse when I took over. I thought they were going to kiss me. But he doesn't really like me. You know that . . ."

"Nonsense, of course he does. He's said so, often."

The lie came over his car phone with gracious ease. The phone embarrassed him: He loved it as much as he loved his own hand. There were times when his feeling for Fiona embarrassed him too, but then he had always been vulnerable to anything he adored with such a passion—such as the telephones that were his business as well as his delight, his childhood toys, and the three-parts Labrador dog he had left at home three years ago with his widowed father. Before then, he'd loved Dad, too, with the same single-mindedness, came home often, all three of them basking in companionship. That was before Fiona routed his twenty-eight-year-old innocence and made him notice the sheer importance of possessions. He still felt vaguely treacherous, as if love were a competition and he were a prize. Rubbish, of course. A hardworking man like himself could have it all. He phoned Fiona four times a day. Her voice was as much like rich velvet as the soft pouches beneath the Labrador's jaw, where Richard tickled until that pink and yellow belly would turn over in ecstasy. Clutching the car phone in lane three of the motorway, checking the mirror at the same time, he saw himself grinning. There was another BMW on his tail. He made it wait.

"You know your father doesn't like me, but I thought I'd better warn you—he's much worse. Swears like a trooper. Says awful things about people, me included—you, even. Much worse than last month. Insists on eating dinner with a spoon. He may not say much this evening because he's very tired, but he might blow bubbles."

"What kind of bubbles?" Richard asked stupidly. Then his car lurched and the line began to crackle. His phone was suddenly dead without apology, the BMW behind suddenly in front as he drifted left. He hadn't had a chance to ask about the silly golden bitch and her late, aberrant pregnancy (a condition that showed more than anything how Dad was losing his touch and Richard himself losing one rudder to replace it with another). He shook his head, spurred the car into life. Fiona was simply a miracle.

The pudding was almost cooked. There was a brace of geese, stuffed and wrapped, in the larder. What an ugly house this is, Fiona thought. No country mansion, but postwar Gothic, stuck on the edge of an awful connubation made rich and now poor by the industries of coal. The town slipped downhill toward unreal countryside reconstituted from opencast mining, leaving odd valleys and bald fields, no trees, but a kind of scrub extending out beyond heavy suburban gardens lush with evergreen. The villa was on the edge with a field sloping down the bank to a pond in a gulley, part of Dad's domain but haunted by local youth who thought it was theirs, a stagnant stretch of water that the romantic owner and his family still described as "the lake." It might have looked larger to kids, Fiona admitted condescendingly, but it was still deep and cold, or so she had discovered as she warmed her hands in the sink after a second brisk walk to the crumbly edge just to get out and see how the ice was doing.

Now she checked her watch. That sister of a sister-in-law should have phoned; the train must be late. Good. Someone else would have to fetch her. There was a keening sound from the dog's basket, a vague noise of distant thumping from the living room reached by a horrible linoleum passage. Granddad's dog regarded Fiona with eyes of helpless misery. The bitch lay on one side with her swollen tits exposed, the blanket beneath her freshly clean as a replacement for the torn and bloody newspaper of yesterday. Fiona strode across and forced a pill between the unresisting pink jaws. The effort left her own fingers damp with saliva. "There, there," she said. "Vet's orders. You mothers are such a trial to the rest of us. Come on, show a leg. Come *on.*"

The almost Labrador obeyed with ponderous reluctance, her unclipped claws clicking on the linoleum, which gave way to tartan carpet. There was no feature here incapable of improvement, Fiona thought. Everything frightful. But this house could make a beautiful and valuable suburban monster if only it were rescued from the early sixties when the last child was born here. Since then, it had lacked a woman's touch. We'd have stone flags for the garden, Fiona thought. Gravel for the driveway. The pond could become a swimming pool. Richard could call me from there on his mobile.

The house did not loom up out of the mist as Sarah approached on foot, passing closed-up dwellings with eyeless windows set back from the road, the odd glimmering of light emphasizing her own exclusion. "Not splendid," Mary had said. "Only big and short of bathrooms." The rutted drive was large enough for three cars in a row, but holding only one: Fiona's. Which meant Sarah was the first and made her reluctant to knock, left her standing in a state of uncertainty by the front door, next to an enormous terracotta pot, pretentiously out of place and housing a small shrub on a bed of fresh compost. The shrub branches were festooned with tiny baubles, tinkling very softly as she breathed, the whole edifice repellent in its tasteful newness, reminding her of a graveyard with fresh flowers. Still reluctant, inhibited by this sign of festivity, Sarah moved to her right and looked into a window for distraction. There were leaded panes through which she could see multicolored fairy bulbs on a Christmas tree, hear muffled sounds, blurred, like the lights, by the distortions of the glass.

An old man was sitting in an armchair, so far upright he might easily have risen with the aid of the stick leaning against the door sixteen feet away. He seemed to be yelling for his prop, screaming with rage and beating his wrists on the arms of his seat. There was a tall young woman about the business of shushing him, followed by a faded yellow dog with a pink underbelly. The leaded panes swam a little: Sarah regretted the wine consumed on the train and the then inevitable sickness at the station. She thought she saw a plastic bib ripped from the creped neck, revealing a clean white shirt; a hearing aid rammed in, the stick strategically placed to allow him to rise, a brush dragged through the thick gray hair, yanking back a full, round face into a scream. He looked like a baby: She felt sick all over again. The bright blue eyes in his face turned to the window as if for redemption, saw the headlights, ceased to stare.

The slim form of the young woman busied itself about the room, the hair of her glowing, the lean rump bent with graceful ease as she stooped over cushions. Sarah scuttled toward the door. Her back was illuminated as she rang the bell, a dinky, irritating chime that defied the last illusion of ancestral splendor and also cut across the modern good taste of the expensive pot. One car pulled up behind her, another more slowly behind that. Fiona flung open the door, framed in the light like an angel, laughing her hellos, uttering warm and lovely platitudes, "Come in, come in, how clever of you all to arrive at once. Come and see Dad . . ."

Richard saw Dad first. He was looking every inch the pristine gentleman of mature years dressed in ancient cavalry twill with the yellow dog at his feet and unshed tears in his eyes. Dad smiled: he was desperate to talk, it seemed, but there wasn't the time. Richard was indulgent, patted Dad's arm, presuming the presence of so many made his father confused, remembered what Fiona had said. Besides, there was homemade soup, sandwiches, biscuits, and pap for the kids. Lots of red wine for the adults. Perfect for a family on Christmas Eve. They settled quickly.

It was Beth, as usual, who sang out the discord by pointing at the almost Labrador with a trembling finger. She did not mean to accuse or criticize the animal, but she simply wanted to know.

"Where are her puppies?" she shouted with polite impatience.

Granddad arched in his chair, looked as if he was about to

shout, but hissed instead. "She didn't want . . ." he began to say. "She didn't want . . ."

"Oh dear," said Fiona, laying a hand on his arm, looking at Beth with profound sympathy. "I think it was a false alarm." She turned to Richard. "Hysterical pregnancy; she's had them before, the vet told me. So I'm sorry, darlings, no puppies this time. The poor thing *thought* she was, her poor old body *thought* she was, but she wasn't. She just got fat." Beth began to weep, slow, solid tears of frustration.

I wish I were like that, Sarah thought wryly. I wish that my condition was the result of hysteria instead of careless fornication, and I wish I did not have a choice. I wish I were not thirty-five years old and seven weeks pregnant at the same time. I do not like spending Christmas considering the appropriate time to have my abortion, but then I detest Christmas anyway.

The dog raised a paw, suddenly acquiescent with a child warm against her throbbing flank. Dad thumped his stick. He shouted for scissors to deal with his sandwiches, ate with voracity the pieces that Fiona had cut so kindly and without comment or condescension, staring at her calm and beautiful face. Yes, you are wonderful, Sarah thought. Mary's eyes were closed again. The children and her sister were all of a heap, as if Sarah had somehow acquired them all. How peculiar it was that little girls and boys should be so like cats, adopting the adult who was not their own and the one who might have liked them least. So it was Sarah who took them to bed soon after Granddad had been shepherded away without protest, as if to give good example. The brothers had opened the next bottle by the time Mary had defected into a greedy sleep with the baby, unable to manage the vestiges of politeness.

The ugly house was strangely silent apart from the plumbing: The children spoke in whispers. They should be more excited, Sarah reflected, suddenly protective of their dreams. They should be in that semihysterical state that comes before Christmas morning, just like I was once, and against her better judgment, which applauded the convenience of their subdued behavior, she found herself trying to stimulate some of the old and naughty fever.

"What's Santa bringing you? Will he be able to get everything down the chimney?"

"He was bringing me a puppy," said Beth savagely. Not as far as Mommy knows, Sarah thought wisely. That's the last thing she'd allow in their little cramped house. Beth eyed her, the glance sliding away as honesty prevailed.

"C'n I tell you som'ink? I don't care. I wanted to *see* a puppy. Tha's all. Granddad said, he said . . . Anyway, he said on the phone it was Dog's last chance. Only Fiona says she didn't have nothing. No puppies."

"Dogs have lots of chances. So do people."

"No, they doesn't. I don't think they does. Granddad said. Will you play with me tomorrow? Will you, will you, will you? Granddad used to throw sticks for Dog, into the lake. You will, won't you?" Sarah found the thought appalling.

"Shush, now. Everyone's tired. Shush . . ." She knew she was using the last excuse ever acceptable to a child. She thought she was clumsy with children, but persevered until she could tiptoe away. Then she hesitated. A light shone beneath Granddad's door, and although she scarcely knew him, it seemed only polite to bid goodnight to the host whose dreadful house it was.

The old man lay on his side, fetally curled with his hand stretched out to a bedside light and a book that seemed too far from his fingers for easy reach, and anyway, Sarah reflected with uneasy pity, he was probably beyond reading. There was something of the stage set about it all—the light, the book, the pristine cleanliness of him that showed Fiona's efficiency. The lamp looked new, as if recently replaced, and Granddad resembled a man to whom replacement parts did not come easy. He turned his face to the door as she entered and all at once she recognized that look of pellucid sanity in his blue eyes that she had perhaps seen before, distorted by the glass.

"Do something," he hissed. "She'll eat him up. Do something." Sarah was embarrassed, arranged his blankets, smiled in the conciliatory way she imagined Fiona would smile, drew the lamp nearer, put his ever elusive stick within reach, listening all the time to the shout of laughter from downstairs that beckoned her to where she really belonged. Amongst the grown-ups, not with a capricious old man and not with tedious, demanding children. None of this had ever been her scene.

"Shall I turn off the light?"

He stuck two fingers in the air, a gesture obscenely at odds with his laundered fragility. Awkward, old cuss, Sarah thought, retreating in good order. Drink beckoned, along with adult conversation. Surely she was not so much of an interloper that she had to tolerate insult. But again, she might have known. Downstairs there was no relief either. They were family: Together they could only speak of their young and the old and this was the season for both.

"Your dad can't cope," Fiona was saying gently, lying like a lioness at rest across Richard's knees. "He's determined he can, but he can't."

Richard bristled. "I could get him a mobile phone," he said pointlessly. "We could get someone in to look after the poor dog—how could he let her get into that state?"

Swiftly, effortlessly, Fiona adjusted their positions so that it was he who lay in her lap, with her hands free to gesture and stroke his hair. "But he should never go into a home, should he darling?" she murmured reassuringly. "*We* could always keep Dog. You'd like that, wouldn't you?"

Richard nodded.

Jonathan considered how far he had grown away from home, distanced into other priorities, grateful if someone else made all the decisions for Dad since he could make no more, even though he still cared as much as he could when half drunk and fascinated by Fiona's long, elegant limbs.

"So I just think we step up the support for now," Fiona continued. "I mean, I know it's difficult for Mary with the kids, but I could come more often. I mean, actually, we could live here, once we're married." She tweaked Richard's ear playfully. He seemed to arch his neck for his chin to be stroked while the other hand reached for the dog.

"Yes," said Jonathan, relieved at the mere suggestion of solutions half as tidy. "Yes." Since the birth of his children, he too, had felt old.

Sarah nodded and smiled. Her contribution was not required. She was the only one distant enough to watch. So she watched.

No snow on Christmas morning. A milky mist melted against the windows, preface to a halfhearted daylight designed to comfort prisoners behind walls by suggesting there was nothing worth missing beyond. It was warmer as the boiler cranked into life and melted the ice on Sarah's window. Seven o'clock when the first piece of chocolate was presented by Beth, eight when Sarah rose, padded toward the Christmas tree like a pilgrim unsure of her religion. The old man was sitting there in his chair, haphazardly dressed, smiling with the fixed smile of a cheerful garden gnome.

"Did it all by myself. Easy, when I can reach the stick. What the hell does he think I normally do? I'm not mad, you know," he added absently. "I don't let on, but I'm not mad at all. Only as mad as a man with sons who are deaf and blind . . . after all I taught them. Listen to me. You didn't listen to me, did you? They don't either."

"When?"

He seemed to slump, then rallied into a murmur.

"I love Richard best. Is that so awful?"

"No. We all love someone best. It's allowed."

"Which is why it's so important for him to know that she is trying . . . to . . ." The voice descended to a mumble as the dog swayed into the room and the old man's hand went out protectively, fondling the underjaw of the golden head laid like a weight on his lap. Spittle landed on the dog's ears. Granddad's face contorted into an inane smile. "She's trying to . . . trying to . . . kiss me! Oh yes, she likes to kiss!" He shouted while his other hand waved in a mockery of greeting.

"Silly old thing," said Fiona's fond voice from the doorway. Her face was perfect, without a trace of tiredness. "Sarah, could you be an angel and help peel a few spuds before all hell starts? Then we can relax." Sarah followed her out, looked back once. Granddad was slightly purple in the face.

"He's better in the morning," Fiona confided. "But he does talk nonsense."

"Some of the time?"

Fiona responded sadly. "No. I daren't tell Richard. All of it."

No one listens to the old, Sarah was thinking, as they all fell into a regime. Of course there was a regime, beginning with no breakfast for anyone except those under ten, strong coffee to stimulate a long salivation in anticipation for lunch for the rest, the opening of presents in between. So, this is what families do, Sarah thought. They produce an over-elaboration of gifts, perhaps had always done so, but it seemed so vulgar now. Mary and Jonathan exchanged books and records with a peck on the cheek and then turned attention to the pleasure of their children. Sarah lingered over the opening of her token gifts to make them last, said thank you politely, delivered hers, then helped a listless Granddad open up a sweater, a shirt, a tie, a watch—all with the same disinterest—while the children tore into parcels like wild beasts. Even they had finished long before Richard and Fiona had ceased presenting to each other gift after perfectly wrapped gift. Oh, darling, you shouldn't! A silk dress. Sweetheart! There was a hunky suede jacket, then more and more until the whole room was ablaze with their luxury. Mary had begun to look a little stiff to remind Richard he seemed to have forgotten his nieces. It took a while for him to remember where he was.

"Oh, I got this for the kids."

Beth perked up, then her face assumed a stony expression of no expectation as Fiona handed her the parcel. Inside was a mobile phone.

"Oh," said Jonathan doubtfully.

"There's another one for Sylvie," said Richard happily. "I get a discount. They can try them in the garden."

"Crap," said Granddad suddenly and distinctly. "What crap."

"Lunch in an hour," Fiona announced brightly, gathering up paper. "Is it worth going out?"

"We'll go," said Sarah, desperate for air, feeling frantic with heat and all the gift wrapping. "Won't we? Come on, Sylvie, we'll take a phone and phone Granddad."

"If you must," said Fiona. "Do be careful with it— they're expensive. I should stay in the garden. If I were you. No, don't take the dog. She's been out already."

The resistance worked the opposite effect on Beth, who had been ready to grumble, ask for television, more chocolate, and full-scale attention until then, but now pushed her sister first and screamed for her outdoor clothes, stamping with impatience. Mary shot Sarah a look of sheer gratitude, held open the back door, and waved them away.

Outside, the mist and the mood cleared. Beth shrieked her way down the long unkempt garden, holding the mobile phone as a kind of balance, yelling, "Yuck," as she skirted the tentacles of a dripping bush, bellowing out of sight. Alarmed, Sarah ran after, remembering the mythical lake and the strange mood of the child, anxiety and resentment dogging her steps. She did not want to be in charge of children. They were not hers. She hated this place and the smell of sweet-scented soap on the living room floor; hated the prospect of dangerous water, thick with ice like the melting lawn and her own mood. Her arms clutched her bosom as she ran through a gap in a hedge, yelling after them, "Wait for me, wait for me!", anxiety lending wings and making her breathless. "Wait for me!"

Cold and Deep

There was no real cause for concern. To the children the lake was a large stretch of water of which they were in awe as they approached, gingerly testing the steep, friable edges with the insensitive toes of Wellington boots, both quieter than before, sulking with their feet because they could go no further and dare not try the ice. To Sarah, this nasty pond looked like a recent and unsuccessful excavation, a laughable thing, deep and cold as it might have been for all she knew. A ridiculous, unromantic, weedy pool with litter around the edge, but all the same, the temptation to scorn made her ashamed and she desperately wanted to revive for them the simple excitement that seemed to die indoors, felt the same desire in herself as the last evening, to make them noisily, joyously responsive. "Let's break the ice," she yelled. "Come on, get stones. We can crack it!"

The ice that had formed leaked around the edge, looked thick but still dangerously unsolid, and became a thing to conquer. Sylvie threw a branch she had lugged to the edge and watched it skitter across the surface. Beth threw lumps of earth with increasing frustration and bloodcurdling yells. Then Sarah found a piece of metal, which made a satisfying sound, but slid, too, and then a large stone, which was an effort even to lift. Beth helped; between them, they dropped rather than threw it, watched it roll heavily down the side, bounce the last yard, and make a hole in the edge of the ice. The water heaved and burped: bubbles rose.

"Yeah, yeah!" Beth howled.

"I hate Fiona!" Sylvie shrieked. She had been the quietest of the two, the least disposed to naughtiness, which was why Sarah failed to move fast enough to stop her, surprised by the speed of her action and what she had said. She did nothing to stop Sylvie picking up the abandoned phone and throwing it toward the hole.

"Stop it," Sarah shouted, far louder than the child, but too late. Sylvie's aim was bad. The phone slid too, three feet distant from the hole. She began to cry. Oh, no, please don't, Sarah thought. I wanted to see you both happy. We were doing so well.

"Silly," she said sternly. "Don't be silly. We'll get it back." It was understated, but by some common instinct they all three knew that the wrath of Fiona would be terrible. None of them thought of anything else. Sarah knew they had no reason for thinking as they did, but they thought it all the same, so she scrambled down the bank and stood in the edge of the water, making an act of it, pretending it was fun. On the very edge, she was safe, until she looked at her feet. A piece of sacking was protruding above the surface and with it the pink snout of a corpse. A pink and yellow body, bloated, pathetic, followed by another. Dead puppies. A whole litter of drowned puppies, the almost Labrador's last chance.

Squatting over her freezing feet, Sarah shielded the sacking, talked brightly to the children over her shoulder to disguise the waves of sheer fury that made her tremble.

"Listen," she said. "Listen, I've got an idea. Aunty Fiona can't get mad at me, right? I'm a guest and a grown-up and I don't care anyway. Right?" They nodded, like two wise owls. "So you go back up to the house now, tell her I was carrying the phone and I dropped it on the ice. Say we don't want to tell Uncle Jonathan, in case he gets upset. Get her in the kitchen, make it sound secret, right? And ask her to come down here with a broom or something, so I can get it back. Then stay inside. It's too cold out here."

They continued nodding. Sylvie opened her mouth. Beth grabbed her by the arm and they both fled, rehearsing lines. Sarah waited. She fished out of the water one of the dead puppies, repelled by the touch but compelled to hold it over her hand and wipe the water away from its blind eyes and feel for the softness under the chin. Then she dragged out the sack containing the rest, looked briefly. The other six were still curled together. There was a pain in her abdomen and a fluttering in her chest. The stone had been too heavy. She felt sick, but she knew she would not wait long. Soon, down the slope, she heard the breathless panting of Fiona, booted, spurred, carrying a yard brush.

"The phone," Fiona said. "How could you? Jonathan lives for phones."

She'll eat him up, was all Sarah thought, seeing in her mind's eye the sanity of the old man that they all ignored, concentrating on his weakness. She'll eat them all up. She likes to kiss. Sarah was halfway up the bank, scrambling with one hand, the other holding the sodden sack behind her back. Fiona saw, stopped.

"How many did the poor bitch have? What a nuisance for you." Sarah tried to sound patient and understanding. Fiona pretended she had not heard, then relented, seduced into a sense of conspiracy by the concern in the other's voice.

"Well, yes, it was, a bit. The *day* I arrived—can you imagine! He can't cope, you know. Jonathan would have wanted to keep them. How awful. You know what I mean?"

"Yes, I do see. Anyway, the phone's more important, isn't it?"

"Of course it is."

"Why don't you try and get it? I'm afraid my feet have gone numb."

"Fine, fine."

Oh, she was such a coper. Sarah squatted, winded with a pain far worse than the sickness outside the station the night before, clutching her belly where the gripe was sharpest, the sackful of sodden babies by her side. She was half weeping, praying madly for the invisible fetus inside her. Oh no, oh no—whatever the punishment to me, please do not die. I want you to live—that is what I want. Whatever the purgatory, don't die on me. Every dog deserves its day, every bitch deserves a baby, heaven help me.

In this kind of daze, like an insect preserved in amber with wide-open eyes, she watched Fiona stand up to her knees in icy water and fish for the phone, which lay like some ghastly talisman on the frozen surface. The slim body of the fiancée leaned forward to sweep the brush over the ice, grunting. Then Sarah watched as Fiona slipped on the clay surface, which was smoothed by the footsteps of her last expedition the day before, when the ice was only paper thin. Then Fiona was sliding under the ice up to the waist, her feet flailing for hold, gasping. Half the bank caved in behind her with a plop. The incline down was now very steep. The ice broke against her back. She slid further, bawling for help, and for more than a moment Sarah was tempted, but it was a passing temptation.

She hurt too much. She had too much to protect to fling herself down a slippery incline toward deep, cold water—could not run for help anyway. So she simply wondered about how to harness her small store of energy to bury the puppies in case the children should see them. She stayed where she was, full of the overpowering desire to preserve her own child and aware of the dimmest possible notion that it was better for a woman like Fiona to go like this. Better in the long run for everyone. Knowing while she thought it how a woman like herself was the slightest bit mad, but also knowing she couldn't, wouldn't, ever quite regret it. It was not as if she was able to move. Would it be better, she asked herself, if Jonathan knew about the puppies? Probably not.

Before the new set of bubbles stopped rising to the surface, Sarah got up. She went around to the front of the house to the enormous planter on which she had stumbled the night before, lifted the tinkling shrub with ease, buried the sack deep in the soft compost, replaced the shrub carefully, went back to the bottom of the lawn behind, and walked to the kitchen door.

"Where's Fiona?" Jonathan demanded.

"What? Isn't she here? I left her trying to fish a phone out of the lake. Went for a walk down the avenue. Isn't it remarkable how everyone's houses look the same but manage to be so different. What's wrong? She said she'd give it five minutes. Isn't she back? Does she like the cold or something?"

He flung out of the house. Sarah washed her hands, went into the living room, where Grandfather sat as before, with the head of the dog on his knee. Jonathan was on the floor, next to his suddenly animated wife as they laid out a game for the children, all four heads together except for the grinning baby in a bassinet, also studiously ignoring Sarah's glance. The atmosphere was suddenly lighter and brighter as though a stone had been removed and daylight was streaming into a cave.

Sarah knelt by the old man's knee, watched while the dog lay down and transferred a trusting head into her own lap. Granddad watched too, with his crepey hand trembling. Her fingers interlaced with his.

"Trust me," she said.

"You'll have a nice pup," he said, "one day."